The
New Girl at St. Chad's

A Story of School Life

Angela Brazil

Illustrated by John Campbell

iBoo Press

London

The New Girl at St. Chad's

A Story of School Life

Angela Brazil

Illustrated by John Campbell

Layout & Cover © Copyright 2020 iBooPress, London

Published by
iBoo Press House

3rd Floor
86-90 Paul Street
London, EC2A4NE UK

t: +44 20 3695 0809
info@iboo.com II iBoo.com

ISBN
978-1-64181-706-6 (h)

The
New Girl at St. Chad's

A Story of School Life

Angela Brazil

Illustrated by John Campbell

A CHANCE FOR RETALIATION

Contents

CHAPTER I

Honor Introduces Herself

Any new girls?"

It was Madge Summers who asked the question, seated on the right-hand corner of Maisie Talbot's bed, munching caramels. It was a very small bed, but at that moment it managed to accommodate no less than seven of Maisie's most particular friends, who were closely watching the progress of her unpacking, and discussing the latest school news, interspersed with remarks on her belongings.

Maisie extricated herself from the depths of her box, and handed a pile of stockings to Lettice, her younger sister.

"What's the use of asking me?" she replied. "Our cab only drove up half an hour ago. I feel almost new myself yet."

"So do I, and horribly in the blues too," said Pauline Reynolds. "It's always a wrench to leave home. I'm perfectly miserable for at least three days at the beginning of each term. I feel as if——"

"Oh, don't all begin to expatiate about your feelings!" broke in Chatty Burns. "We know Pauline's symptoms only too well: the first day she shows aggressively red eyes and a damp pocket-handkerchief; the second day she writes lengthy letters home, begging to be allowed to return immediately and have lessons with a private governess; the third day she wanders about, trying to get sympathy from anyone who is weak-minded enough to listen to her, till in desperation somebody drags her into the playground, and makes her have a round at hockey. That cheers her up, and she begins to think life isn't quite such a desert. By the fourth morning she has recovered her spirits, and come to the conclusion that Chessington College is a very decent kind of place; and she begins to be alarmed lest her mother, on the strength of the pathetic letter, should have decided to let her leave at once, and should have already engaged a private governess."

"You're most unsympathetic, Chatty!" said Pauline, smiling in spite of herself. "You don't know what it is to be home-sick."

"I wouldn't parade such a woebegone face, whatever might be the depths of my misery," returned Chatty briskly.

"I'm always glad to come back," declared Dorothy Arkwright. "I like school. It's fun to meet everybody again, and arrange about cricket, and the Debating Society, and the Natural History Club. There's so much going on at St. Chad's."

"No one has answered my question yet," remarked Madge Summers. "Are there any new girls?"

Chatty wriggled herself into a more comfortable position between Adeline Vaughan and Ruth Latimer.

"I think there are about a dozen altogether. Vivian Holmes says there are four at St. Bride's, three at St. Aldwyth's, two at the School House, and two at St. Hilary's. I saw one of them arriving at the same time as I did, and Miss Cavendish was gushing over another in the library; and Marian Spencer has brought a sister—she introduced her to me just now."

"But what about St. Chad's?"

"We've only one, I believe, though Flossie Taylor, the Hammond-Smiths' cousin, has moved here from St. Bride's. She was always destined for a Chaddite, you know, only there wasn't room for her till the Richardsons left."

"She's no great acquisition," said Dorothy Arkwright. "I hate girls to change their quarters. When once they start at a house, they ought to stick to it."

"Well, she wants to be with her cousins, I suppose," put in Madge Summers. "Who's our new girl?"

"I don't know. I haven't heard anything about her."

"Perhaps she hasn't arrived yet."

"Sh! Sh!" said Pauline Reynolds, squeezing Madge's arm by way of remonstrance, and pointing to the closely-drawn curtains of the cubicle at the farther end of the room. "She's here now."

"Where?"

"There, you goose!"

"What has she shut herself up like that for?"

"How should I know?"

"Perhaps she's unpacking," suggested Dorothy Arkwright.

"If she is, she'll finish it quicker than Lettice and I can," returned Maisie Talbot. "Why can't you be hanging up some of those skirts, instead of sitting staring at me? Yes, this is a whole box of Edinburgh rock, but you shan't have a single piece, any of you, unless you get off my bed at once."

"Poor old Maisie, don't grow excited!" murmured Ruth Latimer, appropriating the box and handing it round, though no one attempted to move.

"But look here! what about this new girl?" persisted Madge. "Hasn't anybody seen her?"

"No. She's been in there ever since she arrived."

"Don't talk so loud; she'll hear you."

"I don't care if she does."

"I want to know what she's doing."

"I can tell you, then," said Chatty Burns, in a whisper that was more audible by far than her ordinary voice.

"What?"

"Crying! New girls always cry, and some old ones too, if you take Pauline as a specimen."

"I'm not crying now!" protested Pauline indignantly. "And how can you tell that the new girl is?"

"I'm as certain as if I'd proved a proposition in Euclid. Why should she have drawn her curtains so closely? If she's not lying on her bed, with a clean pocket-handkerchief to her eyes, I'll give you six caramels in exchange for three peppermint creams!"

"Then you're just mistaken!" cried a voice from the end cubicle. The chintz curtain was pulled aside, and out marched a figure with so jaunty an air as to banish utterly the idea of possible homesickness or tears.

It was a girl of about fifteen, a remarkably pretty girl (so her schoolmates decided, without an instant's hesitation), and rather out of the common. She had a clear, olive complexion, a lovely colour in her cheeks, a bewitching pair of dimples, and a perfect colt's mane of thick, curly, brown hair. Perhaps her nose was a little too tip-tilted, and her mouth a trifle too wide for absolute beauty; but she showed such a nice row of even, white teeth when she laughed that one could overlook the latter deficiency. Her eyes were beyond praise, large and grey, with a dark line round the iris, and shaded by long lashes; and they were so soft, and wistful, and winning, and yet so twinkling and full of fun, that they seemed as if they could compel admiration, and make friends with their first glance. The girl walked across the room in an easy, confident fashion, and stood, with a broad smile on her face, beaming at the seven others seated on Maisie's bed.

"Why shouldn't I pull my curtains?" she asked. "If I'd been pulling faces, now, you might have had some cause for complaint. You look rather a nice set; I think I'm going to like you."

The girls were so surprised that they could only stare. It seemed reversing the usual order of things for a new-comer, who ought to be shy and confused, to be so absolutely and entirely self-possessed, and to pass judgment with such calm assurance upon these old members of St. Chad's, some of whom were already in their third year at Chessington College.

"Perhaps I'd better introduce myself," continued the stranger. "My name is Honor Fitzgerald, and I come from Kilmore, near Ballycroghan, in County Kerry."

"Then you're Irish!" gasped Chatty Burns.

"Quite right. First class for geography! County Kerry is exactly in the bottom left-hand corner of the map of Ireland. It's a more hospitable place than this is. I've been here nearly two hours, and nobody has offered me any refreshments yet. I'm simply starving!"

She looked so humorously and suggestively at the Edinburgh rock that Madge Summers promptly offered it to her, regardless of the fact that the box belonged to Maisie Talbot.

"Come along here," said Ruth Latimer, trying to make a place for the new girl on the bed by pushing the others vigorously nearer the end.

"No room unless I sit on your knee, while you get up and walk about," declared Honor. "There! I knew you would!" as Madge Summers fell with a crash on to the floor.

"Seven little schoolgirls, eating sugar sticks;
One tumbled overboard, and then there were six!"

"Thank you. I think I prefer to 'take the chair', as the dentist says. There only seems to be one in each cubicle, but as I'm the visitor——"

"Take care!" screamed Maisie. "My clean blouses!"

"What am I doing? I declare, I never saw them. There, I'll nurse them for you while I eat this delicious-looking piece of pink rock."

The new girl was so utterly different from anybody else who had ever come to St. Chad's that the others waited with curiosity to hear what she would say next.

"Well?" she enquired coolly at last. "I suppose you're thinking me over. I should like to know your opinion of me. They tell me at home that my nose turns up, and my tongue is too long. But I didn't turn up my nose at the Edinburgh rock, did I?—and as for my tongue, it fits my mouth, as a general rule, though it runs away sometimes."

"When did you come?"

"What class are you in?"

"Have you seen Miss Cavendish yet?"

"How old are you?"

"Have you been to school before?"

"Do you know anyone here?"

"Why did you come to St. Chad's?"

The questions were fired off all together from seven pairs of lips.

"One at a time, please!" returned Honor. "I'm older than I look, and younger than I seem. You mayn't believe me, yet I assure you I've only had three birthdays."

"Rubbish!" said Chatty Burns.

"It's a fact, all the same."

"But how could that be?" demanded Pauline Reynolds incredulously.

"Because I was born on the twenty-ninth of February, and I can't have a birthday except in a leap year. That accounts for anything odd there is about me; so if you find me queer, you must just say: 'She's a twenty-ninth of February girl', and make excuses for me. As for the other questions, I've never been to school before; I've seen Miss Cavendish, but I haven't heard yet what class I'm to be in; five minutes ago I didn't know anybody here, but now I know—how many are there of you?—one, two, three, four, five, six, seven, eight, nine!"

"Have you unpacked yet?" asked Maisie, returning to her box, which Lettice had been steadily emptying.

"Only about half."

"I think we had better come and help you, then."

"Better finish our own first!" grunted Lettice, for which remark she was promptly snubbed by her elder sister.

"Miss Maitland will be up at eight o'clock to look at our drawers," said Chatty Burns. "She'll expect you to have everything put away, and your coats and dresses hung in the wardrobe."

"We have to be so fearfully tidy here!" sighed Adeline Vaughan. "A warden comes round each morning, and woe betide you if you leave hairs in your brush, or have forgotten to fold your nightdress!"

"It's just as bad at St. Hilary's," said Madge.

"And worse at St. Bride's," added Ruth Latimer.

"My father wanted me to be at the School House," said Honor, "but Miss Cavendish wrote that it was full, so I was entered at St. Chad's instead."

"Yes, you generally need to have your name down for two years before you can get a vacancy at the School House," said Dorothy Arkwright. "It's the popular favourite with parents, because Miss Cavendish herself is the Head; but really, St. Chad's is far nicer. We all stand up for our own house, and I know you'll like it."

"There's the tea-bell! Come along! we must go at once," interrupted Chatty Burns.

"Won't they wait for us?" enquired Honor, beginning to wash her hands with much deliberation.

"Wait! She asks if they'll wait!" exclaimed Adeline Vaughan.

"One can see you've never been to school before!" commented Maisie Talbot. "No, you certainly haven't time to comb your hair now. You had better follow the rest of us as fast as you can."

St. Chad's could accommodate forty pupils, and Honor found a place assigned to her in the dining-hall near the end of a long table, which looked very attractive with its clean white cloth, its pretty china, and its vases of flowers in the middle. She had a good view of her schoolfellows, more than half of whom seemed of about the same age as herself, though there were tall girls, with their hair already put up, and a few younger ones who had apparently only just entered their teens. Grace was sung, and then the urns began to fill an almost ceaseless stream of cups, while plates of bread and butter circulated with much rapidity.

"We're late to-day," explained Honor's neighbour, "because the train from the North does not get in until five. Our usual tea-time is four o'clock, after games; then we have supper at half-past seven, when we've finished evening preparation. Did you bring any jam? Your hamper will be unpacked to-morrow, and the pots labelled with your name. I expect you'll find one opposite your plate at breakfast. Jam and marmalade are the only things we're allowed, except plain cakes."

Tea on the first afternoon was generally an exciting occasion at St. Chad's. There were so many greetings between old friends, so much news and such various topics to be discussed, that conversation, in a sufficiently subdued undertone, went on very brisk-ly. The girls had enjoyed their Easter holidays, but most of them seemed pleased to return to school, for the summer term was always the favourite at Chessington College.

"Have you heard who's in the Eleven?" began Madge Summers. "They've actually put in Grace Shaw, and she bowls abominably. I think it's rank favouritism on Miss Young's part. She always gives St. Hilary's a turn when she can."

"She was a Hilaryite herself," returned Adeline Vaughan. "That's the worst of having a games mistress who's been educated at the school; she's sure to show partiality for her old house."

"And yet in one way it's better, because she understands all our customs and private rules. It would be almost impossible to explain everything to a new-comer."

"What about the house team?" asked Ruth Latimer. "Is anything fixed?"

"Not yet. There's to be a practice to-morrow, and it will go by our scores."

"I shall stick to tennis," declared Pauline Reynolds. "One gets a fair chance there, at any rate, and we must keep up the credit of St. Chad's in the courts. I don't know whether we've any chance of winning the shield. I wish we could get a real champion!"

"You should see Flossie Taylor play!" burst out Edith and Claudia Hammond-Smith, who were anxious to bring their cousin forward, and to ensure her popularity among the other girls.

"I've not heard that she made any record at St. Bride's," remarked Dorothy Arkwright, who resented Flossie's removal to St. Chad's.

"She hasn't had an opportunity. She only came to school last Christmas, and it wasn't the tennis season. Wait till you see her serve!"

"Miss Young will have to be judge, not I," replied Dorothy coldly.

"Flossie is in your bedroom, Dorothy," announced Claudia. "She has the cubicle near the fireplace."

"If you're sleeping in the bed next to mine," said Flossie, eyeing Dorothy across the table with a rather patronizing air, "I sincerely hope you don't snore."

"Of course not!" responded Dorothy, in some indignation.

"At St. Bride's," continued Flossie, "one of my room-mates snored atrociously. I used to have to get up and shake her, and pull the pillow from under her head, before I could go to sleep."

"You'd better not try that on with me!"

"I would, in a minute, if you kept me awake."

"It is a shame she's not in our room," interposed Edith. "We've asked Miss Maitland to let her change with Geraldine Saunders, and I think perhaps she may. We want Flossie all to ourselves; I do hope she'll let us!"

"So do I!" retorted Dorothy feelingly. "The Hammond-Smiths are welcome to their cousin, so far as I'm concerned," she whispered to Chatty Burns; "I don't like her. She's trying to show off. Edith and Claudia are making far too much fuss over her."

"They always gush," commented Chatty. "Still, I dare say Flossie will need taking down a little."

"It would do her all the good in the world," replied Dorothy. Then, turning to the Hammond-Smiths, she remarked aloud: "There's a new girl here who may be just as good as your cousin, for anything we know. Honor Fitzgerald, do you play tennis?"

"I can play, but how you'll like it is another story," answered Honor. "We two," nodding at Flossie, "had better try a set by ourselves, and then you can choose the winner."

"I'm sure I don't care about it, thank you." Flossie's tone was supercilious.

"All right! We don't force ourselves where we're not wanted in my part of the world."

"Is that Ireland? Then I suppose your name is Biddy?"

"Certainly not!"

"I thought all Irish girls were called Biddy; are you sure you're not?"

"My name is Honor Fitzgerald."

"Really! I'm astonished it isn't Mulligan, or O'Grady."

The Hammond-Smiths giggled, and poked Effie and Blanche Lawson.

"Isn't Flossie funny?" they whispered delightedly.

"I think she's very rude," observed Dorothy Arkwright. "I call that an extremely cheap form of wit."

"Irish names are often rather peculiar," drawled Claudia Hammond-Smith.

"They're quite as good as English ones, and sometimes a great deal more ancient and aristocratic," returned Honor.

"One for Claudia, and for Flossie Taylor too!" said Dorothy to Chatty Burns.

"Paddy, for instance," interposed Flossie, who saw that the Lawsons were listening, as well as her cousins. "St. Patrick and pigs always go together, in my mind. I suppose you keep a pig in Ireland?"

"Don't answer her!" whispered Honor's neighbour. "They're only teasing you because you're new. They want to see how much you'll stand."

But poor Honor was unaccustomed as yet to schoolgirl banter, and could not abstain from replying:

"Does it matter whether we do or not?"

She spoke quietly, but there was a gleam in her eye, as if her temper were rising.

"Not in the least! I only thought all Irish people cultivated pigs."

"It's no worse than keeping a cat, or a dog."

"My dear Paddy, of course not! Still, I shouldn't care to have the creatures in the drawing-room. Take a little more bread and butter. I'm sorry we've no potatoes to offer you."

The Hammond-Smiths and the Lawsons tittered, and Dorothy Arkwright was about to state her frank opinion of their behaviour when Honor's pent-up wrath exploded.

"We don't keep pigs in the drawing-room," she exclaimed.

"There's a saying that it takes nine tailors to make a man, so if your name is Taylor you can only be the ninth part of a lady!" Then, realizing that her upraised voice had drawn upon her the attention, not only of all the girls, but also of Miss Maitland, she flushed crimson, scraped back her chair, and fled precipitately from the room.

Miss Maitland looked surprised. It was an unheard-of thing for any girl to leave the tea-table without permission. Such a breach of school decorum had surely never been committed before at St. Chad's! There was a very complete code of etiquette observed at the house, and to break one of the laws of politeness was considered an unpardonable offence.

"She's made a bad beginning," whispered Ruth Latimer to Maisie Talbot. "It's most unfortunate. It was really the fault of Flossie Taylor and the Hammond-Smiths. They needn't have teased her so."

"Still, it was silly of her to lose her temper," replied Maisie. "She stalked out of the room like a queen of tragedy. Miss Maitland can't bear girls who give way to their impulses; she despises what she calls 'early Victorian hysterics', and I quite agree with her."

"Yes, we must learn to be stoics here," said Ruth; "and as for teasing, the wisest thing is to take no notice of it."

A monitress had been dispatched to fetch Honor back, but in a short time she returned alone, and reported that she could not find her. Miss Maitland made no comment, and as the meal was now over she gave the signal of dismissal. Most of the girls went to the recreation room, but Maisie Talbot, who had not yet quite concluded her unpacking, ran straight upstairs. Noticing something move behind a curtain in the corner of the bedroom, she pulled it aside. There was Honor, sitting in a queer little heap on the floor, and rubbing her eyes in a very suggestive manner. She jumped up in a moment, however, and pretended that she was only arranging her boots.

"I'd finished tea," she remarked airily, "so I thought I might as well empty my box, and put my dresses away in my wardrobe."

"You'll have to ask Miss Maitland's leave next time, before you march out of the room, or you'll get into trouble," said Maisie. "If it weren't your first evening, you'd be expected to make a public apology. Of course, Flossie Taylor and the Hammond-Smiths were aggravating, but you should just have laughed at them, and then they'd have stopped. We don't behave like kindergarten children here."

Maisie spoke scathingly. She was a girl who had scant sympathy with what she called "babyishness", and disliked any exhibition of feeling. And, after all, she only voiced the general opinion of the school, which, by an unwritten law, had established a calm imperturbation as the height of good breeding.

"I don't care in the least what any of you think!" retorted Honor, and she hung up her skirt with such a jerk that she broke the loop.

Yet, although she spoke lightly, she evidently did care. She was very quiet indeed all the rest of the evening, and hardly spoke at recreation. Chatty Burns sat down next to her and tried to begin a conversation, but Honor answered so briefly that she very soon gave up the effort in despair, and moved away; while the other girls were so interested in their own affairs that they did not trouble to remember their new schoolfellow. At nine o'clock prayers were read, and everybody went upstairs to bed.

When the lights were out, and the room was in perfect silence, a strange, suppressed noise issued from Honor's corner. It might, of course, have been snoring; and Honor explained elaborately next morning that Irish people often have a peculiar way of breathing in their sleep—an affection from which she sometimes suffered herself.

"All the same, I don't quite believe her," confided Pauline Reynolds, who occupied the next cubicle, to Lettice Talbot, a more sympathetic character than her sister Maisie. "I know what it is to feel home-sick, and to smother one's nose in the pillow! If that wasn't sobbing, it was as like it as anything I've ever heard in my life."

CHAPTER II

Honor's Home

For a full understanding of Honor Fitzgerald we must go back a few weeks, and see her in that Irish home which was so far away and so utterly different from Chessington College. Kilmore Castle was a great, rambling, old-fashioned country house, built beside an inland creek of the sea, and sheltered by a range of hills from the wild winds of Kerry. To Honor that was the dearest and most beautiful spot in the world. She loved every inch of it—the silvery strips of water that led between bold, rocky headlands out to the broad Atlantic; the tall mountain peaks that showed so rugged an outline against the sky; the brown, peat-stained river that came brawling down from the uplands, and poured itself noisily into the creek; the wide, lonely moors, with their stretches of brilliant green grass and dark, treacherous bog pools; and the craggy cliffs that made a barrier against the ever-dashing waves, and round which thousands of sea birds flew, with harsh cries and whir of white wings.

Its situation at the end of a long peninsula made Kilmore Castle an isolated little kingdom of its own. On the shore stood a row of low, fishermen's white-washed cabins, dignified by the name of "the village"; but otherwise there was no human habitation in sight, and Ballycroghan, the market town and nearest postal, railway, and telegraph station, was ten miles off.

Trees were rarities at Kilmore; a few stunted specimens, all blown one way by the prevailing gale, grew as if huddled together for protection at the foot of the glen, but they were the exception that proved the rule; nevertheless, under the sheltering walls of the Castle Mrs. Fitzgerald had managed to acclimatize some exotic shrubs, and to cultivate quite a beautiful garden of flowers, for the temperature was uniformly mild, though the winds were boisterous. Brilliant St. Brigid's anemones, the poet's narcissus, tulips, jonquils, and hyacinths bloomed here almost as early as in the Scilly Isles, and made patches of fragrant brightness under the sitting-room windows; while in the crannies of the walls might be seen delicate maidenhair and other ferns, too tender generally to stand a winter in the open.

Born and bred in this far-away corner of the world, Honor had grown up almost a child of nature. Her whole life had been spent as much as possible out-of-doors, boating, fishing, or swimming in the creek; driving in a low-backed car over the rough Kerry roads; galloping her shaggy little pony on the moors; following the otter hounds up the river, and sharing in any sport that her father considered suitable for her age and sex. She was the only girl among five brothers, and in her mother's opinion was by far the most difficult to manage of the whole flock. All the wild Irish blood of the family seemed to have settled in her; the high spirits, the fire, the pride, the quick temper, the impatience of control, the happy-go-lucky, idle, irresponsible ways of a long line of hot-headed ancestors had skipped a generation or two, and, as if they had been bottling themselves up during the interval, had reappeared with renewed force in this particular specimen of the Fitzgerald race.

"She's more trouble than the five boys put together," her mother often declared, and her friends cordially agreed with her. Mrs. Fitzgerald herself was a mild, quiet, nervous, delicate lady, as much astonished at her lively, tempestuous daughter as a meek little hedge-sparrow would be, that had hatched a young cuckoo. Frankly, she did not understand Honor, whose strong, uncontrolled character differed so entirely from her own gentle, clinging, dependent disposition; and whose storms of grief or anger, wild fits of waywardness and equally passionate repentance, and self-willed disobedience, alternating with sudden bursts of reformation, were a constant source of worry and anxiety, and the direct opposite of her ideal of girlhood. Poor Mrs. Fitzgerald would have liked a docile, tractable daughter, who would have been content to sit beside her sofa doing fancy work, instead of riding to hounds; and who would have had more consideration for her weak state of health. She appreciated Honor's warm-hearted affection to the full, but at the same time wished she could make her realize that rough hugs, boisterous kisses, and loud tones were hardly suitable to an invalid. Suffering as she was from a painful and incurable complaint, it was sometimes impossible for her to admit Honor to her sick-room, and for weeks together the girl would hardly see her mother. It was through no lack of love that Honor had failed to give that service and tenderness which, in the circumstances, an only daughter might so fitly have rendered; it was from sheer want of thought, and general heedlessness. Some girls early acquire a sense of responsibility and care for others, but in Honor these qualities were as undeveloped as in a child of six.

Many were the governesses who had attempted to tame the young rebel, and bring her into a state of law and order, but all had been equal failures. She had learnt lessons when she felt inclined, and left them undone when she was idle; and she had managed to make life in the schoolroom such a purgatory that it had been difficult to persuade any teacher to stay long at the Castle, and cope with so thankless a task as her education.

It had been of little use to complain to her father, the only person in the world whose authority she recognized; he was proud of his handsome daughter, and, except when her temper crossed his own, was apt to indulge her in most of her whims. Matters had at last, however, come to a crisis. An act of more than usual assumption on Honor's part had aroused Major Fitzgerald's utmost indignation, and had caused him suddenly to decide that she was spoiling at home, and that the only possible solution of the difficulty was to dispatch her to school as soon as the necessary arrangements could be made for her departure.

The incident that led to this resolution was very characteristic of Honor's headstrong, impulsive nature. She was passionately fond of horses, and for some time had been anxious to possess a new pony. It was not that she loved Pixie, her former favourite, any the less; but he was growing old, and was now scarcely able to take a fence, or carry her in mad career over the moors, being only fit for a sober trot on the high road, or to draw her mother's Bath chair round the garden. To obtain a strong, well-bred, fiery substitute for Pixie was the summit of Honor's ambition. One day, when she was with her father at Ballycroghan, she saw exactly the realization of her ideal. It was a small black cob, which showed a trace of Arab blood in its arching neck, slender limbs, and easy, springy motion. Though its bright eyes proved its high spirit, it was nevertheless as gentle as a lamb, and well accustomed to carrying a lady. Its owner, a local horse-dealer, was anxious to sell it, and pressed Major Fitzgerald to take it as a bargain. Honor simply fell in love with it on the spot. She ascertained that its name was Firefly, and begged and besought her father to buy it for her. But on this occasion he would not yield, even to her utmost coaxing. He did not wish to keep another pony in the stable, and he considered the price asked was excessive, and entirely beyond the present limits of his purse.

"No, Honor, it can't be done," he said. "You must be content with poor old Pixie. I have quite enough expenses just now, without running into such an extravagance."

"But couldn't I have it instead of something else?" pleaded Honor.

"There's nothing we could knock off, dear child," replied her father.

"I could do without a governess," suggested Honor hopefully. "I'd set myself my own lessons, and learn them too. Oh, Daddy, darling, if we gave up Miss Bury, wouldn't you have money enough to buy Firefly?"

Major Fitzgerald laughed in spite of himself.

"I consider Miss Bury a necessity, and not a luxury," he replied. "A governess is the very last person we could dispense with. I should like to see you setting your own lessons! Remarkably short and easy ones they would be! No, little woman, I'm afraid Firefly is an impossibility, and you must just try to forget his existence."

Unfortunately, that was exactly what Honor could not do. She thought continually about the beautiful black cob, and the more she dwelt on her disappointment the more keenly she felt it. She considered, most unreasonably, that her governess was the alternative of the pony, and that if she were without the one she might possibly acquire the other. Her behaviour had never been exemplary, but on the strength of this grievance she grew so unruly, so disrespectful, and so absolutely unmanageable that Miss Bury at length refused to teach her any longer, and, after an interview with Major Fitzgerald in the library, packed her boxes and returned home to England.

Honor viewed her exodus with keen delight. It seemed the removal of an obstacle to her plan. She went in to luncheon determined to broach once more the subject of Firefly, hoping this time to meet with better success. She saw at once, however, from her father's face, that he was not in a suitable mood to grant her any favour. He was much annoyed at the governess's departure, for which he had the justice to blame Honor alone; and he was worried with business matters.

"That tiresome agent has not sent the telegram I expected," he announced. "I shall be obliged to go over to Cork, to consult my solicitor. Tell Murphy to have the trap ready by two o'clock, and let Holmes pack my bag. I shall probably be away until Friday evening."

As soon as her father had started for the station, Honor sauntered out in the direction of the stables. It was one of her mother's bad days. Mrs. Fitzgerald was confined to her room, therefore Honor, released from Miss Bury's authority, felt herself her own mistress. Finding Fergus, the groom, she ordered him to saddle Pixie, and make ready to accompany her on a ride. Fergus was devoted to "Miss Honor", and would never have dreamt of disputing any command she might give him; before three o'clock, therefore, her pony was at the door, and, dressed in her neat blue habit, she was ambling away in the direction of Ballycroghan. It was a leisurely progress, for poor Pixie's gait was slow, in spite of his best endeavours, and Honor loved him too well to urge him hard.

She was determined to call at the horse-dealer's, and to ascertain if Firefly were still for sale. Perhaps, when her father returned home, she might catch him at a favourable moment, and be able to cajole him into changing his mind and buying the cob. Mr. O'Connor, the horse-dealer, lived at a large farm on the way to the town, and, to Honor's intense delight, the first object that met her eyes on approaching the house was Firefly, feeding demurely in a paddock to the left of the road. By an equally lucky chance Mr. O'Connor happened to be at home, and came hurrying out at once when he saw "one of the quality", as he expressed it, drawing bridle at his door.

"Good afternoon! I see you still have the black cob," began Honor eagerly.

"Yes, missy," replied the horse-dealer, "and I was thinking of sending a message to your father about him this very day. It's the good fortune to see you here! I've had a man over from Limerick who's anxious to take him—a tradesman who'd run him in a light cart—but I didn't close the bargain at once. I said to my wife: 'Firefly is too good a breed to carry out groceries. I'd rather be for selling him to the Castle. Miss Fitzgerald took the fancy for him, and I'll not be parting with him till I've had word again from the Major.' Maybe his honour will be wanting him, after all? But sure I must know at once, for the Limerick man will be here at noon to-morrow, and I've promised to tell him one way or another."

"Could you possibly wait until Saturday?" asked Honor.

The dealer shook his head.

"I can't afford to miss a sale," he replied. "I've had the cob on my hands for some time; it's just eating its head off, and it's anxious I am to get rid of it."

Honor was in a fever of excitement. Firefly, so spirited and so aristocratic, whose delicately shaped limbs looked only fit for leaping brooks, or cantering over the short grass on the uplands, to be sold to a tradesman, and to run between the shafts of a cart that delivered groceries! It seemed a degradation and an outrage. She could not dream of allowing it; she must save him at any cost from such a fate.

"Must you absolutely have an answer to-day?" she asked.

"Yes, missy. I fear I couldn't put off Sullivan any longer than noon to-morrow. He's a touchy man, and ready to carry his business elsewhere."

"Very well, then, that settles the matter. We will take the cob. You may send him over to the Castle this evening."

Honor spoke in such a high-handed manner that the dealer never guessed she was acting on her own authority. As she had made a special visit to the farm, accompanied by her groom, he imagined she must have been entrusted by Major Fitzgerald with full powers to buy the pony if she wished.

"Many thanks to you, missy! It's the fine mistress you'll make for Firefly. My respects to his honour, and the price shall be the same as I was asking him before."

The price! Honor had quite forgotten that. Weighed against Firefly's possible future, it had seemed an unimportant detail. She remembered now, however, that her father had considered it extravagant, and declared he could not afford it. The thought was sufficient to check her joy suddenly, and to send her home in a sober frame of mind that was well justified by the sequel.

Major Fitzgerald's wrath, when he arrived on the Friday and found the black cob installed in the stable, was more serious than his daughter had ever experienced before.

"It was a piece of unwarranted presumption!" he declared. "I shall not allow you to keep the pony. It must be sent back to O'Connor's, and resold at the first opportunity. As for you, the sooner you are packed off to school the better. We have indulged you too much at home, and it is time indeed that you learnt to submit to some kind of discipline."

The proposal to send her away to school was a terrible blow to Honor. At first she appealed to her mother, begging her to plead with her father and try to persuade him to alter his resolution. But Mrs. Fitzgerald, while regretting to part with her troublesome daughter, was so convinced of the wisdom of the proceeding that, instead of interceding, she applauded her husband's decision.

"I can't ever like England!" sobbed Honor. "I'd rather have our mountains and lakes and bogs than all the grand streets and houses. I'm Irish to the core, and I don't believe any school over

HONOR CONCLUDES THE PURCHASE OF FIREFLY

the water can change me. There's no place in the world like Kilmore. I love even the cabins, and the peat fires, and the pigs, and the potatoes! I shan't forget a single stick or stone of it, and I shall never know a moment's happiness till I'm home again."

After considerable hesitation, and the examination of a large number of prospectuses, Major and Mrs. Fitzgerald had determined to send Honor to Chessington College. It had a wide and well-deserved reputation, and Miss Cavendish, the principal, was understood to give much individual attention to the characters and dispositions of her pupils. Added to this, it was situated within a few miles of the Naval Preparatory School where Dermot, Honor's younger brother, had been for the last two years; so that they knew from experience that the neighbourhood was bracing and healthy.

"It's a comfort, at any rate, that I shall be near Dermot," said Honor, as she sat watching while her mother superintended the maid who was packing her boxes.

"I'm afraid you won't see much of him, dear, during term-time," replied Mrs. Fitzgerald. "He will not be able to visit you, I'm sure; neither will Miss Cavendish allow you to go out with him."

"Why not?" demanded Honor.

"Because it would be against the rules."

"Then the rules are absurd, and I shan't keep them."

"Honor! Honor! Don't speak like that! You have run wild here, but at Chessington College you will be obliged to fall in with the ordinary regulations."

"They'll have hard work to tame me, Mother!" laughed Honor, jumping up and dancing a little impromptu jig between the boxes. "I don't want to go, but since I must, I mean to get any enjoyment I can out of it. After all, perhaps it may be rather fun. It's deadly dull here sometimes, when the boys are at school, and Father is busy or away."

Mrs. Fitzgerald sighed. In her delicate health she could scarcely expect to be a companion for Honor, yet when she thought of how few years might be left them together, the parting seemed bitter, and she was hurt that her only daughter would evidently miss her so little. Young folks often say cruel things from mere thoughtlessness, and unintentionally grieve those who love them. In after years Honor would keenly regret her tactless speech, and blame herself that she had not spent more hours in trying to be a comfort, instead of a care; but for the present, though she noticed the look of disappointment that passed over the sensitive face, she did not fully realize its cause, and the words that might have healed the wound went unspoken.

At length the preparations were concluded, and the time had almost arrived to bid farewell to Kilmore Castle and the sur-rounding demesne. Honor's friends in the village mourned her approaching departure with characteristic Irish grief.

"Miss Honor, darlint, it's meself that will be hungerin' for a sight of yez!" cried old Mary O'Grady, standing at the doorway of her thatched cabin, from which the blue peat smoke issued like a thin mist.

"And it's grand news entoirely they'll be afther tellin' me too, that ye're lavin' the Castle, and goin' over the seas!" put in Biddy Macarthy, a next-door neighbour of Mary's. "It's fine to think of all the iligant things ye'll be seein' now!"

"Bless your bright eyes, it's many a sad heart ye'll lave behind yez!" added Pat Conolly, the oldest tenant on the estate.

"England can never compare with dear Ireland, in my opin-ion," replied Honor, with a choke in her voice. "There's no spot so sweet as Kilmore, and all the while I'm away I shall be wishing myself back in the 'ould counthree'!"

"Will ye be despisin' this bit of a present, Miss Honor?" said old Mary, producing a cardboard box, from which, out of many folds of tissue paper, she proudly displayed a large bunch of imitation four-leaved shamrock. "My grandson Micky brought it for me all the way from Dublin city, and I've kept it fine and new in its pa-pers. Sure, I know it's not worthy of offerin' to a young lady like yourself, but I'll take it kindly if ye'll deign to accept it."

"Of course I'll accept it!" returned Honor heartily. "It's very kind of you to give it to me. It shall go to school with me, as a remem-brance of Ireland, and of you all."

"The four-leaved shamrock brings good luck to its wearer, mavourneen; may it bring it to you! And whenever ye look at the little green leaves, give a thought to the true hearts that will be ay wishin' ye a speedy return."

The last day came all too soon, and Mrs. Fitzgerald, with tears in her eyes, stood at her window, watching the disappearing carriage in which Honor sat by her father's side, waving an energetic good-bye.

"Surely," she said to herself, "school will have the influence that we expect! The general atmosphere of law and order, the well-ar-ranged rules, the esprit de corps and strict discipline of the games, all cannot fail to have their effect; and among so large a number of companions, and in the midst of so many new and absorbing interests, my wild bird will find her wings clipped, and will settle down sensibly and peaceably among the others."

CHAPTER III

The Wearing of the Green

C hessington College stood on a breezy slope midway between the hills and the sea, and about a mile from the rising watering-place of Dunscar. It was a famous spot for a school, as the fresh winds coming either from the uplands or from the wide expanse of channel were sufficient to blow away all chance of germs, and to ensure a thoroughly wholesome and bracing atmosphere. The College prided itself upon its record of health; Miss Cavendish considered no other girls were so straight and well-grown as hers, with such bright eyes, such clear skins, and such blooming cheeks. Ventilation, sea baths, and suitable diet were her three watchwords, and thanks to them the sanatorium at the farther side of the shrubbery scarcely ever opened its doors to receive a patient, while the hospital nurse who was retained in case of emergencies found her position a sinecure.

The buildings were modern and up-to-date, with all the latest appliances and improvements. They were provided with steam heat and electric light; and the gymnasium, chemical laboratory, and practical demonstration kitchen were on the very newest of educational lines. The school covered a large space, and was built in the form of a square. In the middle was a great, gravelled quadrangle, where hockey could be practised on days when the fields were too wet for playing. At one end stood the big lecture-hall, the chapel, the library, and the various classrooms, the whole surmounted by a handsome clock tower; while opposite was the School House, where Miss Cavendish herself presided over a chosen fifty of her two hundred pupils. The two sides of the square were occupied by four houses, named respectively St. Aldwyth's, St. Hilary's, St. Chad's, and St. Bride's, each being in charge of a mistress, and capable of accommodating from thirty to forty girls. Though the whole school met together every day for lessons, the members of each different house resembled a separate family, and were keenly anxious to maintain the honour of their particular establishment. Miss Cavendish did not wish to excite rivalry, yet she thought a spirit of friendly emulation was on the whole salutary, and encouraged matches between the various house teams, or competitions among the choral and debating societies. The rules for all were exactly similar. Every morning, at a quarter to seven, a clanging bell rang in the passages for a sufficient length of time to disturb even the soundest of slumbers; breakfast was at half-past seven, and at half-past eight everybody was due in chapel for a short service; lectures and classes occupied the morning from nine till one, and the afternoon was devoted to games; tea was at four, and supper at half-past seven, with preparation in between; and after that hour came sewing and recreation, until bedtime. It was a well-arranged and reasonable division of time, calculated to include right proportions of work and play. Mens sana in corpore sano was Miss Cavendish's favourite motto, and the clean bill of health, the successes in examinations, and the high moral tone that prevailed throughout pointed to the fulfilment of her ideal. Most of the girls were thoroughly happy at Chessington College, and, though it is in girl nature to grumble at rules and lessons, there was scarcely one who would have cared to leave it if she had been given the opportunity.

It was to this new, interesting, and exciting world of school that Honor unclosed her eyes on the morning after her arrival. She opened them sleepily, and, I regret to say, promptly shut them again, and turned over comfortably in bed, regardless of the vigorous bell that was delivering its warning in the passage. Punctuality had not been counted a cardinal virtue at Kilmore Castle, and she saw no special necessity for rising until she felt inclined. She had just dropped off again into a delicious doze when once more her peace was rudely disturbed. The curtain of her cubicle was drawn back, and three lively faces made their appearance.

"Look here! Don't you know it's time to get up?" said Maisie Talbot, administering a vigorous poke that would have roused the Seven Sleepers of legendary lore, and caused even Honor to yawn.

"You'll be fined a penny if you're late for breakfast," added Lettice, "and that's a very unsatisfactory way of disposing of one's pocket-money."

"And makes Miss Maitland particularly irate," said Pauline Reynolds.

"Honor Fitzgerald! do you intend to get up, or do you not? Because if you don't, we shall have to try 'cold pig'!" Then, as there were no signs of movement, Lettice carried out her threat by dabbing a wet sponge full in Honor's face, while at the same moment

Maisie wrenched back the bed-clothes with a relentless hand.

"We're doing you a real kindness, so you needn't be cross, Miss Paddy Pepper-box!" said Lettice. "Just wait till you've seen Miss Maitland scowl at a late-comer, and you'll give us a vote of thanks."

"I'm not cross," said Honor, laughing in spite of the violation of her slumbers. Lettice spoke so merrily, it was impossible to take offence, even at the nickname. "But I think you use rather summary measures. The sponge was horribly cold and nasty."

"It's the only way to get people to bestir themselves," said Lettice complacently. "I've had experience with sleepy room-mates before."

"We always try the water cure at St. Chad's," added Maisie. "We've given you quite mild treatment, as it was a first case; we might have used your bedroom jug, instead of a sponge."

Owing to her companions' efforts, Honor was in time for breakfast—a fortunate circumstance for her, as, after the episode at the tea-table on the preceding evening, her house-mistress would not have been ready to overlook any deficiency in punctuality.

There was always a short recess between breakfast and chapel, which the girls called a "breathing space", and during which they could revise exercises, sharpen lead pencils, and take a last peep at lessons. This morning everybody seemed to be assembling in the dressing-room for this brief interval, and there Honor repaired with the others.

"I hear you've been put in the Lower Third, Paddy," said Lettice Talbot. "Vivian Holmes told me so just now. It's my form. Maisie and Pauline are in it too."

"Isn't Maisie above you?" asked Honor, looking at the sisters, the elder of whom overtopped the younger by nearly a head. "She is in inches, at any rate."

"I'm only a year older than Lettice, though I am so much taller," explained Maisie. "I suppose I ought to be in a higher form, but she always manages to catch me up. I make up my mind every term I'm going to win a double remove and leave her behind, yet somehow it never happens to come off. I'm much better at cricket and hockey than at French and algebra. But after all, it's rather convenient to have her in the same form: she's sure to remember what the lesson is when I forget, and I can borrow her books if I lose my own."

"Yes, I have to work for both," complained Lettice. "Maisie won't even copy her exercise questions; she always relies on me."

Maisie certainly made her younger sister useful. She expected her to fetch and carry, tidy both their cubicles, and generally maintain a very subservient and inferior position. On the other hand, though she tyrannized over Lettice herself, she would not allow anybody else to do so, and was ready to take her part and fight her battles against the whole school.

"I'm glad we're in the same class," remarked Honor, with an approving glance at Lettice's round, smiling face. "Perhaps I shall ask you to copy the exercise questions too. My memory is not particularly good where lessons are concerned. Who else is in the Lower Third?"

"Ruth Latimer, my greatest chum."

"We allow ourselves chums," put in Maisie, "but we're not at all romantic at Chessington. We don't swear eternal friendships, and exchange locks of hair, and walk about the College with our arms clasped round each other's necks, and write each other sentimental notes, with 'sweetest' and 'darling' and 'fondest love' in them. That's what Miss Maitland calls 'early Victorian'. We're very matter of fact here. Still, when we choose a chum we generally stick to her, and don't go in for all that nonsense of 'getting out of friends', or not speaking, as they do at some schools."

Honor was about to ask more questions, but at that moment Vivian Holmes, the monitress and head girl of the house, came bustling into the room.

"You haven't got your sailor and jersey yet, Honor Fitzgerald," she said. "Miss Maitland asked me to give them to you. Here they are, both marked with your name, so that they needn't be mixed up with anybody else's. You're to take this hook, and this compartment for your shoes, and this locker to keep your books in. I've put labels on them all."

Honor looked without enthusiasm at the knitted woollen coat, and with marked disfavour at the white sailor hat, with its band of orange ribbon.

"I can't wear that!" she ejaculated.

"Why not?" enquired Vivian, in surprise.

"There's an orange band round it."

"Orange is the St. Chad's colour," explained Vivian. "We all have exactly the same hats at Chessington, but each house has its own special ribbon—blue for the School House, pink for St. Aldwyth's, scarlet for St. Hilary's, and violet for St. Bride's. I thought you knew that already."

"If I had, I'd have insisted upon going to another house," declared Honor tragically. "You ask me to wear orange? Why, the very name of 'Orangeman' sets my teeth on edge. I'm a Nationalist to the last drop of my blood; we all are, down in Kerry."

Vivian smiled.

"Don't be absurd!" she said, in rather an off-hand manner. "Our hats have nothing whatever to do with politics. Here are two long pins, but if you prefer an elastic you can stitch one on," and without deigning to argue further she walked away.

Honor stood turning the hat round and round, with a very queer expression on her face. She was a devoted daughter of Erin. Her country's former glories and the possible brilliance of its future as a separate kingdom could always provoke her wildest enthusiasm; to be asked, therefore, to don the colour which in her native land stood as the symbol of the union with England, and for direct opposition to national independence, seemed to her little short of an insult to her dear Emerald Isle. There were still five minutes left before she need start for chapel, so, making up her mind suddenly, she rushed upstairs to her bedroom. She would show these Saxons that she was a true Celt! They might compel her to wear their emblem of bondage, but it should be with an addition that would proclaim her patriotic sentiments to the world.

Hurriedly hunting in her top drawer, she produced a yard of vivid green ribbon and the bunch of imitation shamrock that old Mary O'Grady had given her as a parting present. Then she set to work on a piece of amateur millinery. There was little time to use needle and thread, but with the aid of pins she managed to twist the ribbon into several loops, and to fasten the shamrock conspicuously in front. She looked at the result of her labours with great approval.

"One could almost imagine it was St. Patrick's Day," she said to herself. "Nobody could possibly mistake me now for a Unionist. I'm labelled 'Home Rule' as plainly as can be." Then, hastily pinning on her hat before the mirror, she ran downstairs, humming under her breath:

"So we'll bide our time; our banner yet
And motto shall be seen,
And voices shout the chorus out,
'The Wearin' o' the Green'!"

The girls at Chessington College were all dressed exactly alike, in a uniform costume of blue serge skirts, with blue or white cotton blouses for summer, and flannel ones for winter. On Sundays they wore white serge coats and skirts, and for evenings white muslin or nuns' veiling. They were allowed a little latitude in the way of embroideries with respect to best frocks, but their everyday, ordinary clothes were required to be of the school pattern, with the addition of sailor hats and knitted coats, for use in running across the quadrangle on wet or cold days. Miss Cavendish considered that this rule encouraged simplicity, and provided against any undue extravagance in the matter of dress. She did not allow rings or bracelets to be worn, and the sole vanity permitted to the girls was in the choice of their hair ribbons.

Punctually at twenty-five minutes past eight each morning the bell in the little chapel began to give warning, and by half-past every member of the school was expected to have taken her seat, and to be ready for the short service held there daily by the senior curate of the parish church at Dunscar. In twos and threes and small groups the girls came hurrying in answer to the call of the tinkling bell. Though they laughed and talked as they ran across the quadrangle, they sobered down as they neared the door, and, each taking a Prayer Book from a pile laid ready in the porch, passed silently and reverently into the chapel. Every house had its own special rows of seats, and the sailor hats that mingled like a kaleidoscope in the grounds were here divided into their several sets of colours, though sometimes varied by a gleam of ruby or amber falling from the stained-glass windows above. The singing was musical and the responses hearty, while into his five minutes' explanation of the lesson for the day the clergyman generally managed to compress much helpful thought, sending away some, at least, of his hearers braced up for the duties that awaited them.

On this particular morning anyone accustomed to the ordinary atmosphere of the place might have been aware that something of an unusual character was in the air.

There was an undercurrent of unrest, a turning of heads, a subdued rustling, even an occasional whisper; and the head mistress, realizing at last that some outside cause must be distracting the minds of her pupils, glanced up, and, following the direction of all eyes, saw a sight that filled her with unfeigned astonishment. Among the neat rows of orange-banded sailor hats in the benches marked "St. Chad's" was one trimmed with large and obtrusive knots of emerald-green ribbon, which drooped over the brim, while a bunch of imitation shamrock finished the front. It seemed to stand out so conspicuously from its fellows that it resembled a succulent palm tree growing in the midst of a sandy desert, and could not fail to attract the attention of the whole school. How such an irregularity had crept in amongst the uniforms of the college Miss Cavendish could not comprehend; it must form the subject of an after enquiry, and in the meantime, stilling with a reproachful glance a faint whisper in her vicinity, she joined in the singing of a psalm with her usual clear intonation. When the service was over, however, and the girls began to file away in orderly line, she spoke a few, rapid words to a monitress, who at once passed quickly out by a side door.

As the extraordinary green hat made its appearance in the quadrangle it was greeted with quite a buzz of excitement by the girls assembled outside. Only a few of them, comparatively, knew Honor by sight, and the rest were asking who she was, and to which house she belonged. The common feeling was distinctly unfavourable. Apart from the unseemliness of such an exhibition in a sacred place, new girls were not expected to make themselves conspicuous, or to introduce innovations; either was considered an impertinence on their part: so the general verdict was that Honor had done a dreadful thing, and public opinion was dead against her. She, however, held up her head as proudly as though her absurd hat had been the latest creation from Bond Street.

"It's a tribute to my native land!" she said airily, in response to a chorus of questions. "Sorry you don't like it, but it's my first attempt at hat-trimming, and I flattered myself it wasn't bad for a beginner. St. Patrick for ever! I made up my mind before I started that I'd keep up the credit of the shamrock on this side of the water, and I've done my best. Hurrah for old Ireland!" Then, as if her feelings were absolutely too much for her, she took her skirt in her hands, and began to dance an old-fashioned Kerry hornpipe, humming a lively Irish tune to supply the music.

The girls stared in amazement at the mad performance. "She's showing off!" declared some, but others laughed, and watched with a kind of fascination, for the dance was striking and original, and the movements were unusually graceful.

Honor's triumph, however, was short-lived. Vivian Holmes forced her way through the crowd, and, laying her hand on the shoulder of the obstreperous new-comer, told her to report herself at once in Miss Cavendish's study. The lookers-on scuttled away to their classes without being told; they were half-ashamed of having taken so much notice of a new girl. Lettice Talbot, turning round, caught a glimpse of Honor walking blithely away, with a jaunty smile on her face.

"As if a visit to the head mistress meant nothing at all!" she gasped.

"She'll soon find out her mistake," replied Ruth Latimer grimly. "Miss Cavendish can reduce one to a quaking jelly when she feels inclined."

AN INTERVIEW WITH MISS CAVENDISH

Honor was in one of her wildest, most reckless moods, and the prospect of a passage of arms with the principal of the College was as the call of battle to a knight of old. In her conflicts with her governesses at home she had invariably come off best, and it pleased her to think she had now the opportunity of trying her will in opposition to that of the ruler of this little kingdom.

Miss Cavendish's study was a beautiful and unusual room. It was built in accordance with an old-world design, and in shape resembled an ancient chapter-house. The richly carved chimney-piece, the dark panelling of the walls, and the straight-backed oak chairs helped to carry out the prevailing note of mediaevalism, which was further enhanced by a large, stained-glass window, filled with figures of saints, that faced the doorway. To enter was like going into the peace and serenity of some old cathedral, and, notwithstanding her defiant frame of mind, a feeling of something akin to reverence crept over Honor as she crossed the threshold. Her impressionable Celtic temperament could not fail to be influenced by outward surroundings: she had a great love of the beautiful, and this room satisfied her æsthetic tastes.

The head mistress was standing beside the hearth, which, though devoid of fire at this season of the year, was piled up with newly cut logs. In her long, clinging black dress, the light from the halo of St. Aldwyth in the window falling on her regular Greek features, and touching with a ruddier gleam the pale gold of her rippling hair, Miss Cavendish looked an imposing and commanding figure. Born of a good family, the daughter of a high dignitary of the Church, she was by nature a student, and after a brilliant career at Girton she had for a time devoted herself to scientific research, arousing much interest by her clever articles in various periodicals; but feeling that her true vocation was teaching, she had turned her attention to education, and, gaining a reputation in the scholastic world, had in course of time been elected as the principal of Chessington College, a post which she filled with dignity, and greatly to the satisfaction of both governors and parents. Not a remarkably tender woman, she was perhaps more respected than loved by her pupils; but she had great powers of administration, and managed to impress upon her girls a strict sense of duty and responsibility, a love of work, a fine perception of honour, and a desire to keep up the high tone and prestige of the school.

She turned her clear, cold blue eyes on Honor, as the latter entered the room, with a scrutinizing gaze, so comprehensive and so full of authority that, despite her intention of showing a bold front, the girl involuntarily quailed.

"Come here, Honor Fitzgerald," began Miss Cavendish, in a calm, measured tone. "I wish you to explain to me why you have taken it upon yourself to alter the costume which, you are well aware, is obligatory for all attending the College."

"I can't wear orange," replied Honor, plucking up her courage for the battle; "it's against my principles."

"There are right principles and wrong principles; we will decide presently to which class yours belong. On what grounds do you raise your objection?"

"I'm Irish," said Honor briefly, "so I prefer green."

"That is no reason. We have many nationalities here, and do you imagine that every girl can be permitted to carry out her individual taste? Tell me why you suppose such a rule was framed."

"I don't know," returned Honor rebelliously.

"Then you must think, for I require an answer."

Honor stared at the fireplace, at the bookcase, with its richly bound volumes; at the window, where the red robe of St. Hilary made such a glorious spot of colour; at the table, covered with books and papers; and finally her glance went back to the head mistress, whose eyes were still fixed on her with that steady, embarrassing gaze.

"Was it to make everybody look alike?" she replied at last, almost as if the words were dragged from her lips.

"Exactly! Then, to return to my original question, why, knowing this fact, did you presume to break the rule?"

Honor was again silent. Somehow her intended bravery seemed to desert her.

"I met your father, Major Fitzgerald, yesterday," continued Miss Cavendish. "I understand that he held a command in the Royal Munster Fusiliers, and did splendid service in the Boer War. Kindly tell me what explanation he would have given to his general if he had appeared at church parade minus his uniform."

"Oh, but he wouldn't have done that!" exclaimed Honor in horror.

"Why not?"

"Why! because he is a soldier. How could he? The uniform is part of the service."

"And what is the first duty of a soldier?"

"To obey orders," answered Honor, with a spark of apprehension in her eyes.

"You are right. Now, what would happen to a regiment if each individual, instead of obeying his superior officer, were to follow his own inclinations?"

"It would go to pieces."

"And what occurs when a soldier commits any breach of regulations?"

"He is court-martialled and punished."

"Is that just?"

"Yes."

"But why?"

"Oh, because—because—it's the Army, and they must! There couldn't be any discipline without."

"Exactly! You are an officer's daughter, and you evidently appreciate the vast importance of good discipline. Now, we are a little army here. Every girl, as a member of this community, is bound to preserve its rules, which have been wisely framed, and deserve to be faithfully kept. You have been guilty of a very grave breach of our regulations, and by your own showing you merit punishment. Do you consider this to be just?"

"Yes," returned Honor, meeting the head mistress's look firmly.

"We have an esprit de corps at the College," continued Miss Cavendish, "which makes each girl anxious to keep up the credit and prestige of the school. When you have been here a short time, and have learnt the tone of the place, I believe and trust that you will be truly ashamed of the remembrance of your appearance in chapel this morning. It is for this reason I shall not punish you, though you have yourself acknowledged that punishment would be only an act of justice. As for the matter of principle to which you referred, so far from advancing the good fame of your country, you were bringing it into disrepute. If you imagine it was a particularly patriotic deed to flaunt the shamrock in a wrong place you are much mistaken. We have had Irish girls here before, and I have always been able to rely upon them for the maintenance of our high standard. You may go now, Honor, and remove that foolish trimming from your hat; and remember that, as you have been christened 'Honor', I shall expect you to live up to your name."

Honor left the room more subdued than she would have cared to acknowledge. The calm, well-balanced arguments had completely disarmed her. She had entered in a reckless mood, almost anxious to be scolded, that she might have the chance of showing how little she cared; and now, for perhaps the first time in her life, she had been compelled to think seriously and sensibly upon a subject.

Very few teachers would have taken the trouble to reason thus

with a pupil, but Miss Cavendish had her special method of education, and believed in paying particular attention to each girl's
individuality. "Different plants require different cultivation, if
you are to obtain good results," was one of her axioms. "You cannot successfully grow roses and carnations with the same treatment." She had seen at once, partly from her own observation and
partly as the result of a talk with Major Fitzgerald, that Honor
was an unusual and difficult character; and she wished to obtain
a hold over the girl's mind from the very outset. It was part of
her system to train her pupils to keep rules rather from a recognition of their justice and value than from a fear of punishment;
therefore she regarded the ten minutes spent in the study as, not
wasted time, but an opportunity of sowing good seed on hitherto
neglected ground.

Vivian Holmes was waiting for Honor outside the door of the
study. After conducting her to the school dressing-room, she produced a pair of scissors and ripped the offending green trimming
from the hat in stony silence.

"May I keep them?" Honor ventured to ask, for it went to her
heart to see her bunch of cherished shamrock torn ruthlessly from
its place and flung aside.

"As you like," replied Vivian, "so long as they are not seen here
again." Then, with a look of utterly crushing scorn, she burst out:
"You needn't think that what you have done is at all clever. It's
not the place of a new girl to show off in this way, and you'll gain
nothing by it. I am responsible for St. Chad's, and I don't mean to
have this kind of nonsense going on there; so please understand,
Honor Fitzgerald, that if you give any more trouble, you may expect to find yourself thoroughly well sat upon!"

CHAPTER IV

Janie's Charge

The four-leaved shamrock having so far belied its reputation, and brought bad luck instead of good upon its wearer, Honor put it away in her drawer, with the resolve not to test its powers again until she was back in her own Emerald Isle, where, perhaps, it could exercise its magic more freely than in the land of the stranger.

Her first day at school was satisfactory, in spite of its bad beginning. She took her place in her new class, and made the acquaintance of Miss Farrar, her Form mistress, and all the seventeen girls who composed the Lower Third Form.

After the quiet and solitude of Kilmore Castle, to be at Chessington College seemed like plunging into the world. It was almost bewildering to meet so many companions, all of whom were busily occupied with employments into which she had not yet been initiated. It was an especially fresh experience for Honor to belong to a class, instead of learning from a private governess, and she much appreciated the change. It interested her to watch the faces of her schoolfellows, and to listen to their recitations, or their replies to Miss Farrar's questions. The strict discipline of the place astonished her: the ready answers, the total lack of whispering, the way in which each girl sat straight at her desk, giving her whole attention to the subject in hand; the prompt obedience, even the orderly manner of filing out of the room for lunch, all were as unusual as they were amazing to one who had hitherto behaved as she liked during lessons. She felt for the first time that she was a unit in a large community, and began to have some dim perception of that esprit de corps to which Miss Cavendish had referred during their interview in the study.

In spite of her previous laziness and neglect of work, Honor was a very bright girl, and she contrived even in that first morning to satisfy Miss Farrar that she was capable of doing well if she wished. Perhaps, after all, the four-leaved shamrock had sent her a little luck, for she happened to remember a date which the rest of the Form had forgotten, and won corresponding credit in consequence. When one o'clock arrived she arranged her new textbooks and notebooks in the desk that had been allotted to her next to Lettice Talbot.

"Did you get into a fearful scrape with Miss Cavendish, Paddy?" whispered the latter eagerly. "Do tell me about it!"

But Honor pursed up her mouth and looked inscrutable. She was unwilling to divulge what had passed in the study, and Lettice's curiosity had perforce to go unsatisfied.

On her arrival at St. Chad's Honor had been given a spare cubicle in the bedroom occupied by the Talbots and Pauline Reynolds. On the following afternoon, however, Miss Maitland sent for Janie Henderson, a girl of nearly sixteen, and informed her that a fresh arrangement had been made.

"I am going to put you and Honor Fitzgerald together in the room over the porch," she said. "I hope that you will get on nicely, and become friends. I want you, Janie, to have a good influence over Honor, and help her to keep school rules. She does not yet know our St. Chad's standards, and has very much to learn. I give her into your charge because I am sure you are conscientious, and will try your best to make her wish to improve and turn out a worthy Chaddite. You may carry your things into your new quarters during recreation-time."

"Yes, Miss Maitland," answered Janie, with due respect. She dared not dispute the mistress's orders, but inwardly she was anything but pleased. She did not wish to leave her present cubicle, and looked with dismay at the prospect of having to share a bedroom with this wild Irish girl, towards whom as yet she certainly felt no attraction.

Janie Henderson had a painfully shy and reserved disposition. Hitherto she had made no friends, invited no confidences, and "kept herself to herself" at St. Chad's. She was seldom seen walking with a companion, and during recreation generally buried herself in a book. Slight, pale, and narrow-chested, her constitution was not robust; and though a year and a half at Chessington College had already worked a wonderful improvement, she was still far below the ordinary average of good health. She was a quiet, mouse-like girl, who seldom obtruded herself, or took any prominent part in the life of St. Chad's—a girl who was continually in the background, and passed almost unnoticed among her schoolfellows. She had little self-confidence and a sensitive dread of being laughed at, so for this reason she rarely offered a suggestion, or an opinion, unless invited. She often felt lonely at school, but her shyness prevented her from making advances, and so far nobody had offered her even the elements of friendship. It some-times hurt her to be thus entirely ignored and left out, but she had grown accustomed to it, and, shutting herself up in her shell, she followed the motto of the Miller of Dee:

"I care for nobody, no, not I,
Since nobody cares for me."

She was obliged to share in the daily games, which were com-pulsory for all; but she never joined in the voluntary ones unless she were specially asked to do so, to make up a side, and then she played with an utter lack of enthusiasm. "Moonie", as the girls called her, was a bookworm pure and simple. She had read al-most every volume in the school library; it did not matter wheth-er it were biography, travels, poetry, essays, or fiction, she would devour any literature that came her way. She lived in an imag-inary world, peopled by heroes and heroines of romance, who often seemed more real to her than her schoolmates, and certainly twice as interesting. Half the time she went about in a dream, and even during lesson hours she would let her thoughts drift far away to some exciting incident in a story, or some mental picture of her own. It appeared as if Miss Maitland could not have picked out two more opposite and unsuitable girls to share a bedroom than Honor Fitzgerald and Janie Henderson; but she had good reasons for her choice. Not only did she hope that Janie's sober ways would steady Honor, but she also thought that Honor's high spirits would have a leavening effect upon Janie, who was sadly in need of stirring up.

"I wish I could shake the pair in a bag!" she confided to a fel-low-teacher. "It would be of the greatest advantage to both."

There was at least one compensation to Janie for being obliged to change her quarters. No. 8, the room over the porch, was a special sanctum, much coveted by all the other Chaddites. It was arranged to accommodate only two, instead of four, and was the beau-ideal of every pair of chums. It had a French window open-ing out on to a tiny balcony, and, having been originally intended for one of the mistresses, was furnished rather more luxuriously than the rest of the bedrooms. There was a handsome wall-paper, a full-length mirror in the wardrobe, a comfortable basket-chair, and also what appealed particularly to Janie—a large and invit-ing bookcase, with glass doors. She conducted her removal, there-fore, with less dissatisfaction than she had at first anticipated.

"I call you lucky," declared Lettice Talbot. "I only wish I could go instead. Everyone on our landing is envying you. I shall be rather sorry to lose Paddy—I think she's a joke."

"Especially as we're to have Flossie Taylor instead," said Pauline Reynolds. "It's a poor exchange. I can't stand Flossie; she gives herself airs."

"She needn't put them on with us," observed Maisie. "I've had a quarrel with her already. She was actually trying to make Lettice pick up her balls for her at tennis!"

"Lettice always picks up yours," suggested Pauline.

"That's a totally different matter," declared Maisie.

"I wish Miss Maitland would have let Flossie join the Hammond-Smiths," said Lettice. "I can't imagine why she is making such changes. Oh, here's Honor! Do you know, Paddy, you have got notice to quit?—in fact, you're going to be evicted from No. 13."

Honor had already been informed of the fact by the house-mistress herself. She appeared to take the news with the utmost sangfroid.

"I don't care in the least which room I have," she replied. "All I bargain for is a room-mate who doesn't use 'cold pig' in the mornings. I haven't forgotten your wet sponge."

"You ungrateful Paddy! It was for your good."

"If you call me Paddy I shall call you Salad!"

"You can if you like. It's rather a pretty name, and has a juicy, succulent sound about it."

"Make haste, Honor, and clear your drawers," grunted Maisie. "Here's Flossie Taylor coming down the passage with her arms full of under-linen."

No. 8, like all other bedrooms at St. Chad's, was divided by a curtain that could be drawn at pleasure. At present, however, this was pulled aside for the mutual convenience of the occupants of both cubicles. To Janie the burning question to be decided was the possession of the bookcase. She tried to imagine that it was nearer her bed than Honor's, but justice forced her to come to the conclusion that it stood exactly in the middle, between the two. With heroic self-denial she offered her companion the first choice of its shelves before she put away her own little library.

"But I haven't brought any books with me," declared Honor. "You're welcome to the bookcase, so far as I'm concerned. We can take turns at this luxury," sinking into the basket-chair.

"Don't you ever read?"

"Very seldom."

Janie went on arranging her volumes in silence, the poets on the top shelf, by the side of her edition of Scott's novels, and the miscellaneous authors below. She touched each book tenderly, as though it were an old and dear friend, opening one occasionally to glance at a favourite passage; and she became so absorbed in her occupation that she utterly forgot Honor's presence.

"There! I've stowed away all my possessions," remarked the latter at last. "I don't know whether Miss Maitland judges a room by a tidy bookcase. She said she was coming up presently, to see if we had put our things straight."

Janie started guiltily. She, who was expected to be the mentor and to keep her companion up to the mark, was certainly the defaulter in this instance. Her bed and the chairs were strewn with various articles, and nothing seemed as yet in its right place.

"I couldn't help dipping into that book," she confessed. "It's a collection of old Irish fairy tales and legends. It was given me yesterday, before I left home, and I've scarcely had time even to look at it."

"Are they nice?"

"Lovely, to judge by the one I've just sampled!"

"Then do tell it to me! I hate reading, but I'm an absolute baby for loving to be told old tales."

"I? Oh, I couldn't!" exclaimed Janie.

"Yes, you can—while I'm helping you to put all these things into your drawers. Do, mavourneen! I want to hear the Irish story."

When Honor's grey eyes looked pleadingly from under their long, dark lashes, and a soft blarney crept into her voice, there were few people who could resist her. Janie flushed pink; she was so seldom asked to do anything for anybody! She had no natural gift for narrative, but she made an effort.

"There was once an Irishman called Murtagh O'Neil," she began, "and he was walking over London Bridge, with a hazel staff in his hand, when an Englishman met him and told him that the stick he carried grew on a spot under which were hidden great treasures. The Englishman was a wizard, and he promised that if Murtagh would go with him to Ireland, and show him the place, he would gain as much gold as he could carry. Murtagh consented, so they went over to Bronbhearg, in Kerry, where there was a big green mound; and there they dug up the hazel tree on which the staff had grown. Under it they found a broad, flat stone, and this covered the entrance to a cavern where thousands of warriors lay in a circle, sleeping beside their shields, with their swords clasped in their hands. Their arms were so brightly polished that they illuminated the whole cave; and one of them had a shield that outshone the rest, and a crown of gold on his head. In the centre of the cave hung a bell, which the wizard told Murtagh to beware of touching; but, if at any time he did so, and one of the warriors were to ask: 'Is it day?' he was to answer without hesitation: 'No, sleep thou on!' The two men took as much as they could carry from a heap of gold pieces that lay amidst the warriors, and Murtagh managed accidentally to touch the bell. It rang, and one of the warriors immediately asked: 'Is it day?' when Murtagh answered promptly: 'No, sleep thou on!' The wizard told him that the company he had seen were King Brien Borombe and his knights, who lay asleep ready for the dawn of a new day. When the right time should come the bell would ring loudly, and the warriors would start up and destroy the enemies of Erin, and once more the descendants of the Tuatha di Danan should rule the isle in peace. When Murtagh's treasure was all finished, he went back to the cave and helped himself to more. On his way out he touched the bell, and again it rang; but this time he was not so ready with his answer, and some of the warriors rose up, took the gold from him, beat him, and flung him out of the cave. He never recovered from the beating, but was a cripple to the end of his days."

"And serve him right, too!" declared Honor. "Brien Borombe was a great hero of Ireland."

"Yes, there's one of Moore's Irish Melodies that begins: 'Remember the glories of Brien the brave'," said Janie.

"Are there any more stories about him in that book?"

"I'm not sure, but there are tales about fairy raths and changelings and leprechauns and pookas and banshees, and all kinds of extraordinary creatures."

"Then we'll have one every day, please! I think you're a first-rate story-teller. You're almost as good as old Mary O'Grady. I've often sat by her peat fire and heard about the banshee and the leprechaun; only, she believes in them. I'm so glad I've moved into this bedroom! I like you far better than those girls in No. 13."

When Miss Maitland came upstairs to inspect No. 8, she found Honor and Janie already on a more favourable footing than she had dared to hope, the latter chatting with a vivacity that no one at St. Chad's had hitherto imagined she possessed. Once she had broken the ice of her shyness, and had broached her beloved topic of books, Janie had plenty to say; and, as Honor was also in a communicative mood, the pair seemed well started on the high road to friendship.

It was fortunate for Honor that she had found a congenial room-mate, as her first days at Chessington proved rather a time of trial. She was woefully and terribly home-sick. It seemed an absolute uprooting to have been torn away from Kerry, and she considered that nothing in her new surroundings could make amends for the change. Her pride upheld her sufficiently to prevent her from showing any outward signs of misery before the inquisitive eyes of her schoolfellows, but every now and then the yearning for Kilmore would rise with an almost unbearable pain, and she would have to fight hard to keep her self-control. Maisie Talbot, she was sure, would regard home-sickness as "early Victorian", and consequently worthy of contempt; and she was determined not to give either Maisie or any of the others an opportunity of laughing at her.

She felt very keenly the confinement and restraint of school life. To be obliged to study lessons and play games at specified hours, all within a certain limited area, seemed an utter contrast to the freedom in which she had hitherto revelled; and she would long for a scamper with Bute and Barney, her two terriers, or a sail with her father down the creek and out into the Atlantic. She would pour enthusiastic descriptions of her home into Janie's ears, until the latter felt she knew Kilmore Castle and its demesne, and the little fishing village, with its peat smoke and its warm-hearted peasants; and the rocks and the moors and the stream, and the green, treacherous bogs, almost as well as Honor herself.

Notwithstanding her former reputation for unsociability, Janie, at the end of three days, had completely lost her heart to this wayward, impulsive daughter of Erin. It was true, Honor was apt to be trying at times. Her gusts of hot temper, petulance, or utter unreasonableness were rather disconcerting to anyone unaccustomed to the Celtic disposition; but they never lasted long, and Janie soon found out that her friend rarely meant what she then said, and was generally particularly lovable after an outburst, with a winsome look on her face and a beguiling, endearing tone in her voice that would have gained forgiveness from a stone.

With the rest of the members of St. Chad's Honor was also on good terms. She could be very amusing and full of racy Irish humour when she liked, and would send the girls into fits of laughter with her quaint sayings and funny stories. Her nickname of "Paddy Pepper-box" stuck to her, and she certainly justified it occasionally.

"She's like a volcano," declared Lettice Talbot. "Sometimes if you tease her she starts with a bang, and lets off steam for five minutes. Then it's all over, and she's quite pleasant again, until next time."

"I'd rather have that than sulking, at any rate," said Dorothy Arkwright. "A storm often clears the air."

"It's not much use chaffing her, either," said Madge Summers, "for she always seems to get the best of it."

"Yes; if she's down one minute she'll bob up again the next, like a cork."

Honor's humours were apt to overflow into the region of practical jokes. These were generally played on such genial recipients as Lettice Talbot and Madge Summers, but occasionally she would venture on more dangerous ground. One afternoon, at the end of her first week at Chessington, she was in the dressing-room, changing her shoes in preparation for cricket, when Ruth Latimer interposed.

"I forgot to tell you, Paddy! Games are off to-day."

"Why?" asked Honor in astonishment, for the hour and a half in the playing-fields was as strict a part of the college curriculum as the morning lessons.

"Because it's the Health Testing."

"What's that?"

"A kind of medical examination," explained Dorothy Arkwright. "We always have it at the beginning of each term, to make sure that, as Miss Cavendish expresses it, we are 'physically fit for the duties of school life'."

"Oh!" said Honor, looking rather aghast at the prospect.

"You needn't pull such a long face, Paddy," said Lettice. "We none of us mind; indeed, we think it's a joke."

"We have a lady doctor, you see," said Ruth, "and she's so jolly, she keeps one laughing all the time."

"What does she do?"

"Oh! weighs us, and sounds our lungs, and tests our eyes, and measures our chests."

"You'll have to draw a deep breath, and to put out your tongue, and to let her look at your teeth," added Lettice.

"And if any girl is really very much below standard," said Dorothy, "she is 'turned out to grass'. That means that she only does half-lessons."

"Of course, she has to be rather bad for that," remarked Ruth.

"It's never been my luck yet!" lamented Lettice.

"I should think not, with those fat, red cheeks! You couldn't look delicate, however hard you tried."

"It happened to Janie Henderson, though, in her first term. How little did you weigh, Moonie?"

"I'm sure I forget," returned Janie, who had joined the group.

"But you had to be fed up on cream and beaten eggs and all kinds of things. I remember how we envied you."

"Are you weighed in stones or pounds here?" asked Honor.

"In stones. It's very puzzling to some of the Colonials, because they're accustomed to American machines that register in pounds. They have to do a sum before they can calculate the result."

"When does this exam. come off?"

"Some time this afternoon. We go up in relays. It's St. Chad's turn to-day. On Wednesday it was the School House, and on Thursday, St. Aldwyth's. Then on Saturday it will be St. Hilary's and St. Bride's. It takes nearly a week to get through the whole school."

The medical examination was to be conducted at the sanatorium, and Dr. Mary Forbes was already installed there, and busily employed, when Honor and her classmates arrived.

"She begins with monitresses, and then works downwards," explained Dorothy. "I don't expect it will be our turn for half an hour yet, but we're obliged to stay here, to be ready in case we're called."

"It's not nearly so alarming as the dentist's," said Ruth.

The waiting-room was full of girls, who were beguiling the time with jokes and banter and lively chatter. Lettice, Ruth, and Dorothy soon mingled in the crowd, and forgot all about their Irish companion until the voice of Vivian Holmes was heard announcing:

"Next—Ruth Latimer, Chatty Burns, Madge Summers, and Honor Fitzgerald."

"Where's Honor?" asked Lettice. "She was here just now."

"Why, she's there!—actually outside in the garden," replied Dorothy.

"What's she doing, dodging about the rockery?"

"Someone call her—quick!"

Honor came running in, looking rather flushed and hot, and with a curious, bulgy appearance about her blouse.

"Where have you been?" demanded Ruth, but her question went unanswered, for Vivian whisked the four girls with scant ceremony into Dr. Mary Forbes's consulting-room. Time was too precious to be wasted, and the monitress was something of a disciplinarian. Honor sat watching with deep interest while first Ruth, then Chatty, and finally Madge were duly examined and passed as "sound". She was called then, and after her name and age had been entered on her chart, and her height taken, she was told to step on to the weighing machine. Round swung the pointer, and stopped at 8 stone 4 lb. Dr. Mary looked at the dial almost incredulously. She thought there must be something wrong with the machine.

"Stand off for a minute," she said, "while I examine the weights. I must have made a mistake."

Honor obeyed, with a very solemn face. She appeared to be taking the matter with unusual seriousness. Dr. Mary readjusted the lever, and even oiled the machine; but when Honor stepped on to it again it registered exactly the same.

"It's most extraordinary!" exclaimed the lady doctor. "For a girl of your height and slight build I have never known such a record," and she gazed at Honor's rather slender proportions in amazement.

"I expect it's bones," volunteered Honor. "The Fitzgeralds are a big-boned family."

"Your bones would have to be of cast iron, to bring you up to eight stone odd," cried Dr. Mary. "The machine must be at fault. It's absurd, on the face of it—a small, slim girl like you!"

"Perhaps it's the change of air since I arrived," said Honor innocently, but at the same time she looked at Madge Summers with a very mischievous expression on her face.

"She's up to something!" thought Madge, and nudged Ruth, though she dared not venture to whisper.

"Of course, we eat a great deal over in Ireland," continued Honor. "There is nothing like potatoes for making one grow. I saw in the British Almanac that they were twice as nourishing as anything, except herrings and oatmeal; and we have those too in Kerry."

"I think, in that case, we must try Banting," said Dr. Mary, who must have caught Honor's glance, for she suddenly took hold of her, and began feeling her carefully.

"Ah!" she exclaimed; "so these are the extra bones, are they?" and diving into her patient's pocket, she drew out stone after stone, and as many more again that had been tucked down in the front of the white flannel blouse.

The doctor was a good-tempered woman, with a strong sense of humour, and, instead of scolding, she laughed heartily at having been taken in by such a trick.

"I've had patients who shammed ill before," she declared, "but never such a scandalous case of imposition as this."

"Well, the girls told me the weight was to be reckoned by stones," said Honor, with a twinkle in her eye, "so I thought I'd better come well provided. I'm not at all sorry to be rid of them, if they're not wanted."

"Get on to that machine again immediately!" commanded Dr. Mary, with an effort to be severe. "Ah! 6 stone 5 lb. is rather a difference. It's lucky for you I didn't put you on starvation diet to reduce you. Don't try to be so clever again, or I shall have to perform an operation to get rid of your cheek!"

Madge, Ruth, and Chatty had sat chuckling with subdued delight during the interview, and the moment they were out of the room they published the story abroad, for the edification of the others.

"She thinks of such funny things!" laughed Madge, "things that nobody else would ever dream of doing."

"I was afraid she'd get into a fearful scrape," confessed Chatty.

"Oh, Dr. Mary Forbes is too jolly to mind!" said Ruth. "She was far more amused than cross. If it had been Miss Maitland, or Miss Cavendish, now! But I should imagine that even Honor Fitzgerald would scarcely dare to play a practical joke upon either of them!"

CHAPTER V

A Riding Lesson

The College had reopened on a Tuesday, so that by her first Sunday Honor had been at school five days. In her own estimation it seemed more like five months, but as she had left home on 24th April, and the Shakespeare calendar in the recreation room (a leaf of which was torn off punctually each morning by the monitress) only recorded 29th April, she was obliged reluctantly to acknowledge the evidence of the almanac, and realized that twelve whole weeks must intervene before the joyful termination of what she considered her banishment from Erin.

Sundays were made very pleasant at Chessington. In the morning the girls attended the parish church at Dunscar. In the afternoon they might read, or stroll about the grounds where they pleased, an indulgence not permitted on weekdays. During the summer term they were allowed to carry their four-o'clock tea into the garden. All was laid ready by the servants in the dining-hall, and each girl might pour out her own cup, and, taking what bread and butter she wished, retire with a few select companions to some nook under the trees, or a seat in an ivy-covered arbour.

From half-past four to half-past five was "silence hour", which everyone was required to devote to reading from a special library of books carefully chosen for the purpose by Miss Cavendish.

"I won't call them Sunday books," she sometimes said, "because I consider our religion would be a very poor thing if it were only kept for one day in the week. What we learn in this quiet time we must apply in our busy hours, and let the helpful words we read influence our ordinary life and go towards the building of character, which is the most invaluable of all possessions."

At half-past six there was a short service in chapel; and the rest of the evening, after supper, was given up to the writing of home letters.

All the routine of the school was still new to Honor, and she felt very strange and unusual as, precisely at ten o'clock, she took her place among the lines of Chessingtonians marshalled in the quadrangle preparatory to setting off for church. Miss Cavendish gave the signal to start, and the two hundred girls filed along two and two, all dressed alike in white serge coats and skirts and best sailor hats, with their house colours, the blue ribbons of the School House leading the way, followed by the pink of St. Aldwyth's, and the orange, violet, and scarlet of St. Chad's, St. Bride's, and St. Hilary's, respectively.

"I believe it's considered one of the sights of the neighbourhood to see us parade through the lich-gate," said Lettice Talbot, who happened to be walking with Honor. "Visitors stand in the churchyard and try to count us. They make the most absurd remarks sometimes; I suppose they think we shan't overhear what they say. Really, they seem to look upon us as a kind of show, and I quite expect we shall be put down in the next edition of the guide-book as one of the attractions of Dunscar. Of course, we take no notice. We walk along with our noses in the air, as if we weren't aware that anyone was even thinking of us; but all the same we feel giggles inside when we catch a whisper: 'They look like angels dressed in white!' or, 'What a pile of washing they must make!'"

Honor had been looking forward immensely to this Sunday morning, for she hoped she might have an opportunity of seeing her brother Dermot, who was at Dr. Winterton's school. Dermot was her favourite among her five brothers, and the thought that Orley Grange and Chessington stood only a mile and a half apart had so far been her one thread of comfort. To catch even a distant glimpse of Dermot would be like a peep at home, and she felt that a moment's talk with him would be sufficient to send her back to St. Chad's rejoicing.

The students of the College occupied the whole of the left aisle of the church, and the right aisle was reserved for Dr. Winterton's pupils. As a rule, the girls arrived early and took their seats first; and they always passed out by a side door, so that they seldom met the boys in the churchyard. Should they happen to do so, however, it was etiquette to take no notice of them, even though some might be relations, or intimate friends. Honor was unaware of this rule, which her classmates, not knowing she had a brother at the Grange, had not thought of mentioning to her.

On this particular Sunday either Miss Cavendish or Dr. Winterton had slightly miscalculated the time, for the two schools arrived at exactly the same minute. As there was not room for all to march in together through the lich-gate, the boys were drawn up like a regiment, and waited for the College to go by. The girls sailed past with well-bred unconsciousness, their eyes fixed discreetly upon the Prayer Books and hymn-books that they carried—all except poor impulsive, unconventional Honor, who made a sudden dart out of the line, and snatched rapturously at a brown-faced, curly-headed boy, by his coat sleeve.

"Dermot! Dermot! I am glad to see you!" she exclaimed, in a voice that could be heard from end to end of the ranks.

"Oh, I say, Honor! Stow it!" murmured the boy in an agonized tone, turning as red as fire, and trying to back away from her.

Naturally Honor's unexpected and unprecedented act caused a great sensation. Lettice Talbot stopped when deserted by her partner, and the girls behind her were obliged to halt too. All wondered what had happened, and, in spite of their excellent training and good discipline, their curiosity got the better of them, and they craned their necks to look. Miss Farrar saved the situation by hurrying to Honor, seizing her by the shoulder, and forcing her back into her place; then the long line once more moved forward, and the Chessingtonians, slightly ruffled, but trying to carry off the affair in a dignified fashion, marched with admirable coolness into the church. If Honor had a little, surreptitious cry behind her Prayer Book, she managed to conceal the fact from the neighbours on either side of her in the pew; and if her eyes looked suspiciously red, and there was a slight tendency to chokiness in her voice she walked home after service, Lettice Talbot, at any rate, was tactful enough to take no notice, though she seized the opportunity of explaining the school code of decorum, and was severe in her censure.

"You ought to have told me before," said Honor. "How could I know that I mustn't speak to my own brother?"

"I didn't even know you had a brother," returned Lettice; "and I never dreamt you'd do such an idiotic thing as rush at him like that. He evidently didn't appreciate it."

"No! I thought he'd be more glad to see me," gulped Honor, not the least part of whose trouble had been Dermot's cold reception of her enthusiastic greeting.

"How silly you are! Does any boy care to parade his sister before his whole school? I expect he'll get tremendously chaffed about this, poor fellow! Really, Paddy, you ought to know better!"

Considerably chastened by Lettice's crushing remarks, Honor subsided into silence, and only reopened the subject when, in company with Janie Henderson, she had retired after dinner to a spot overlooking the playing-fields. It was a warm, beautiful afternoon, a day when you could almost hear the buds bursting and the flowers opening. The two girls spread their jerseys on the grass, and sat basking in the sunshine, watching a lark soar up into the blue overhead, or the seagulls flapping leisurely round the cliffs; or listening to the caw of the jackdaws that, in company with a flock of starlings, were feeding in a neighbouring ploughed field. The sea lay a sparkling sheet of pearly grey, and Honor looked wistfully at its broad expanse when she remembered that its farther waves washed the rocky shores of Ireland.

Janie was the only girl at St. Chad's to whom she cared to mention her home. With the others she could exchange jokes, but not confidences; and though she returned their banter with interest, she did not look to them for sympathy. Janie seemed altogether different from the rest; she never laughed at Honor, and even if she remonstrated, it was in such a gentle, apologetic way that the most touchy of Celtic natures could not have taken offence.

Miss Maitland had not overlooked the episode of the morning. She had had a few words to say after their return from church, and Honor, in consequence, was feeling rather sore, and ready to pour out her grievances into her friend's ears.

"It's too bad!" she declared. "If you can't speak to your own brother, to whom may you speak, I should like to know? It seems absurd that Dermot should be living at the Grange, not two miles off, and yet we're never to see one another. I thought I should at least meet him once a week, and now I mayn't even say, 'How do you do?' without being scolded as if I had committed a highway robbery."

"Is he your favourite brother?" asked Janie.

"Yes; he's the nearest in age to me, and we're great chums. We have the wildest fun during the holidays—we dare each other to do the maddest things we can think of!"

"What kind of things?"

"Well, one day, when old Biddy Macarthy was ill with quinsy, we got up early and took her cart to Ballycroghan market, and Dermot sold all her chickens for her. He talked away like a Cheap Jack, and made such fun, people nearly died with laughing. You see, most of them knew who he was, and it seemed so absurd to hear him proclaiming the virtues of Biddy's fowls. Then we filled the cart with seed potatoes, as a present for her; and tore home so fast that the traces broke, and the donkey ran straight out of the shafts. We fell on the road, nearly buried in potatoes, but luckily we weren't hurt. We managed to catch the donkey, and to mend the traces with a piece of string; then we had to put all the potatoes back. Biddy laughed so much when we told her about the adventure that it cured her quinsy; and she said she never had such a splendid crop of potatoes as from those we brought her that day from Ballycroghan. That was Dermot's joke; but I think mine was quite as much fun."

"What was yours?"

"I saved up my pocket-money to get a little pig, to give to old Micky, the cobbler. Dermot and I walked over to Ennisfellen fair to buy it, and drove it home with a string tied to its leg. As fast as we pulled one way it ran another, and just as we got to Micky's cabin the string snapped, and off the pig bolted down the village, and ran straight into the open door of the school. The children chased it round and round beneath the forms, and caught it at last under the master's desk. Oh, we have lively times at Kilmore! Then once Dermot and I ran away, and went to see Cousin Theresa at Slieve Donnell. Nobody knew where we were for two days, and people were hunting all over the country for us. They thought we must have been drowned, or have fallen into the bog."

"But weren't your father and mother fearfully anxious?" asked Janie, who had listened almost aghast to the recital of those wild escapades.

"Well, Father was rather cross about that, certainly. He was never really very angry, though, until the last time, when I——"

But here Honor stopped. On the whole, she decided she would not relate the story of Firefly. She could not quite understand the expression on Janie's face, and she began to doubt whether her friend would altogether sympathize with her. Instead, she plunged into a detailed description of her elder brothers, telling how two were preparing for the Army at Sandhurst, how another was at Oxford, and the fourth was studying law.

"I suppose you are nearly always with your mother, as you are the only girl," said Janie.

"Well, no," admitted Honor. "She's so delicate, and so often ill. I'm afraid I give her a headache."

"My mother is delicate too," confided Janie. "She has most dreadful neuralgia sometimes. I bathe her head with eau-de-cologne, mixed with very hot water, and it always does her good. She calls me her little nurse. Have you ever tried hot water with eau-de-cologne for your mother's headaches?"

Honor had never dreamt of offering any help or assistance to anyone in sickness. The idea was quite new to her, and that Janie evidently expected her to be her mother's companion and right hand surprised her. She had already met with many astonishments at St. Chad's, where most of the views of life seemed different from her old standards. She scarcely liked to confess that she was of so little use at home, and hastily turned the conversation back to her brother Dermot.

"Do you think if I were to ask Miss Cavendish, she would let him call to see me?" she suggested.

Janie shook her head.

"I'm quite sure she wouldn't," she replied. "The rules are so strict about visitors. Nobody but our parents is allowed, except an occasional uncle or aunt—never a brother. You'd better not suggest it."

"Then I shall have to go and see him."

"How could you, Honor? Don't be so unreasonable!"

"I thought I might find an opportunity some day," said Honor reflectively. "One never knows what may turn up. Dear old Dermot! It would be hard luck to be within two miles of him for a whole term, without exchanging a single word."

"Well, if you do, you'll get into a far bigger scrape than you'll like. You'd much better wait until the holidays, when you'll probably both travel home together," advised Janie.

There certainly were no opportunities at Chessington College for paying calls. Except on half-holidays, the girls seldom went beyond the school grounds, the large playing-fields providing a wide enough area for exercise. The members of the Fifth and Sixth Forms were allowed to go out occasionally, within specified bounds, if they went three together; but the younger ones had not attained to such a privilege.

"We mayn't even put our noses through the gate of the quad," said Lettice Talbot, in reply to a question from Honor, who chafed sorely against the rule; "not unless we can get a special exeat from Miss Cavendish, and that's only given once in a blue moon. It's no use looking volcanic, Paddy! You'll have to grin and bear it."

"It's as bad as being in prison," grumbled Honor.

"Nonsense!" snapped Maisie Talbot. "You have cricket or tennis for nearly two hours every afternoon. What more can you want? I'd rather play games myself than do anything else."

"You can't expect to do just as you like at school," remarked Dorothy Arkwright, who sometimes joined with Maisie in "squashing" Honor.

"The riding lessons begin next Thursday," said Lettice, with an attempt at consolation. "They are very jolly. Mr. Townsend always takes the class a trot over the Tor. You said you were to learn riding?"

"It's the one lesson I begged for," replied Honor. "I could have dispensed with Latin, or German, or mathematics."

"Maisie and I are to begin this term; we're looking forward to it tremendously!"

"You are lucky," said Pauline Reynolds enviously. "I'd give all I possess to be going with you. I've never ridden anything more interesting than a rocking-horse, or a donkey on the sands; and one doesn't get much of a canter for six-pence!"

"I believe I'm horribly nervous, and I don't mind confessing it," declared Lettice. "The idea of being perched on a great, tall horse makes me shake in my shoes. When it begins to trot I shall drop off—I know I shall!"

"Don't be so silly!" protested Maisie. "You can stick on to Teddie at home all right. Honor Fitzgerald, can you ride?"

"Bareback, if you like," said Honor. "Dermot and I used to take our old pony and practise what we called 'circus performances'. Pixie quite entered into the spirit of the thing, and would walk along gently while we stood on his back."

"I hear Mr. Townsend brings very fresh horses," said Lettice, with a shiver of apprehension. "I do hope he'll choose me a quiet one!"

"The fresher the better for me," said Honor. "I'm just longing for a good gallop."

"But suppose it runs away?"

"Then it will have to take me with it. If it's any kind of a beast with four legs, I'll undertake to make it fly."

"I heard that Mr. Townsend's horses aren't worth the fag of riding," observed Flossie Taylor, who had joined the group.

"There speaks the voice of envy! You wouldn't say so if you were taking the lessons," retorted Maisie.

"People who are accustomed to hunt at home don't care about hired hacks," drawled Flossie, in her most supercilious manner.

"It all depends on the sort of hunting," returned Honor, who was never at a loss. "If it's only 'hunt the slipper', I'll admit it's not much of a training, and you might be afraid of your seat."

The riding course was a special feature of the summer term at Chessington. It was an "extra", not part of the ordinary school curriculum, as were the games. A master came from Dunscar, and would escort select little parties of girls for a trot upon the Tor, a stretch of moorland not far from the College. Mr. Townsend did not care to take out many pupils at once, so on the following Thursday afternoon only seven horses were waiting in the quadrangle. The Talbots, Ruth Latimer, and Honor represented St. Chad's, while two girls from St. Hilary's and one from St. Bride's completed the party. Lettice confessed to a very superior and elated feeling as the reins were laid in her hand and the cavalcade began to move, particularly as Flossie Taylor and the Hammond-Smiths were just setting off for tennis, and could not help witnessing the start, though they resolutely looked the opposite way.

"Flossie always tries to be extremely grand herself, and make other people seem small," whispered Lettice.

"Fortunately, one needn't take people at their own estimate," replied Maisie, whose downright nature much disliked Flossie's habit of bragging.

To all the seven girls it was a delight to find themselves passing under the archway of the big gate, and away along the road towards the Tor. A chestnut called Victor had fallen to Honor's share, and though he was very tall in comparison with her old favourite Pixie, she nevertheless sat him well.

"She looks just like the picture of Diana Vernon in our Rob Roy," remarked Lettice to Maisie, gazing with admiration at the upright, graceful figure of her schoolmate, who seemed perfectly at home in the saddle.

Lettice was getting on much better than her modest protestations beforehand would have led her friends to expect. Violet Wright, the girl from St. Bride's, was quite a beginner, and Mr. Townsend held her horse by a leading rein; while Gwen Roby, from St. Hilary's, looked rather solemn, as if she were not altogether sure that she was enjoying the experience.

"I've ridden before," she explained, "but only on a small pony, and this feels so very different."

At first the party went at a walking pace, but on coming to a good, level stretch of road the master gave the order to trot, and his pupils were able to test the capacities of their steeds. Honor, at least, was most unwilling to pull up when Mr. Townsend called out "Halt!" I am afraid she did not want a lesson, only a scamper through the fresh air; and she listened impatiently while the master explained the right position of the whip, the hold on the snaffle, and the principle of rising elegantly in the saddle.

"It's all very well to talk of principles," said poor Violet, who happened to find herself next to Lettice; "I expect a little practice will be of more use to me. At present I jog up and down like a sack of flour, and it's all I can manage to stick on anyhow. I know I shall be as stiff as a board to-morrow!"

"When we reach the Tor we may manage a short canter," said Mr. Townsend, "but for the present I wish you to keep together. Now then, young ladies, please, elbows in and heads up! Hold the reins rather short in the hand, and take care not to bear on the curb!"

"It's no fun, is it?" remarked Honor, as she passed Ruth Latimer. "Are we only going to walk in a stupid row, and then trot for about ten yards? I thought we should be flying along, like a hunt. I'd rather be on Pixie at home; I could always make him go when I tickled his ears. If we don't hurry up a little more I shall try it on this horse, and see if he won't break into something more interesting than a snail's pace."

"Oh, Honor, do take care!" remonstrated prudent Ruth.

But Honor did not stop to listen, and pushed on ahead of the others, swishing her whip about in a manner that drew instant reproof from the master. They had left the highway, and were now on a road leading across the open moor. On one side the cliffs descended steeply to the sea, and on the other rose bare, rolling hills, covered with short, fine grass, the sails of a windmill or an occasional storm-swept tree alone breaking the line of the horizon. It was a very suitable place for a canter, and after a few preliminary remarks Mr. Townsend started his flock on what seemed to most of them a rather mad career, following closely himself in their wake, to continue his instructions:

"Courage, Miss Roby! Miss Talbot, you are leaning over in your saddle! Miss Lettice, your elbows again! Miss Wright, you must learn not to grasp the pommel. Don't drag the rein! Miss Latimer, keep a light hand! What, tired already? Well, I won't work you too hard just at first."

A little shaken and agitated by the unwonted exercise, the girls checked their horses to a walk. They were none of them practised riders, and all were glad that no more was expected from them for the present. Honor, however, was some way on in front, and, instead of pulling up, as she was told, she gave her horse a switch across the flank and a tweak on the ear, such as she had been accustomed to bestow on her old pony at home. The effect was magical. Seaside hacks are not generally prone to run away, but this one had a little spirit left in him; he resented his rider's liberties, and, feeling the soft grass under his feet, fled as if he were on a racecourse.

"Miss Fitzgerald! Miss Fitzgerald!" shouted Mr. Townsend, but he might as well have spoken to the wind. Honor had found her opportunity, and was quick to seize it. Instead of attempting to pull up Victor, she let him have his head. She had no desire to check his pace, the motion was so exhilarating; and she could not resist the temptation to display her horsemanship before the rest of the class. The unfortunate master dared not desert his other nervous and inexperienced pupils to give chase, and in a few minutes she had left the remainder of the party a mile behind. They could see her tearing past the coastguard station, where an old man with a telescope yelled wildly to her to stop; past a windmill, where children and chickens scrambled in hot haste out of her path; and away over the moor, until she quite disappeared from sight.

The girls were in a panic of alarm. Mr. Townsend turned rather white, but preserved his presence of mind, and, leading his little company straight to the coastguard station, made all dismount, and tied up the horses. Then he set out himself in pursuit of the runaway.

Honor, meanwhile, continued her "John Gilpin" galop. On and on she flew, her hair, as the fairy tales say, "whistling in the wind". It occurred to her at last that she might be going too far, and she made an effort to pull up. But it was of no avail; Victor had got the bit firmly between his teeth, and nothing could hold him. Luckily, the girl did not lose her nerve, but waited until she could tire him out, and get him in hand again; and I verily believe she would have succeeded in mastering him, and turning him safely on his homeward course, had not the way been unexpectedly barred by a fence. The poor old horse must have been a hunter during some period of his life; he went at the fence like a greyhound, and cleared it nimbly: but there were a trench and a rough bank on the farther side, and as he alighted he stumbled, flinging Honor violently from the saddle. Mercifully, her foot came clear of the stirrup, and she rolled safely into a bed of nettles, while Victor, scrambling up again, made off without her over the crest of the hill.

Honor picked herself out of the nettles as quickly as she could. No bones were broken, and, except for some painful stings, she was none the worse for her adventure.

Nevertheless, the situation was awkward. There she was on the open moor, many miles away from Chessington, and obliged to make her way home to St. Chad's as best she could. She climbed over the fence, and, holding up her habit, set out to walk back in the direction in which she had come.

It seemed slow progress compared with riding, and she began to wonder how long it would take her to retrace her steps. She had not gone more than half a mile, however, when she met Mr. Townsend, who had at last succeeded in reaching her. His relief at finding her alive and unhurt was almost too great for words. He put her quietly on his own horse, and led it by the bridle back to the coastguard station, where the rest of the girls were waiting, very anxious to know what had become of Honor, and very rejoiced when they saw she was safe.

There was no further riding lesson that day. As Maisie Talbot explained afterwards to a select company of interested friends: "I'm sure Mr. Townsend was frightfully angry, but he scarcely said a word. He only took us straight home at once, in a kind of solemn procession. He had to walk himself, leading Honor's and Violet's horses, so of course we went horribly slowly; and he looked so savage that nobody dared to speak."

"What possessed you, Paddy?" asked Lettice.

"I had an idea of going to see Dermot," confessed Honor. "I thought if I rode straight up to the Grange, and asked leave from Dr. Winterton, perhaps he'd let us have half an hour together."

"Well, you are the silliest goose! Why, the Grange is in exactly the opposite direction! Will you never learn sense?" and Lettice collapsed with laughter.

"Mr. Townsend is having a long talk with Miss Maitland at this present moment," announced Ruth Latimer.

"Then I'm glad I'm not you, Paddy!" chuckled Lettice.

Nobody ever knew the details of Mr. Townsend's interview with the house-mistress, or what explanation he gave of the affair. Though he was perfectly persuaded that it was Honor's own fault, it was difficult for him to blame her for what might, after all, have been a mere accident; so, beyond a few words of warning about the danger of whipping her horse without proper orders, she did not on this occasion receive the scolding that she certainly merited.

Victor was found on the hills six miles away from Chessington, gently cropping the grass, and allowed himself to be caught by a passing farmer. He was not used at the riding lessons again. Honor was in future given the tamest and least-spirited of the mounts, and for the next two lessons was even kept strictly to the leading rein.

"She's fearfully disgusted about it," said Lettice, "and it certainly is a humiliation, when she can ride so well. It's quite the worst punishment Mr. Townsend could possibly have given her, and I expect he knows it!"

CHAPTER VI

The Lower Third

The Lower Third Form at Chessington College numbered seventeen pupils, eight of whom were members of St. Chad's. In addition to Honor, these included Maisie and Lettice Talbot, Ruth Latimer, Pauline Reynolds, Janie Henderson, Effie Lawson, and Flossie Taylor. The teacher, Miss Farrar, was rather a favourite with her class. Though she could well uphold her authority, and maintain the good discipline that was universal in the school, she was not so strict as some of the other mistresses. She had a very pleasant, genial manner; she was a capital tennis player, and no mean figure at hockey and cricket; she was a prominent supporter of the Debating Society and the Natural History Union; and was altogether so cheerful and brisk that "jolly" was the word generally applied to her. Honor liked Miss Farrar, and, according to her lights, really made a heroic effort in the direction of good behaviour. Her conduct was certainly immeasurably superior to what it had been with her governesses at home, and yet, judged by Chessington standards, it was frequently irregular and unorthodox. With her best endeavours, she could not grasp the fact that education is a very solemn affair, and a school-room about the last place in the world where one should try to be funny. She never seemed able to be absolutely serious, and at the least opportunity her Celtic humour would flash out, and not only upset the gravity of the class, but sometimes even cause Miss Farrar to have a difficulty in keeping her countenance.

She was a slightly disturbing element in the Form. When it was her turn to answer there would be an air of general expectancy in the room; the didactic language of the textbooks was often paraphrased by her lips into something of a more racy description, and even her mistakes were as delicious as her quaint methods of stating facts. Miss Farrar occasionally suspected her of intentionally giving wrong replies, for the sheer satisfaction of causing amusement; but it was difficult to prove the charge, since, however ludicrous her statements might be, she never under any circumstances laughed at them herself, and all the while her large, grey Irish eyes would be fixed upon her teacher with the innocence of a baby.

Thanks to Janie Henderson's assiduity, Honor conformed tolerably well to the ordinary rules. Mindful of Miss Maitland's charge, Janie considered herself responsible for Honor, and was continually ready to jog her memory about what exercises must be written, what lessons learnt, and what books brought to class, all of which were details that her friend would not have troubled about on her own account; but in spite of her exertions the poor girl often saw her protégée in trouble.

"The worst of it is," she admitted to herself, "that one never knows what to expect. Honor is a darling, but she does such peculiar and extraordinary things, she almost takes one's breath away. If I could be prepared for them beforehand, and warn her, it might be of some use; but I can't, so she's bound to get into scrapes."

Undoubtedly, very unprecedented happenings took place in the Lower Third—happenings such as had never occurred before Honor's advent. Who but she would have thought of tilting two books together and emptying the inkpot on the top of them, when asked to describe a watershed? Yet she looked genuinely astonished when the vials of Miss Farrar's wrath descended upon her, and said almost reproachfully that she was only trying to give a practical illustration.

One day she smuggled Pete, the kitten from St. Chad's, into class, and shut him inside her desk, where he settled down quite comfortably, and slept peacefully through the French lesson. But in the middle of algebra, Honor, who hated mathematics, managed to give him a surreptitious pinch, with the result that a long-drawn, impatient, objecting "miau" suddenly resounded through the room. Miss Farrar gave quite a jump, and looked round, but could see nothing. Honor sat bolt upright, with arms folded and eyes fixed attentively on the blackboard, as if she were sublimely unconscious of any noise in her vicinity.

"What can it be? It sounds like a cat," said Miss Farrar, peering about on the floor, and even peeping into the cupboard where the chalk and the new books were kept.

The girls jumped up, and pretended to look under their desks. Most of them had an inkling of the situation, but they were human enough to enjoy an interruption in the midst of difficult equations.

"Perhaps it's a mouse in the wainscot that's not feeling quite well this morning," suggested Honor, though it would have needed an absolute giant of a mouse to give vent to the unearthly yowl in which Pete had indulged. She said it, however, rather too innocently on this occasion. Miss Farrar was not dull, and had suspected from the beginning who was at the bottom of the mischief; indeed, it was easy enough by this time to trace the noise to the right spot, for the kitten had begun to scratch, and lifted up its voice in a series of emphatic wails, evidently protesting vigorously against solitary confinement.

Miss Farrar walked straight to Honor's desk and opened it, when out jumped Pete, purring with satisfaction, and arching his back as if in expectation of petting. The teacher seized him by the scruff of the neck and gave him to Janie Henderson, at the same time quelling the unseemly mirth of her class with a withering glance.

"Carry this kitten back at once to St. Chad's," she commanded. "Honor Fitzgerald, you will learn two pages of Greek chronology, and repeat them to me before school to-morrow morning. Lettice Talbot, take a forfeit! Girls, I am astonished at you! Open your books instantly, every one of you! Gwen Roby, read out your answer to Example 37."

Though Honor was popular with most of the members of her Form, she was never on very good terms with Flossie Taylor. Flossie had a sharp tongue, and liked to make sarcastic remarks; and though Honor would promptly return the compliment, and often "squash" the other completely, continual bickering did not promote harmony between the pair. Flossie was occasionally capable of certain dishonourable acts, which always drew upon her Honor's utmost indignation and scorn. The latter could not tolerate cheating or copying, and spoke her mind freely on the subject.

"Well, I'm sure I'm not nearly as bad as you!" Flossie retorted once. "You do the most outrageous things. I never mixed the French and history exercises, nor dipped the chalk into the red ink!"

"It's worse to crib someone else's work," protested Honor, "because that's sneaky and underhand. What would Miss Farrar say if she knew you wrote dates on a slip of paper and put it inside your dictionary, and then copied them when you pretended you were only looking how to spell a word?"

"Miss Farrar won't find out, and what the eye doesn't see the heart doesn't grieve for!"

"But it's so mean!"

THE LIBERATION OF PETE

"You turning Mentor!" sneered Flossie. "Really! I wonder what we may expect next? Come, girls, and hear our most righteous and well-conducted Paddy preach a homily on 'How to be the pattern pupil'!"

"Paddy is quite right," declared Maisie Talbot, taking up the cudgels for once on Honor's behalf. "There's a difference between her way of breaking rules and yours. She mayn't be exactly a shining example to the class, but, at any rate, she's always square and above-board, and that's more than I can say for you!"

"We're none of us saints," added Lettice, "but we've never gone in for cribbing at Chessington. No other girl in the Form ever does it."

It was not only as regards the question of fairness in her work that Flossie failed to reach the standard of honour current in the Lower Third. She had many little meannesses, so small in themselves as to be hardly worthy of notice, yet enough in the aggregate to exhibit her character unfavourably.

One morning, just as the girls were going to their desks, Maisie Talbot suddenly remembered that it was Miss Farrar's birthday.

"We ought to say something about it," she whispered to Lettice. "I wish we had thought of it before, and bought her some flowers. How stupid we were to forget!"

"Are you sure it's her birthday? How do you know?" asked Flossie, who was standing near, and overheard.

"I'm absolutely certain. I have her name in my birthday book," replied Maisie.

Flossie said no more just then, but the moment Miss Farrar came into the room she stood up and wished her "Many happy returns", in the name of the whole Form, before either Maisie or Lettice had the opportunity to say a word.

They were most annoyed to be thus forestalled.

"It was our idea," protested Lettice afterwards. "You didn't even know it was Miss Farrar's birthday before we mentioned it."

"And yet you calmly took all the credit, and made yourself the mouthpiece of the class!" exclaimed the equally indignant Maisie.

"I suppose I had as good a right as anybody else to offer congratulations," laughed Flossie. "You should have brought yours out a little quicker."

Flossie might be appreciated by her cousins, the Hammond-Smiths, and their particular friends, the Lawsons and the Palmers, but she was certainly not a favourite in her own Form. Nearly everybody had a squabble with her upon some pretext. Even Janie Henderson, whose retiring disposition involved her in few disputes with her schoolfellows, found a cause for complaint. It was one of the ordinary regulations that the girls should each take the office of warden for a week in turn, the duties being to give out any necessary books, clean the blackboard, distribute fresh pens and blotting-paper, and collect any articles that might be left in the room after lesson hours. By general custom all pencils, india-rubbers, or other stray possessions were put into what was known as the forfeit tray, whence their owners might reclaim them by paying the penalty of the loss of an order mark. Each girl had her pencil-box, in which she was expected to keep her own property; but many things were usually left lying about, and the warden always made a careful search at one o'clock.

The most cherished object in Janie's desk was a little, pearl-handled penknife, which she greatly valued. She guarded it zealously, lending it as seldom as she could, and taking good care that it was always returned to her immediately. One unfortunate day, however, she had been sharpening her pencil at the close of the arithmetic lesson, and in the preoccupation of correcting her answers she laid her treasure down, and forgot all about it. She remembered it after dinner, and ran back to the schoolroom to rescue it, but it was nowhere to be found.

"It must have been put in the forfeit tray," she said to herself. "I shall get it to-morrow, though it will cost me an order mark, worse luck!"

She looked eagerly next morning when Miss Farrar produced the tray, but her penknife was not among the lost property. She made a few enquiries in the class, but nobody professed to have seen it, and she was obliged to abandon it as hopelessly gone.

It must have been quite a week after this that one evening, when the St. Chad's girls were sitting in the recreation room, Flossie pulled her handkerchief from her pocket, and in so doing whisked out a pearl-handled penknife. She stooped in a hurry to recover it, but it had fallen under a little table, close to where Pauline Reynolds was sitting, and the latter picked it up instead.

"Hello! This is Janie Henderson's knife," exclaimed Pauline. "Look here, Janie! Isn't this the one you lost?"

"Of course it is," affirmed Janie. "I can tell it by the small blade. There's a tiny piece broken off at the end."

"Where did you get it, Flossie?" enquired
"I found it when I was warden," replied Flossie. "How should I know it was Janie's?"

"You might have asked whose it was," said Maisie. "You've no right to pocket things when you're warden!"

"I wrote a 'Found' notice about it," declared Flossie.

"I never saw any notice," put in Janie.

"Where did you pin this wonderful paper?" asked Pauline.

"On the dressing-room door."

"Where nobody would ever dream of looking!" returned Maisie. "Why couldn't you put the knife on the forfeit tray?"

"I really don't know! What's the use of making such an absurd fuss about trifles?" said Flossie, linking her arm in Norah Palmer's, and turning away.

"I call them principles, not trifles," murmured Maisie; "it's just on the same lines as the cribbing, not quite open and square. I wish Flossie had stayed at St. Bride's; I certainly don't consider her a credit to St. Chad's."

The quarrels between Honor and Flossie occasionally rose to the level of a miniature war. The latter never lost any opportunity of flinging ridicule and contempt on all things Irish, and Honor, who resented a slur on her native land more than a personal injury, could not keep her hot temper within bounds. It was, of course, very foolish to take any notice of Flossie's taunts, and so her friends reminded her.

"The more you blaze up, the more she'll tease, of course," said Maisie.

"Why can't you keep calm, and pretend you don't hear her?" said Pauline. "She doesn't try it on with us."

"You're such a set of stolid Anglo-Saxons!" declared Honor. "You never get roused about anything."

"It's bad form, my dear girl! Hysterics are out of fashion. We don't go in for them at Chessington."

"But you really are entertaining when you're aggressively Celtic, Paddy!" said Lettice. "I own I can't resist taking a rise out of you myself sometimes, just for the fun of seeing you explode."

"You ought to have been born Red Indians!" retorted Honor. "I like people with a little fire. What's the good of having feelings, if one's not to show them?"

"You show them so hard," laughed Lettice, "you make yourself quite ridiculous! I'm sure I shouldn't think one of Flossie's silly jokes was worth making any fuss about."

This was very excellent and practical schoolgirl wisdom, but unfortunately Lettice preached a philosophy of stoicism to which Honor had not yet attained. At the least provocation her fiery Irish blood always asserted itself, and she would flare up, albeit she was conscious that, by so doing, she was affording her enemy the keenest satisfaction, and was providing amusement for the other girls, who enjoyed "hearing Paddy break out".

One morning the feud came to a crisis. When Honor opened her desk she found inside a neat little collection of new potatoes, and on the top, pinned to the biggest, a paper in Flossie's handwriting, bearing these lines:

Honor's Wish

Oh, Erin, moist Erin, how damp are thy showers!

I would I were back 'mid thy pigs and thy rills!

The "tater" to me is more dear than thy flowers,

And I relish the rain on thy ever-wet hills.

Honor could not help laughing at this, in spite of the aspersion on the climate of her country. Such a quip, however, could not go unrequited, and she sought for means of retaliation. She decided that Flossie deserved a "booby trap", and fled back early to the classroom after lunch, to set it for her. It was a rather difficult and delicate operation, for she did not wish to catch anybody else by mistake. She balanced a big dictionary so that it rested on the top of the door and the lintel of the doorway; then, stationing herself inside the room, she held the handle firmly, lest someone should disturb her arrangement by flinging back the door, which was just sufficiently wide open to allow a single person to enter. She peeped every now and then into the passage, on the look-out for Flossie, and admitted each returning girl with caution and due warning.

"Here she is at last!" whispered Lettice, who was naughty enough to enjoy practical jokes, and, after admiring the preparations, had offered to act scout.

"Is she really coming in next?"

"Yes; she's walking in front of May Thurston and Dorothea Chambers."

"Are you certain?"

"Absolutely."

"Then tell me when!"

"Now!"

Honor pulled open the door, and down crashed the dictionary, tumbling full on the head, not of Flossie Taylor, but (oh! horrible miscarriage of justice!) of Miss Farrar herself. At exactly the wrong moment the teacher had popped out of the next classroom, and, as Flossie had stood politely aside to give her precedence, she had walked straight into the trap destined for her pupil.

The dictionary was heavy, and in its fall its sharp corner caught Miss Farrar on the cheek. She stopped, almost dazed by the sudden blow, and, pressing her handkerchief to her face, drew it back marked with a red stain. At the sight of the blood Honor uttered a shriek, and, rushing from the room, fled down the passage, as if to escape from the horror of what she had done. In almost a state of panic she ran across the quadrangle, and, turning into the garden, sought refuge inside the tool-shed. Here she was found some time afterwards by Janie, who had been sent to look for her, and had vainly searched St. Chad's and every other likely spot of which she could think.

Honor never did things by halves; if she wept, she wept, and at present she was a perfect Niobe, almost drowned in tears. When she saw Janie she gave her streaming eyes a hasty mop with a very wet pocket-handkerchief.

"Have I killed her?" she asked, in a tragic whisper.

"Of course not!" replied Janie. "It was only a small cut on the cheek. It's all right now it has been bathed with cold water."

"I was afraid they'd bring it in murder," groaned Honor. "Oh, the ill luck of it, that it should have been Miss Farrar! And the dictionary came down with such a frightful bang! I can never look her in the face again."

"You'll have to!" said Janie. "I was sent to fetch you back at once. You needn't be afraid, Miss Farrar has taken it so nicely."

Poor Honor's apologies and the depths of her genuine remorse would have melted the hardest of hearts, much more that of her teacher.

"We'll say no more about it," declared Miss Farrar. "All the same, remember that I cannot allow such things to happen in the classroom. You might have hurt Flossie very seriously. No, my scratch is nothing! It will be healed directly. But if you are really sorry, Honor, you must give me your most solemn promise that you will never play such a dangerous practical joke again."

CHAPTER VII

St. Chad's Celebrates an Occasion

During her first few days at Chessington, Honor had considered the College as little better than a prison; but as time went on and she grew more accustomed to the routine, she began to reverse her opinion. After all, it was pleasant to have companionship. The various fresh interests, the many jokes, amusements, and constant small excitements inseparable from a large community of girls seemed to open out a new phase of existence for her.

"I'd no idea what school was like before I came," she confided to Janie. "Of course, the boys were always talking of the things they did, and of the fagging and bullying and ragging that went on, but I was sure they were piling on the horror for my benefit, and that it wasn't really as bad as they pretended."

"Why, no one bullies at girls' schools," said Janie.

"I know they don't; but Derrick and Dermot stuffed me with all kinds of ridiculous tales, just for the sake of teasing. They said that Chessington was exactly on the model of a boys' college, and that if girls learnt Latin and mathematics, and played cricket and hockey, and had a gymnasium and a debating society, it put such a masculine element into them that they couldn't refrain from using brute force, instead of any other means of persuasion. They declared it was a natural sequence, and I must make up my mind to it. Derrick even offered to teach me to box before I came, as a useful accomplishment!"

"Did you accept?"

"No, thank you!—not after the way I'd seen him knock Brian about. I suppose brothers are always teases."

"I've no experience, because I haven't any brothers. I've nobody except Mother; but she's as good as a whole family combined." When Janie mentioned her mother her eyes always shone, and her face would light up. It was evident the two were everything to one another, and that the separation during term-time was a hardship.

"I didn't want to go to school at all," continued Honor; "not, of course, because I believed Derrick's absurd stories, but simply because I was so fond of home that I hated to leave."

"That's just how I felt. Mother and I had such a delightful time together, I was sure Chessington couldn't be half so nice."

"What used you to do? You've scarcely told me anything about your home, though I often talk about Kilmore."

"We live in quite a quiet place," began Janie, "though it's not so out-of-the-world as Kerry. Our house is at Redcliffe, a village a few miles from Tewkesminster. It's a beautiful country. There are lovely farms, with red-tiled roofs and big orchards and picturesque barns; and there's a splendid old castle overlooking the river. And then the trees! You ought to see our trees! These about Chessington look the most wretched, stunted things, after our grand oaks and elms. It's a great fruit-growing neighbourhood; we have heaps and heaps of apples and pears and plums and apricots in our garden. They're simply delicious when they're ripe. Then Tewkesminster is so quaint! There are all kinds of funny little side streets, with cottages built at odd angles; and there's a market cross and several old churches, as well as the Minster. Mother is extremely fond of painting, and sometimes she takes me out sketching with her. I can't draw very well yet—most of my attempts are horrid daubs! but Mother is such a good teacher, she always makes one want to try."

"Hadn't you a governess?" asked Honor.

"Yes. Miss Hall used to come every day from Tewkesminster; but I had a few lessons from Mother as well, in drawing, and Greek history, and English literature. We used to read books aloud in the evenings—Shakespeare, or Dickens, or sometimes Tennyson or Wordsworth. We got through a tremendous amount of poetry in the winter, when it was dark early, and we had nothing else to do, except sit by the fire. We read all Marmion and the Idylls of the King and Lalla Rookh, as well as shorter pieces. Mother reads aloud most beautifully; it's delightful to listen to her. Then in summer-time we used to go country walks, and find wild flowers, and bring them back and hunt out their names in the botany book. I kept a Nature Calendar, and put down everything I noted—when the first violets were out, and when I heard the cuckoo, or saw a swallow for the first time in the year; and what birds' nests I found, or butterflies, or moths, or caterpillars. Sometimes I drew pictures of them as well. I had a whole row of specimen sheets pinned round the school-room at home. Then one day a wretched doctor told Mother that Tewkesminster was too relaxing a place for me, and recommended Chessington. I begged and implored not to be sent away, but Mother said the doctor was quite right, and that I was far too grown-up for my age, and an only child ought to have young companions, so I must certainly go to school at once. I was absolutely miserable my first term. I'm a little more used to it now, but I begin to count the days to the holidays directly I get back to St. Chad's. There are still eight weeks before we break up!"

Janie spoke of home with the intense longing of a girl who is not naturally fond of the social side of life. She was out of her element at Chessington, and the strenuous bustle and stimulating whirl of the place, which began to mean so much to Honor, were repugnant to her quiet, reserved disposition. In every big school there are Janies, isolated characters not quite able to run the pace required by the inexorable code of public opinion, interesting to the one or two who may happen to discover their good points, but to the mass of their companions merely names and faces in class. Some of them do fine work in the world afterwards, yet the very qualities that help them to future success are not those to bring present popularity. They are not for the many, but for the few, and only show their best to an occasional friend whose sympathy can overstep the wall of shyness that fences them round.

With Honor alone Janie was at her ease, and she would chat away in their bedroom with a sprightliness that would have amazed the other members of St. Chad's, if they could have heard her. The two girls got on well together. Their opposite dispositions seemed to dovetail into one another, and so to cause little friction; and Miss Maitland, whose observant eyes noticed more than her pupils imagined, was well satisfied with the result of her experiment. Janie kept Honor up to the mark in the way of work; she would generally go over dates or difficult points in the lessons while they were dressing each morning, and it was chiefly owing to her efforts that Honor held a tolerably high place in her class. The latter often wished that she could have performed a like service for her friend in respect of athletics, but Janie was hopeless at physical sports, and endured them only under compulsion.

Every afternoon, from two o'clock till a quarter to four, all the girls were required to take part in organized games, under the direction of Miss Young, the gymnastic mistress. They were allowed their choice between cricket and tennis, but during the specified hours they must not be absent from the playing-fields, as this systematic outdoor exercise formed part of the ordinary course of the school. Now and then it was varied by a walk, and occasionally by an archery or croquet tournament; but these were reserved for insufferably hot days, and the time, as a rule, was devoted to more active pursuits. The cricket pitch lay to the west of the College, a splendid, level tract of ground, commanding a glorious prospect of low, undulating hills, cliffs bordering a shingly beach, and the long, blue stretch of the Channel beyond. All the healthy moorland and sea breezes seemed to blow there, filling the lungs with pure, fresh air, and well justifying Miss Cavendish's boast that Chessington was the most bracing place in the kingdom for growing girls. Even Janie's pale cheeks would take a tinge of pink as she ran, unwillingly enough, in chase of a ball; and the majority of the school would come in at four o'clock flushed and rosy, and very ready indeed for the piles of thick bread and butter that awaited them in the various dining-halls.

Honor took to the games with enthusiasm. Having served an apprenticeship in the Beginners' Division at cricket, and having shown Miss Young her capacity in the way of batting and bowling, she was allowed a place in the St. Chad's team.

It happened that on the very day of her promotion her house played St. Hilary's, and there was great excitement about the match, because the latter was generally considered the crack team of the College. That afternoon, however, the Hilaryites did not quite justify their reputation. Perhaps the St. Chad's bowling had been extra good; at all events, the St. Hilary side was dismissed for sixty-seven.

Honor's heart was beating fast when at length her innings arrived, and, taking her bat, she walked to the wicket. Every eye, she knew, would be fixed upon her play. A new girl, she was standing her trial before the school, and on the result of this match would largely depend her position during the term. She had played cricket during the holidays with her brothers, and all Derrick's rules came crowding into her mind as she tried to imagine that she was on the dear, rough old field at home, with Brian to bowl, and Fergus for long-stop, and Dermot and Osmond to field, and criticize her strokes afterwards.

She held her bat well, keeping her left shoulder to the bowler and her eye on the ball. The bat was a light, new one, which the boys had given her as a parting present, and she felt she could wield it easily. During the first over she played steadily, but did not attempt to score. It was one of Derrick's pet maxims that it was folly to try to do so until you had taken the measure of your opponent, and she wished to gain confidence.

In the next over her partner, Chatty Burns, made a single, which brought Honor to the opposite wicket. Gertrude Humphreys's bowling was more to her taste; it might be described as fast and loose, and Honor, unlike most girls, did not object to swift bowling, having been accustomed to it from Brian and Derrick. The first ball she received came down at a good pace, but well on the off side of the wicket. This was just the chance she had been waiting for, and a well-timed cut sent it flying to the boundary for three. The rest of the over was uneventful, Chatty having evidently made up her mind to be careful. Winnie Sutcliffe now took up the bowling at the other end, but her first ball, being a wide, served to increase the confidence that Honor had felt in breaking her duck. The next ball, though straight on middle stump, was a half-volley; Honor stepped out to it with a feeling of exultation, and a moment later it was soaring over the bowler's head for four.

"Good!" "Well hit, Honor!" "St. Chad's for ever!" "Hurrah!" ejaculated the Chaddites.

Success like this often turns the batter's head, but Honor remembered in time the many cautions she had received from her critical brothers, and the next ball, being of good length, she played quietly to long off for one. Chatty now received the bowling, and, encouraged by Honor's success, made what the girls afterwards described as the finest leg hit they had ever seen. Certainly it was a good stroke, taken quite clean and square, and as it cleared the boards it was marked down six amid rapturous applause. After that runs came more slowly for a time, and neither girl appeared inclined to take any risks. This careful play, however, began to wear down the bowling, especially Gertrude Humphreys's, which became decidedly loose. Honor, seeing her chance, suddenly began hitting about her with a spirit and vigour that almost sent the Chaddites delirious with delight, while even Miss Young was seen laughing and smiling with Miss Maitland in a manner that seemed to imply no small self-congratulation on her choice for the last vacancy in the team.

The Hilaryites were looking decidedly glum at this marked change in the fortunes of the game. Grace Ward, their captain, at the end of the over quietly rolled the ball to Ida Bellamy, famed for her slow "twisters". Her first essay pitched well to the leg side, and Honor, who rather despised "slows", made a mighty stroke at it, not allowing for the break, and missed it altogether. With her heart in her mouth she glanced rapidly round at the wicket, expecting to see her bails fly; but luck was on her side, for the break had been a little too great, and the ball just cleared the off stump.

"A good thing Derrick isn't here," said Honor to herself. "I should never have heard the end of that!"

It was very hard to resist the temptation to hit out, dangerous though she knew it to be, and it was with a sensation of relief that she saw the ball travelling off for a single to long field, thus leaving the rest of the over to Chatty, who, neither so ambitious nor so impatient, played it out without giving the much-longed-for chance of a catch. By this time sixty was up on the board, of which Honor had contributed twenty-eight, to the great satisfaction of all concerned.

But Grace had not played her last card. She had evidently decided on a double change of bowling; for, when the fielders had crossed, Irene Richmond was seen at the wicket. Irene's bowling was peculiar; it was left-handed, which is quite uncommon in a girl, and the more difficult on that account. The Chaddites looked at one another with smiles that were less spontaneous.

Certainly Irene might with advantage have been put on before. Her style, though by no means swift, was most awkward to play. Chatty received the first ball, which beat her completely, though luckily it did not touch the wicket. A minute later she made a single, and Honor felt rather blank, as it was now her turn to face the bowling. One of Derrick's pet rules, however, came into her mind: "When you're in doubt, watch each ball carefully, till you get your eye in"; and by dint of adherence to this, she played out the over with safety.

The slow bowling at the other end, though it looked so simple, was full of weird pitfalls, into one of which Chatty fell an easy victim. She played too soon at a short-pitched ball, and spooned a catch to mid-on, who took good care not to drop it. Chatty retired rather ruefully, but was consoled by the applause she received from the pavilion, her twenty-three runs being regarded as a handsome contribution.

Maisie Talbot came in next. Being tall and athletic for her age, she had a long reach, which she employed successfully in driving the first ball she received right along the ground into "the country" for three. This seemed to disconcert the bowler; the next one she sent down was an easy full pitch. Honor waited till just the right moment, and then, with a fine swing of her bat, sent the ball clean over the boundary for six, a performance that quite "brought down the house", even the Hilaryites joining in the cheering. For a moment no one seemed to have realized how the score was going, but when seventy went up on the board there was a wild rush for the pavilion, for the match was won.

Honor's friends were loud in their congratulations, and Janie, who had been an excited spectator, was almost as proud as if the success had been her own. Vivian Holmes herself actually expressed approval.

"Well played, Honor Fitzgerald!" she said. "I expect some day you'll be a credit to St. Chad's."

As Vivian was generally more ready to "squash" new-comers than to encourage them, this was indeed high praise, and Honor felt inspired to continue her exertions, having the white ribbon of the College team as the object of her ambition.

Great were the rejoicings of the Chaddites at their triumph over St. Hilary's. Something in the way of a celebration seemed necessary to immortalize the occasion, and that evening, after a hurried conference among the elder girls, it was given out that, with Miss Maitland's permission, an impromptu fancy-dress ball would take place in the recreation room at 8.30 precisely.

"We're just to come in any kind of costumes we can manage to contrive," said Lettice Talbot, who, wild with excitement, had carried the thrilling tidings to the younger contingent. "Miss Maitland is going to dress up, and so is Miss Parkinson. The cook is making some lemonade; I hope it will be cold in time, but even if it isn't it will be rather nice hot. Oh, would you advise me to go as a flower-girl, or do you think Queen Elizabeth would be better?"

"I should suggest a Merry-andrew at the present moment," said Ruth Latimer, as Lettice, unable to contain her glee, went hopping round the room. "You could easily put a different coloured stocking on each leg, cut sheets of tissue paper to make a short, frilled, sticking-out skirt, borrow the toasting-fork from the kitchen and hang it with ribbons for your bauble, and there you are!"

"Jolly!" exclaimed Lettice. "I'll do it. Will you lend me your scarlet sponge-bag? It would make the very cap I want."

It was fortunate that Vivian Holmes and her fellow-workers had reserved the announcement of the proposed fête until after preparation, otherwise very few lessons would have been learnt at St. Chad's. The girls finished supper with record speed, and filed out of the dining-hall at least ten minutes earlier than usual, all anxious to flee upstairs and begin the delightful but arduous task of robing themselves in character.

Miss Maitland was the owner of what she called a "theatrical property-box". It held a store of most invaluable possessions, which she had collected from time to time and put by to serve for charades or tableaux. There were old evening dresses and cloaks, feathers, shawls, a few hats, artificial flowers, bright-coloured scarves, beads, bangles, and cracker jewellery, even some false moustaches and beards, a horse pistol, and a pair of top-boots. These she placed entirely at the disposal of the girls, telling Vivian Holmes to distribute them so as to allow as many as possible to have a share. Vivian was strictly impartial, and doled out the treasures with the stern justice of a Roman tribune. They did not go very far, however, among forty Chaddites; so, of necessity, at least half of the costumes had to be composed hastily of anything that came to hand.

The apparelling was a lively process, to judge from the sounds of mirth that issued from the various cubicles; and so many different articles were borrowed, lent, and exchanged that it was a wonder their respective owners ever managed to claim them again. Strict secrecy was observed, the occupants of each bedroom denying even a peep to their next-door neighbours, who, though full of their own preparations, could not fail to exhibit curiosity when such exclamations as, "Oh, how lovely!" or, "It's simply screaming!" were wafted down the passage.

Nowhere was the excitement keener than in No. 8, though Honor and Janie had the fun all to themselves. The latter had decided to go as a friar. She had contrived a capital monk's habit out of her waterproof, tied round the waist with the cord that held back the window curtains. The hood formed the cowl, a dictionary made a very passable breviary, and a hockey stick served as a pilgrim's staff.

"You're just like a palmer returning from the Holy Land," declared Honor.

"Or the 'Friar of Orders Grey'," said Janie, "who—

"'Walked forth to tell his beads,

And he met with a lady fair

Clad in a pilgrim's weeds!'

"I ought to have a rosary, but there isn't anything that would do in the least for it."

"Never mind! One must imagine it is in your pocket. Even palmers couldn't tell their beads all day long. You look a most unsuitable figure to dance! I'm afraid they would turn you out of your monastery, if they caught you."

Honor was determined to enact the part of Dick Turpin. She had corked herself the most ferocious moustaches, and made a cocked hat out of brown paper; and was now only waiting for a certain cloak, the horse pistol, and the pair of top-boots, which Vivian had promised to bring her if Barbara Russell, one of the elder girls, did not want them.

"I heard Barbara say she meant to be a shepherdess," she said, "so she couldn't possibly wear top-boots. I don't believe anybody else has thought of a highwayman. I wish Vivian would be quick!"

She was in a ferment of excitement. A festivity such as this was an event in her life. She could hardly bear to wait, and would have been down the passage in search of the missing properties, only she did not wish to exhibit her beautiful moustaches before the right time.

"Vivian won't be long," Janie assured her. "She is the most dependable person I know; when she says she'll do a thing, she does it. Oh, here she is now!"

Honor sprang to the door, but her face fell as she saw the monitress arrive empty-handed.

"I'm dreadfully sorry!" announced Vivian. "Barbara decided, after all, to be Oliver Cromwell, so of course she wanted the cloak, boots, and pistol. I've brought you a few bangles and a wreath of flowers, if they'll be of any use to you; I've nothing else left. I must fly! I've to get into my own costume."

Poor Honor! It was a bitter disappointment. She had counted so much on representing Dick Turpin that to have to forgo the part seemed little short of a tragedy.

"I can't do a highwayman in nothing but a pair of corked moustaches!" she exclaimed dolefully.

"It is a pity," sympathized Janie, "but of course it can't be helped. If we're very quick we shall just have time to think of something else. Could you manage a fairy, with the bangles and the wreath and a white petticoat?"

"A fairy! No! Do I look like a fairy? I'm so cross, it would have to be a goblin. I know what I'll do; I shall go as an Arab."

"With the towels wound round you, I suppose?"

"They're not big enough; I must use my sheets," and Honor, suiting her action to her words, ruthlessly disarranged her bed.

If the towels were too small, the sheets proved too large. In spite of Janie's efforts (much hampered by her cassock and cowl) they refused to drape elegantly. Honor lost all patience at last, and, seizing her scissors, ripped the offending sheets in halves with uncompromising fingers.

"Oh, Honor, what have you done? How could you? Oh, what will Miss Maitland say?" shrieked Janie, almost in tears.

"I don't care!" declared Honor recklessly.

In her present excited state she would have torn up her best dress with equal readiness. She was elated with her success in the

cricket field—what the Scotch call "fey"; and so long as she grat-
ified her present whim, she had no thought at all for the future.

"I must have some costume," she continued, "and we ought to
go downstairs at once. They're my own sheets, so what does it
matter? It isn't as if they were school property; I brought them
from home with the rest of my linen—they're marked 'H. Fitzgerald' in the corner."

"You'll get into a shocking scrape, all the same," said Janie, who
was horror-stricken at her friend's lawlessness.

There was no time, however, to think about consequences. The
gong was giving the signal for the parade to begin, and various
gigglings and exclamations in the passage warned them that the
other girls were already issuing from their rooms. Honor hastily
finished her Arab toilet, and without further delay the pair joined
the rest of the masqueraders in the hall.

Here a brilliant scene awaited them. Considering the scanty
materials at command, quite marvellous results had been accomplished. The costumes were most gay and varied, and many
of them showed extreme ingenuity on the part of their wearers.
Lettice Talbot had carried out Ruth Latimer's idea for a Merry-andrew with great success, and was evidently endeavouring
to sustain the character by firing off bad puns, or facetious remarks on the appearance of her friends. Dorothy Arkwright, in a
blue evening dress and a black velvet hat with feathers, made a
dignified Duchess of Devonshire; and Pauline Reynolds, whose
long, golden hair hung below her waist, came arrayed as Fair
Rosamond. There were several Italian peasants, a Cavalier, a
Roundhead, and a matador. Agnes Bennett, one of the elder girls,
impersonated the Pied Piper of Hamelin. By pinning two dress-
ing-gowns (one of red and one of buff) together, she had well
imitated the "queer long coat from heel to head, half of yellow
and half of red", worn by the mysterious stranger; and, with her
pipe, hung with ribbons, at her lips, seemed ready to charm either rats into the Weser, or children into the hillside. Edith Hammond-Smith was a fairy, and Claudia a pierrot; while Flossie Taylor, in an Eastern shawl, and with bangles tied on for ear-rings,
looked a gorgeous Cleopatra.

Chatty Burns, in a tartan plaid, made a typical "Highland las-
sie". Effie Lawson, with her hair plaited in a tight pigtail, and
her eyebrows corked aslant, had, with the aid of a coloured bed-
spread and a Japanese umbrella, turned herself into a very cred-
itable "Heathen Chinee"; and Maisie Talbot, who found materials
waxing scarce after she had finished arraying Lettice, had flung a

skin rug over her shoulders, painted her face in streaks of red and black, and come as a savage. Adeline Vaughan had an original and rather striking costume. She called herself "Scholastica", and had decorated herself with a double row of exercise books, suspended by ribbons round her waist. Pencils, india-rubbers, pens, and rulers were fastened to all parts of her dress; and a College cap, borrowed from Miss Maitland, completed the effect.

The funniest of all, however, was Madge Summers, who represented a sausage. She had been elaborately got up for the part by her room-mates. They borrowed a coloured table-cloth from the kitchen, the reverse side of which was a pinky-fawn shade; then they padded Madge carefully all over, so as to make her the right shape, swathed her in the table-cloth, and fastened it down the back with safety-pins, tying it tightly round her neck and ankles. She could scarcely manage to walk, much less dance; and she was so hot in her many wrappings that her face burnt—so she assured her friends—as if she were already on the frying-pan: but if she could not take an active part in the proceedings, she had the satisfaction of attracting an immense amount of attention.

The girls chose partners in the hall, and marched in procession into the recreation room, where Miss Maitland (a stately Marie Antoinette) acted hostess, and received her guests with the assistance of Miss Parkinson (a Spanish gipsy) and Vivian Holmes (hastily attired as a troubadour).

"It is indeed a carnival," said Miss Maitland. "The costumes are splendid, and all deserve hearty congratulations. We shall have to take votes as to which is the best. We haven't thought of the music yet; it seems almost presumptuous to ask Queen Cleopatra to play a waltz for us, but perhaps she will condescend thus far. We can't ask the sausage, for she hasn't any arms! The troubadour and the Pied Piper ought to do their share, and the Merry-andrew must give us a pas seul."

Everybody declared the evening to be the greatest success. The lemonade, fortunately cold, was delicious, and so were the biscuits that Miss Maitland, through lack of any other dainties, had provided as refreshments. Half-past nine came far too soon, and the dancers, hot, flushed, and excited, were forced reluctantly to abandon the festivities and betake themselves upstairs to tear off their grandeur.

Honor slept between the blankets that night, and her slumbers were haunted by a vision of Miss Maitland, as an avenging spectre, arrayed in the mutilated sheets. The dream was certainly prophetic, for the house-mistress was extremely angry on discovering the damage done, and gave Honor a lecture such as she richly deserved.

"You will stay in from cricket to-day, and mend the sheets," she decreed, at the conclusion of the scolding. "You will find them ready fixed by two o'clock. I shall expect the seams to be neatly run, and the edges turned over and hemmed."

Honor groaned. After the excitement of yesterday's match, she had been looking forward to the cricket practice; moreover, she hated sewing. But there was no appeal. Each house-mistress had authority to suspend games, if necessary, so she was compelled to pass a weary afternoon at a most uncongenial occupation.

"It's hard labour!" she exclaimed, when Janie ran in at four o'clock. "Finished! No! I've only run one seam, and hemmed about six inches. I feel like the 'Song of the shirt' (only it's the song of the sheet instead). 'Stitch, stitch, stitch', and 'work, work, work'! My fingers are getting quite 'weary and worn'. There's one comfort, at any rate: Miss Maitland won't be likely to keep me away from preparation, and as the clothes go to the wash to-morrow, perhaps she'll let one of the maids do the rest of this, and give me some other penance instead. I'd rather learn five chapters of history, or a scene from Shakespeare; and I'd welcome a whole page of equations—I would indeed!"

"I'm afraid it's a vain hope," said Janie. "Miss Maitland always sticks to her word."

She proved right; Miss Maitland was inexorable. The discipline at Chessington was strict, and any mistress who gave an order was accustomed to enforce it rigorously. Honor was obliged to forgo the triumphs of the playing-fields until the very last stitch had been put in her sheets—a punishment which was severe enough, if not entirely to work a reform, at any rate to sober her considerably for the present.

CHAPTER VIII

A Mysterious Happening

I wonder how it is," philosophized Ruth Latimer, "that one always seems to like some girls so much, and detest others? There are certain people who, no matter what they do, or even if their intentions are good, always rub one up the wrong way."

"Natural affinity, or the reverse, I suppose," answered Maisie Talbot. "I'm a great believer in first impressions. I can generally tell in five minutes whether I'm going to be friends with anyone or not; and I find I'm nearly certain to be right in the long run."

"I suppose I must have a natural antipathy, then, against Flossie Taylor," confessed Honor candidly. "It didn't take me as long as five minutes to discover my sentiments towards her."

"I don't wonder," said Lettice. "Flossie is a bounder!"

"What's that?"

"Oh, Paddy! You've lived at the back of beyond! A bounder means—well—just a bounder; putting on side, you know."

"How particularly lucid and enlightening!"

"It means someone who tries to make herself out of more consequence than she really is," explained Maisie. "Flossie is continually dragging into her conversation the grand things she has at home, and the grand people she stays with."

"She doesn't mention them naturally, as anyone might do without being offensive," said Ruth Latimer. "She parades them just to show off, in a particularly obtrusive and objectionable manner."

"And we think that very bad taste at Chessington, because, of course, almost all of us have quite as nice homes and friends, only we don't care to boast about them."

"It looks as if you hadn't been accustomed to decent things, if you're always wanting to let people know you possess them," added Lettice.

"The worst of it is," continued Maisie, "that she's having a bad influence at St. Chad's. The Hammond-Smiths and the Lawsons and the Palmers follow her lead implicitly, and she's completely spoiling Rhoda Cunliffe and Hope Robertson. They used to be quite different before Flossie came. I don't think Jessie Gray and Gladys Chesters have improved either lately. It seems such a pity, because we've always prided ourselves that St. Chad's was the best house in the College, and we don't want this kind of element to creep in."

"What can we do?" asked Ruth Latimer.

"Suppose we form a league against it! All the nicer girls would join, and if Flossie and her set see that we really vote them bad style, perhaps they'll have the sense to drop it."

"All right. Put me down as your first member. What's the name of the Society?"

"We might call it the 'Anti-Bounders'. It has a brisk, rolling sound that's rather jolly."

"The A.B.S. for short," suggested Honor.

"And the rules?" asked Ruth.

"Those could be short and sweet—something on these lines:

"1. No member is to make an unnecessary or ostentatious display of wealth or valuables.

"2. No member is to brag constantly of high connections or titled friends.

"3. Members are to consider, not money, but culture, as the standard of public estimation at St. Chad's; and to remember that the essence of good breeding is simplicity.

"4. Any member transgressing any of these rules will be black-balled."

"Excellent!" said Ruth. "It puts what we mean in a nutshell. Now, we must write that out, and try to get signatures. We might add a fifth rule, about not doing sneaking tricks; it's decidedly necessary."

"And our motto could be Noblesse oblige," proposed Honor.

The "Anti-Bounders" met with favour among a large proportion of the Chaddites, but with much derision from Flossie and her friends, who lost no opportunity of ridiculing the league, nicknamed its members "The Pharisees", and threw open scorn upon its rules. Nevertheless, in spite of their opposition, the society was strong enough to work a decided improvement, particularly among a certain section who were ready to trim their sails according to the prevailing wind, and to follow blindly the general consensus of public opinion. In future any girl guilty of inordinate bragging was christened "Chanticler", and a warning "Cock-a-doodle-doo!" would advise her of the fact without further explanation.

"It's quite enough!" said Maisie. "We don't want to rub it in too hard, but just to let them see that we notice. Jessie Gray is better already, and although Flossie and Claudia make so much fun of us they're really extremely nettled, because they thought themselves the absolute perfection of good style, and it has been a great blow to them to discover that three-quarters of the house consider them bad form."

It was a constant annoyance to Maisie, Lettice, and Pauline that Flossie should occupy the fourth cubicle in No. 13 bedroom, and they often wondered why Miss Maitland had placed so uncongenial a companion in their midst—"especially when Adeline Vaughan is with the Hammond-Smiths in No. 10," said Lettice. "If we might only make an exchange, everybody would be satisfied."

Miss Maitland, however, had reasons for her arrangements, which she did not care to explain. She knew far more of the inner life of the house than the girls suspected, and hoped that by a judicious sandwiching of different elements certain undesirable traits might be eliminated, and the general tone raised. Though she was often aware of things that were not entirely to her satisfaction, she was wise enough not to interfere directly, but by careful tactics to allow the reformation to work from within, experience having taught her that codes fixed by the girls themselves were twice as binding as those enforced by the authorities.

The bedrooms at St. Chad's were on two floors, Nos. 9 to 16 being on the upper story, and Nos. 1 to 7 on the lower. No. 8, occupied by Honor and Janie, was the higher of two small rooms built over the porch, and occupied a position midway between the two floors, being reached by a short flight of steps from the landing below. In No. 4 slept Evelyn Fletcher, the youngest girl in the house. She shared the room with an elder sister and two cousins, all three members of the Sixth Form. Though Evelyn was thirteen, she was very small and childish for her age, and was treated rather as a pet by the Chaddites. She was a pretty little thing, with appealing blue eyes, fluffy hair, and a helpless, dependent manner. It was the great trial of her life that she was obliged to go to bed more than an hour before the other occupants of No. 4. She had a morbid horror of being alone in the dark—a horror that, through a sensitive dread of being laughed at, she had so far confessed to no one, but which, all the same, was very real and overwhelming. Night after night she would lie with the curtain of her cubicle half-drawn, and the door ajar so as to catch a gleam of light from the landing, listening with every nerve on the alert for she knew not what, and enduring agonies until the welcome moment when her sister Meta came upstairs. It was, of course, very foolish, but her terror was probably due to a dangerous illness from which she had suffered some years before, and which had left a permanent delicacy.

One evening the younger girls had retired as usual, and everything was very quiet in the upper stories. Evelyn lay wide-awake, sometimes straining her ears to catch a sound from the ground floor below, and sometimes burying her head in her pillow. Suddenly she sat up in bed, with wide-open, terror-stricken eyes. On the opposite wall there gleamed a strange, dancing light, which appeared and disappeared and reappeared again, flickering faintly from floor to ceiling. There seemed no explainable origin for it, and Evelyn's mind at once turned to the supernatural. A silly maidservant at home had been accustomed to ply her with ghost stories, all of which now recurred to her memory. What was it, that unnatural, luminous halo on the opposite wall? It was moving nearer to her, and had almost reached the curtain of her cubicle, when, with a choking little gasp, she sprang out of bed, and darting into the corridor ran shrieking upstairs, her one idea being to escape from the mysterious apparition.

Her screams not only roused all the girls on the higher rooms, but brought up Vivian Holmes, who had been crossing the hall at the moment, and felt it her duty as monitress to go and investigate.

"What's all this noise about?" she asked. "Evelyn, what's the matter? Has anything frightened you?"

"It's something on my wall," panted Evelyn; "something white, that moves."

"What was it like?"

"I don't know—I can't describe it."

"Perhaps it was a ghost," said Honor, in a hollow voice; "they come softly, this way," and, pulling a horrible face, she moved slowly forward with a gliding motion, her white night-dress completing the illusion.

Trembling from head to foot, Evelyn turned and clung to the monitress.

"Stop that, Honor!" exclaimed Vivian sharply. "It's a wicked thing to frighten anybody. Come along, Evie! I'll go with you to your room, and we'll try to find out what this mysterious 'something' is. Go back to bed at once, all the rest of you!"

After making a thorough inspection of No. 4, Vivian found that the uncanny light was, after all, very easy of explanation. It was nothing but the reflection from a lamp outside, and the swaying of the blind had been responsible for the movement. Having shown Evelyn the unromantic origin of her spectre, the monitress left her, apparently pacified, and went downstairs.

In the upper rooms all was soon in absolute stillness. The girls took Vivian's advice and retired to bed again, laughing at having been disturbed for so trivial a cause.

"Evelyn Fletcher is a goose!" said Flossie Taylor. "She'd run away from her own shadow."

"She is rather silly," agreed Maisie Talbot. "I've no patience with people who imagine ghosts!"

Maisie's own nerves were of the stoutest. She certainly could not sympathize with superstitious fears, and neither flickering lights nor possible spectres would have distressed her in the least.

"When people shriek at nothing and rouse the whole house, they deserve to have something to shriek at," remarked Flossie.

But Maisie was in the act of hopping into bed, and only grunted in reply, while Pauline and Lettice were already half-asleep. Flossie lay for a minute or two pondering over the affair, then got up again very softly. First, she felt on her washstand for her tooth powder, and dabbed her face plentifully with it till she was sure it must be white all over; then she took the towel, and arranged it over her head, to hide her hair. In every bedroom at St. Chad's there were a candle and a box of matches, in case the electric light should suddenly fail; Flossie groped for these and found them, and, taking them in her hand, left the room on tiptoe.

"Where are you going?" asked Maisie drowsily, but receiving no reply, she did not even trouble to open her eyes.

Once outside the door, Flossie lighted her candle. She was determined, in spite of Vivian's warning, to play a trick upon Evelyn.

"She needs teasing out of such rubbish," she said to herself. "Vivian Holmes always makes an absurd fuss of her—quite spoils her, in fact. I think the best way to cure people is to laugh at them."

Creeping softly downstairs, she switched off the electric light at the end of the lower landing, and, shading her candle with her hand, passed along in the darkness to No. 4. Without pausing a moment she entered, holding up one arm in a dramatic attitude, and making her eyes glare wildly from her whitened face. The effect was beyond all that she had anticipated. Such a scream of agonized fear came from the bed in the corner that, alarmed at what she had done, Flossie turned and fled. As she ran through the door she realized that somebody was hastening along the dark passage, and, afraid of being discovered, she turned suddenly and rushed up the short flight of steps that led to Honor's bedroom, blowing out her candle as she went. She crouched for a few moments outside the door of No. 8, then, hearing no footsteps pursuing her, she ventured to steal down again and make a dash for the stairs and the upper landing, where she whisked into No. 13 with all possible speed.

"It was a narrow shave!" she said to herself. "If that was Vivian, and she had caught me, I expect she'd have made herself uncommonly disagreeable."

In the meantime, Vivian had returned to the recreation room, and told the story of Evelyn's groundless fears to the elder girls assembled there.

"A shock of this kind is extremely bad for Evie," said Meta. "She had a nervous fever four years ago, and has been so fragile and highly-strung ever since. She was sent to Chessington because we hoped the bracing air might do her good. I remember she used to have night terrors when she was a wee child, but we thought she had quite got over them."

"She looks very white and delicate," said Vivian. "She's all eyes. If she were my sister, I should like to see her less 'nervy'."

"Perhaps I had better run upstairs to her," said Meta, rather anxiously. "Now I think of it, I remember she always seems most relieved when May and Trissie and I make our appearance at nine-thirty."

Meta found the landing in total darkness, a most unusual occurrence, as the electric light was always left on there. She felt her way along by the wall, and as she did so she was aware of somebody coming towards her from the opposite end of the long corridor. Whoever it was carried a light in her hand, so small as to make only a faint glimmer, but enough to allow Meta to perceive that she turned into No. 4. The next moment a cry of frantic fear issued from the room. Meta hurried forward, her heart throbbing wildly, while the figure, rushing from the room, and showing in its hasty flight a white-veiled head, darted up the steps to No. 8, and disappeared, light and all.

It did not take Meta more than three seconds to reach her sister's bedside. Strangled sounds issued from under the clothes, where Evelyn lay cowering in mortal terror; and again, as Meta placed her hand on the bed, came that convulsive, half-stifled cry.

"Evie! Evie dear! Don't you know me?" exclaimed Meta.

Realizing at last who stood near, Evelyn sat up and flung her arms round her sister. She was in a most agitated, hysterical condition, trembling and quivering with sobs. Meta soothed her as well as she could, and requested Vivian, who had followed to see that all was right, to switch on the bedroom light, and also the one in the passage.

"Someone must have intentionally turned it off," she said, "on purpose to play this trick."

"I know I'm silly!" choked Evelyn, more reassured now that the room was no longer in darkness, "but I can't help it. I really thought it was a ghost."

"Who is responsible for this?" asked Vivian indignantly.

"Honor Fitzgerald," replied Meta, without hesitation.

"Are you sure?"

"Whoever it was ran back into No. 8. Janie Henderson would never dream of doing such a thing, so it must have been Honor."

"She certainly was pretending to be a ghost upstairs," said Vivian. "I shall go and tell her my opinion of her," and she departed with a very grim expression on her face.

Janie and Honor were half-asleep when Vivian, like an avenging angel, entered No. 8.

"Look here, Honor Fitzgerald!" she began, "if you try any more of those senseless practical jokes, I shall report you to Miss Maitland. I'm monitress here, and I don't intend to have this kind of thing going on at St. Chad's."

"What's the matter?" asked Honor, rubbing her eyes.

"Matter, indeed! You know as well as I do. It was a cruel, mean trick to play upon a nervous, delicate girl like Evie Fletcher."

Honor was considerably astonished. She, of course, knew nothing of Flossie's escapade, and imagined that the monitress must be referring to the few words she had said on the upper landing.

"Why, Evie didn't seem to mind all that much!" she retorted.

"You've frightened her most seriously, and I consider it so dangerous that I'd rather you were expelled from the school than that it should happen again. I don't want to get you into trouble at head-quarters if I can help it, so I'll say nothing if you'll promise me faithfully that this is absolutely the last time you'll ever act ghost."

"Of course I'll promise. I didn't intend to upset Evie. I think both you and she are making a great fuss about nothing," replied Honor, lying down once more.

"I'm disgusted with you, Honor Fitzgerald! If you can't realize the mischief your thoughtlessness has done, you might at least have the grace to be sorry for it! To amuse yourself by playing on the fears of a timid girl, younger than you, is the work of a coward—yes, a coward! That's what I consider you!" and Vivian turned away, full of righteous wrath, and wondering whether she had adequately fulfilled her monitorial duty, or whether she ought to have said even more.

CHAPTER IX

Diamond cut Diamond

Honor was both amazed and indignant at Vivian's stern rebuke. She appealed to Janie in self-justification.

"I don't understand it," she declared. "I only screwed up my face, and said ghosts glided. I stopped at once when Vivian asked me. How could Evelyn have been so fearfully frightened just at that?"

"I can't imagine," said Janie, "except that she's such an extremely nervous girl."

"It's too bad to blame me on that account."

"Vivian is generally very severe."

"She's always down on me! I'm continually in hot water, and half the time I don't know exactly why."

It was not until the next afternoon that Honor learnt of the practical joke that had been practised upon her schoolfellow. As she was washing her hands in the dressing-room she chanced to overhear a few remarks between two or three girls who were discussing the affair, and at once questioned them about it.

"Of course Meta knew it was you, Honor!" said Ruth Latimer, rather reproachfully.

"Why of course?" asked Honor.

"Because it couldn't be anyone else. You're always playing tricks upon someone."

"It's a case of 'give a dog a bad name', then. I'm innocent for once."

"But the ghost ran up the steps to No. 8!"

"That's only 'circumstantial evidence'. I certainly didn't do it. Janie can tell you that I never left the bedroom."

"Yes, I could take my oath in a law court, as a reliable witness," vouched Janie.

"Then who was it?"

Honor shook her head.

"Ask me a harder!" she said briefly.

Flossie, who was standing near, looked rather conscious, but volunteered no explanation.

"It's a most peculiar thing," said Ruth. "Somebody must have been the ghost, I suppose."

"Unless it were a real one!" suggested Flossie. "It might——"

"What nonsense! Nobody believes in ghosts, except, perhaps, Evelyn," interrupted Ruth scornfully. "Of course, it was a girl playing a trick. The only question is, who?"

"Could it be May or Trissie Turner?" suggested Flossie.

"Impossible! Evelyn's own cousins—and in the Sixth Form, too!"

"It's very extraordinary!"

"It ought to be properly cleared up," said Lettice Talbot.

"Suppose we ask every girl in the house if she knows anything," proposed Dorothy Arkwright.

"No; Meta begged us to let the matter drop," replied Ruth. "She says Evelyn is extremely sensitive about it, and can't bear the subject alluded to."

"Evelyn looked very ill this morning," observed Dorothy.

"Yes; Meta says she has had a severe shock, and the least reference to it might upset her again."

"So it will have to remain unexplained?"

"I suppose so," said Flossie. "It seems a complete mystery."

"Why, Flossie!" exclaimed Maisie Talbot suddenly, "didn't I hear you get up last night, after Vivian had gone downstairs and we had marched off to bed again? I remember I called out to you, but I was too sleepy to wake up properly. I verily believe it must have been you who frightened Evelyn. Honestly now, was it?"

Flossie turned very red. She would have continued to shield herself at Honor's expense if it had been any longer possible, but she was not prepared to tell a direct falsehood. There was no way out of it but to confess.

"What a storm in a teacup!" she replied, shrugging her shoulders. "It's absurd if one can't play the least joke without a monitress interfering and making a ridiculous fuss. It was only meant for fun; I should have laughed if anybody had done it to me."

"It's no laughing matter," said Maisie gravely. "In the first place, though Evelyn may be silly, you had no right to frighten her; and in the second place, you deliberately let the blame rest on Honor's shoulders."

"Vivian ought to be told of this," declared Dorothy.

"Yes, she must know at once," added Ruth.

"Oh, please don't go sneaking to the monitress on my account!" interposed Honor. "If Meta wants the affair to drop, it shall. Both she and Vivian took it for granted last night that I had acted the ghost in No. 4; they never asked me, or gave me a chance of denying it, so I shan't trouble to undeceive them. If Vivian has such a poor opinion of me already, she shan't think me a tell-tale in addition. As for Flossie, she's not worth noticing."

"But telling a monitress isn't like telling a teacher," objected Ruth.

"It savours of sneaking, and I prefer to leave it alone. What does it matter? I don't care about anybody's opinion!"

Honor was on her high horse. She had been much hurt by Vivian's injustice, and all the Fitzgerald pride was roused within her. Notwithstanding the girls' remonstrances, she would not allow herself to be cleared of the false charge.

"The whole thing is altogether beneath me," she remarked, as she stalked haughtily away.

"It's no good trying to persuade her," said Lettice. "When she puts that set look on her face, arguments are absolutely useless."

"On the whole, I think I rather admire her for saying nothing," commented Maisie. "It's more dignified than making a fuss. I can't tolerate tale-bearing myself. It would have got Flossie into a terrific scrape with Vivian, and probably with Miss Maitland as well."

"Flossie doesn't deserve to go scot-free," said Ruth, with a glance at the flaxen head that was discreetly disappearing through the door.

"She won't!" asserted Lettice. "Honor is the most contrary, queer, impossible, perverse girl I've ever met. She'll let Flossie off easily now, but she'll make her pay for it in some other way. I could see it in her eye. She was as cool as a cucumber outside, but I'm sure that was only the crust over the crater, and that there was the usual volcano inside. It's bound to find a safety-valve, so Flossie had better look out for squalls!"

Lettice was right. Honor was certainly in a most unenviable frame of mind. She considered that Vivian had treated her unfairly in assuming her to be guilty without making any proper investigation.

"It's the first time a Fitzgerald has ever been called a coward!" she said to Janie.

The word rankled in her memory even more than the monitress's high-handed manner.

"Then you must use every opportunity of showing that you're the reverse," replied Janie. "You'll have to live the thing down. I expect the truth will come round to Vivian's ears in course of time, and I'm sure that she'll think far better of you than if we had gone at once to her with a long accusation against Flossie. If

Flossie herself had offered to tell, that would have been different; but she didn't rise to such a pitch of heroism."

"One wouldn't expect it from Flossie Taylor!" said Honor contemptuously, as she hurried off to her music lesson.

I am afraid Honor's scales that day were anything but a satisfaction to Fräulein Bernhardt, the piano teacher. Her mind was so abstracted that she kept continually playing wrong fingering, or even an occasional wrong note in the harmonic minors. Her study was little better, and her piece a dead failure. The mistress, with characteristic German patience, set her to work to try to conquer a couple of difficult phrases, through which Honor stumbled again and again, each time with the same old mistakes, until the end of the half-hour.

"I find you not yet fit to take share in ze evening pairformance!" sighed poor Fräulein, whose musical ear had been much distressed by this mangling of her favourite tarantella. "Zere must be more of improvement before ve render ze piece to Mees Maitland. You say you not vish to play in publique? Ach, so! Zat is vat zey all say; but it is good to begin young to get over ze fear—vat you call ze 'shyness'—is it not so?"

Fräulein Bernhardt was an excellent teacher—patient, conscientious, and enthusiastic. She tried to inspire all her pupils with her own love for music, and with some indeed she succeeded, though with others it proved a more difficult task.

"I'm almost impossible!" avowed Lettice Talbot. "I believe I'm nearly as bad as the old fellow who declared he only knew two tunes—one was 'God Save the King', and the other wasn't."

"You certainly have a particularly leaden touch," agreed Dorothy Arkwright. "The way you hammer out Mendelssohn is enough to try my nerves, so I'm sure it must be an offence to Fräulein."

"I think it's stupid to be obliged to learn the piano when you've absolutely no taste for it," yawned Lettice. "I'm going to ask Father to let me give it up next term."

"Don't!" interposed Vivian Holmes, who happened to overhear Lettice's remark. "I went through that same phase myself, when I was fourteen. I implored my mother to allow me to stop music, and she had nearly consented when I met a lady who advised me most strongly to go on. She said she couldn't play herself, and regretted it immensely now she was grown-up, and would be thankful if she could manage even a hymn tune. So I did go on, and now I'm very glad. I'm certain you'll like it better, Lettice, when you've got over more of the drudgery."

"Perhaps it will never be anything but drudgery for me!"

"Oh, yes, it will! We shall have you taking part in the 'Friday firsts' yet."

On the first Friday in every month Miss Maitland held a "Mutual Improvement Evening", at which all who were sufficiently advanced were expected to contribute by playing, singing, or reciting. These were quite informal gatherings, only Chaddites being present. Miss Cavendish considered it good for teachers and pupils to meet thus socially, and a similar arrangement obtained at each house. To many of the girls, however, it was more of an ordeal to be obliged to perform before their schoolfellows than it would have been to play to strangers.

"I'm always nervous, in any case," said Pauline Reynolds; "but strangers don't criticize one openly afterwards, whatever they may think in private. I feel it's perfectly dreadful to have Fräulein and Miss Maitland and Miss Parkinson sitting on one side, and all of you in a row on the other!"

"But we're very polite," urged Lettice. "We say, 'Thank you!'"

Honor had not yet been considered proficient enough to take an active part in the monthly entertainment, but Flossie's name was one of the first on the list. She played the violin remarkably well, better than almost anybody else at Chessington; and as she was seldom nervous, her pieces were generally very successful. The day following Evelyn Fletcher's fright happened to be "Mutual Improvement Friday". The girls only spent a short time at preparation, and then went upstairs to change their dresses. The meetings were always held in the drawing-room, and were rather festive in character. Miss Maitland tried to make them as much as possible like ordinary parties; she received the girls as guests, encouraged them to converse with herself and the other teachers, and had coffee served to them during the evening.

On this particular occasion Flossie made a very careful toilet, and she certainly looked nice in her pretty, embroidered white muslin dress, her fair hair tied with big bows of palest blue ribbon. She took a last glance at herself in the looking-glass, then, seizing her violin, which she had brought to her cubicle, she prepared to go downstairs.

In passing Miss Maitland's bedroom on the lower landing, she noticed that the door stood open, and that no one was within. There was a large mirror in the wardrobe, and, catching a glimpse of her own reflection as she went by, she stopped suddenly, and could not resist the temptation to run in for a moment and take a full-length view of herself as she would appear when she was playing her piece. She raised her violin and struck a suitable attitude, and was immensely pleased with the result that faced her—the dainty dress, the blue bows, the coral cheeks, flaxen hair, and bright eyes all made a charming picture, and the position in which she held her instrument was particularly graceful. She drew her bow gently over the strings, to observe the curve of her slender wrist and well-shaped arm. It was gratifying to know that she would make such a good appearance before her schoolfellows. Once again she played a few notes, for the sheer satisfaction of watching her slim, white fingers in the glass.

Alas for Flossie! That single bar of Schubert's Serenade was her undoing. Honor chanced to be passing the door at the identical moment, and, hearing the strain of music, peeped inside. She grasped the situation at a glance.

"Oho, Miss Flossie! So I've caught you prinking!" she said to herself. "You're evidently practising your very best company smile for this evening. What a disappointment it would be to you, now, if you were not able to play that piece after all!"

Honor had a resourceful mind. Very gently she put her hand inside the door and abstracted the key, which, with equal caution, she fitted into the keyhole on the outside; then, quickly shutting the door, she locked it, and ran away before Flossie had even discovered that anybody Was there. The latter naturally noticed the slight noise and turned round, but she was too late; and though she rattled the handle, and knocked and called, it was of no avail. Honor, as it happened, had been the last girl to go downstairs, and there was nobody left on either landing to hear even the most frantic thumps. Flossie rushed to the electric bell, hoping to bring a servant to her assistance; but it was out of order, and would not ring. She was in a terrible dilemma: if she made too much noise one of the teachers, or even Miss Maitland herself, might come upstairs to see what was the matter; on the other hand, there she was locked up fast and secure, missing the "evening", and with an equal chance of being found out in the end, and asked to give some explanation of her presence in the mistress's room.

In the meantime, Honor went downstairs chuckling. She entered the drawing-room in the highest of spirits, paid her respects to Miss Maitland, and found a seat close to the door. The musical part of the performance, she ascertained, was to come first, and after coffee there were to be recitations, and a dialogue in French. A neat programme had been written out and was laid on the top of the piano, so that it could be referred to by Vivian Holmes, who was conductress of the ceremonies.

It was late already, and the proceedings began immediately. The room was crowded, and amongst the forty girls nobody seemed to have particularly remarked Flossie's absence, and no enquiry was made for her, until the close of the song that preceded her violin solo.

"Where is Flossie Taylor?" whispered Vivian then, with a look of marked annoyance on her face. "Her Serenade comes next. She ought to be standing by the piano. Has anybody seen her? Please pass the question on."

She paused a moment or two in great impatience; then, as no Flossie put in an appearance, she turned to Meta Fletcher and May Turner, who followed on the programme, and asked them to begin their duet.

"I can't wait for anybody," she remarked. "If Flossie isn't ready, I must simply miss her out. We've almost too many pieces to get through in the time."

The rest of the music went off successfully. Nobody broke down, or even made a bad stumble, a subject of much self-congratulation to several nervous performers and of great relief to Vivian, who, as monitress of the house, always arranged the little concerts as a surprise for Miss Maitland, the latter preferring that the girls should settle all details amongst themselves, instead of leaving matters to a teacher.

Coffee was brought in at eight o'clock, after which the recitations began immediately. At this state of the entertainment Honor felt magnanimous. She did not want to involve Flossie in serious trouble, so, slipping quietly away, she ran upstairs, unlocked the door of Miss Maitland's bedroom, and released her prisoner.

The disappointed violinist emerged looking decidedly glum.

"It's a nasty, mean trick you've played me, Honor Fitzgerald!" she burst out.

"No meaner than you played on Evelyn Fletcher—not half so bad, in my opinion. I'm sorry to say you're too late for your solo. The music's over long ago, and they're hard at work reciting Shakespeare at present."

"Just what I expected! And it's all your fault!"

"You're very ungrateful! You ought to be most relieved to be let out before Miss Maitland caught you," retorted Honor. "What an opportunity to point a moral on the fatal consequences of vanity!" Then, as Flossie flounced angrily away: "You've never thanked me for unlocking this door yet. I thought we were supposed to cultivate manners at St. Chad's. If Vivian asks where you've been, I suppose you'll tell her?"

"I certainly shan't! And you'll be a sneak if you do."

"All right, all right! Keep your little temper! You may make your mind easy; I don't intend to do anything of the sort," called Honor, watching Flossie's back as her victim hurried out of earshot down the passage. "It has been a delightful evening," she continued to herself; "really quite the jolliest since I came to Chessington. I'm afraid I've had the lion's share of the enjoyment, but that couldn't be helped. It certainly is a most immense satisfaction to feel that Flossie Taylor and I are now exactly quits!"

CHAPTER X

Honor Finds Favour

Honor was undoubtedly finding Chessington College a totally different place from Kilmore Castle, and in the six weeks she had spent there she had already learnt many lessons quite apart from textbooks. The wildest bird cannot fly with its wings clipped, and at school Honor was so bound round with conventionalities and restrictions that she never dreamt of raising such turbulent scenes as had sometimes been her wont at home. The calm, firm administration of Miss Cavendish, Miss Maitland's wise control, and Miss Farrar's brisk authority, all seemed indisputable; and even the regulations of Vivian Holmes might not be defied with impunity. The Fitzgerald pride could not tolerate a low place in class, therefore Honor prepared her work carefully, so that she might be above Flossie Taylor and Effie Lawson, emulation urging her to efforts which love of learning alone would not have effected. She did not indulge so frequently as before in either "tantrums" or bursts of temper, for these provoked such ridicule from the other girls that she felt rather ashamed of them; and even her overflowing spirits began to be modified to the level of what was considered "good form" at Chessington.

There is a vast power in public opinion, and Honor, who at Kilmore had lived according to a model of her own choosing, now found herself insensibly falling in with the general tone of the College, and acquiring the mental shibboleths of her schoolfellows. Naturally all this was not accomplished at once, and "Paddy Pepper-box", as she was still nicknamed, had many outbreaks and relapses; but by the time the half-term arrived, Miss Maitland, in a long talk with Miss Cavendish, was able to report that "Honor Fitzgerald was marvellously improved".

"She has the elements of a very fine character," said the house-mistress, "though at present it is like a statue that is still in the rough block of marble: it will take much shaping and carving before the real beauty appears. There is sterling good in her, in spite of certain glaring faults. She is at a most critical, impressionable age, and will require careful management. Everything depends upon what standards she forms now."

Though the whole atmosphere of St. Chad's had its effect upon Honor, she owed more than even Miss Maitland guessed to the influence of Janie Henderson. Janie seemed to have the power of drawing out all that was best in her friend's disposition. In some subtle fashion she appeared to demand the good, and, by presupposing it was there, to bring it actually into existence. Many new ideas of duty, consideration for others, and self-restraint, that had never before occurred to Honor, now began to take root and grow—feebly at first, but the seed was there, and the fruit would come afterwards. It was Janie who put the first suggestion into her mind that life was more than a mere playground, and that other people have paramount claims on us, the fulfilling of which can bring a purer joy than that of pleasing ourselves; Janie who, by implying what a comfort an only daughter might be to father, mother, and brothers, made her realize how utterly she had so far failed to be anything but a care; and Janie whose high ideals and aspirations raised future possibilities of helpfulness of which she had not hitherto dreamt, for until she came to St. Chad's Honor had not heard of girls taking up careers, or fitting themselves for any special work.

"I don't mean earning one's own living," said Janie. "Neither you nor I will probably ever have to do that, and Mother says it is hardly right for women who have independent incomes to overcrowd professions, and drive out those who are obliged to keep themselves. What I want is to settle on some useful thing, and then to do it thoroughly. I've a large family of cousins in town, and they all are so busy, each in a different way. One has trained as a Princess Christian nurse, and now goes three days a week to give help at a crèche. She took me once to see the babies; they were the very poorest of the poor, but were beautifully clean, and so good. Beatrice simply loves them. Then Millicent, the second girl, has learnt wood-carving and metal-work, and takes a class at a Lads' Recreation Club. One of her boys has turned out so clever that he has been sent to the Technical Schools to study 'applied arts'. Milly is tremendously proud of him, particularly as he comes from such a wretched, lost, drunken home. Barbara is very musical—she teaches singing at a Factory Girls' Club; and Mabel helps with a Children's Happy Evening Society."

"But can you do those kinds of things in the country?" asked Honor.

"I'm going to try, when I leave school. I thought if I could learn ambulance work I could have a 'First Aid' class for the village girls. Most of them don't know how to dress a burn, or bind up a wound. I have another scheme too."

"What's that?"

"It's so ambitious, I'd better not talk about it. Perhaps the ambulance work will be enough for a beginning, and the other could follow. Well, if you insist upon my telling you, I should like to get up a lace-making industry among the girls in our village. I read an article in a magazine about someone who had revived the old Honiton patterns at a place in Devonshire."

"A few of the women make lace in our neighbourhood," said Honor.

"How splendid! Then you could start the same at Kilmore, and we could keep comparing notes, and get specimens sent to exhibitions—the 'Irish Industries', you know, or 'Peasants' Handicrafts'. It's such a pity that everything should be done by machinery nowadays! Why, you might have quite a thriving colony of lacemakers at Kilmore—the women could be working at their 'pillows' while the men are out fishing. If I begin at Redcliffe, will you promise to try the experiment too?"

Such a proposal as introducing a new occupation for the tenants on her father's demesne almost took Honor's breath away; yet to her active mind it was rather attractive, and she drew a rapid mental picture of the little barefooted colleens of Kilmore seated at their cabin doors, plying the bobbins with deft fingers. Janie's ardour was infectious, and if Honor were not yet ready to agree to all her plans, at least she caught enough enthusiasm to be interested in the subject, and to admit that it was a dream worthy some day of realization.

In the meantime, the ordinary school course gave ample scope for the energies of both girls. Janie, though a great reader, was backward in many subjects, and was obliged to study hard to keep up with the rest of the class; while Honor, naturally far more clever, had not been accustomed to apply her brains in any systematic fashion. The work of the Lower Third was stiff enough to need constant application, unless the girls wished to earn the reputation of "slackers", a distinction which neither coveted. Besides their mental exertions, Honor, at any rate, wished to maintain her credit in the playing-fields. Janie had long ago given up all hope of becoming a good cricketer, or even a moderate tennis player. She was not fond of exercise. To use her own phrase, she "hated to be made to run about". Her ideal of bliss was to be left to wander round the grounds with a book; but as this was permitted only on Sundays, she was forced on weekdays, much against her inclination, to take her due part in the games. She even went the length of envying Muriel Cunliffe, whose sprained ankle did not allow her to hobble farther than the garden for five weeks; and hailed with delight the occasions when the school filed out for a walk on the moors, instead of the usual routine of fielding, batting, or bowling, all of which she equally detested.

During the latter part of the summer term, when the weather was sufficiently warm, swimming was included among the outdoor sports. There was a large bath behind the gymnasium, and here every girl was obliged to learn her strokes, and to be reported as "proficient", before she was allowed to venture on a dip in the ocean. Those who reached the required stage of independence were taken in classes of about twelve to practise under the critical superintendence of Miss Young. The bathing-place was a sheltered cove among the cliffs, not far from the College, and reached by a footpath and a flight of steps cut in the rock. On the strip of shore stood a big wooden hut, partitioned off into small dressing-rooms; and a causeway of flat stones had been made down to the water, to avoid the sharp flints of the shingly beach.

Janie, though not an expert swimmer, had passed her novitiate, and thoroughly enjoyed a leisurely round of the bay, with as much floating included as Miss Young would allow. To Honor the sea was as a second element. She had been accustomed to it from her babyhood, and was as fearless as any of her brothers. She soon gave proof of her ability in the bath, and was straightway placed among those Chaddites who were privileged to visit the sea.

It was a glorious afternoon in the middle of June when she started for her first trial of the waves of the Channel.

"It can't be anything like so rough as the Atlantic," she declared. "I've swum out sometimes when there was a swell on, and it was quite difficult to get back."

"Of course, we're not allowed to go when it's rough," said Janie. "To-day I expect it will be as smooth as a millpond. I'm so glad you're not a beginner, and only learning to struggle round the bath!"

"So am I. To judge from Madge Summers's achievements yesterday, it doesn't look like a pleasant performance. She appeared to be trying to drown herself."

"Madge is horribly clumsy! I don't believe she'll ever manage to keep afloat properly. She always flounders unless she has one foot at the bottom. Pauline Reynolds wouldn't venture into the water at all at first; Miss Young had to push her in. I shall never forget how she shrieked; and she was so frightened, she actually swam three strokes!"

"Poor old Pauline! It was hard luck on her."

"Yes, it couldn't have been particularly nice. I didn't altogether appreciate learning myself, with a row of horrid Hilaryites sitting on the diving-board and jeering at my best efforts. However, 'those bright days are o'er', and now 'I hear the ocean roar', as the poem says."

Each Chaddite was required to carry her own bathing costume and towel, and to wait in the quadrangle for Vivian Holmes, who was to escort the party down to the cove. Miss Young was already on duty, superintending a batch of Aldwythites, who were to have the first half-hour in the water, and who must vacate the dressing-hut before the second contingent arrived.

"I wonder if there'll be any trippers to-day," said Lettice Talbot, winding her towel artistically round her hat, and letting the ends fall like a pugaree. "Sometimes excursionists from Dunscar walk along the beach, and insist upon stopping to look at us."

"Are they allowed?" asked Honor.

"We can't help it. The beach is common property, and though the College got permission to put up a wooden shanty, it has no power to prevent anybody who likes from coming past. Some people are the greatest nuisance. They bring cakes and bags of shrimps, and sit down on the rocks to eat them while they watch us."

"What cheek!"

"Yes; we glower at them in as withering a manner as we can, but they don't seem to mind in the least. I suppose they think we're part of the seaside amusements, like the niggers, or the pierrots."

"Fortunately, that doesn't happen often," said Ruth Latimer. "We've only been really annoyed once or twice; Lettice loves to exaggerate. The cove is about the quietest spot on the whole shore. Here's Vivian; it must be time to set off."

Honor was in her liveliest spirits as they walked along the cliffs. She was overflowing with Irish blarney and nonsense, asking absurd riddles and making bad puns, and sending the other girls into such fits of laughter that Vivian called them to order.

"Don't be so horribly noisy!" she said. "Honor Fitzgerald, I wish you were more sensible."

"I'm very contrite," replied Honor cheerfully. "You see, I've never been taught to be serious-minded. I'm quite ready to learn, though, if you'll set me someone to copy. Would this be better?"

and she put on an expression of such lugubrious gloom that the rest could not suppress their mirth.

Vivian did not seem to appreciate equally the humour of the situation. She was rather jealous of her position as monitress, and not unwilling to show her authority. Moreover, she was responsible for the conduct of the girls, who were expected to comport themselves discreetly on a public footpath.

Honor was not a favourite of hers. Vivian considered her too forward, and thought she made a troublesome element at St. Chad's. In her opinion, a new-comer in her first term ought not to attempt to obtrude herself, but should follow the lead of those who had been some years at the school. She told her rather sharply, therefore, to come and walk with her, and made the others go two and two, in a due and orderly fashion.

"I see some people coming along the cliffs," she said, "and I should be most ashamed if it were reported that the Chessington girls don't know how to behave themselves."

"I wonder whether she's taking the opportunity to try to improve Paddy's mind on the way," laughed Lettice to Ruth Latimer.

"She'll have a difficult task, then," remarked Ruth. "I can't imagine Paddy engaged in very deep and serious discourse."

By the time the St. Chad's party had climbed down the rocky steps on to the beach, the Aldwythites were just emerging from the hut, a lively, bareheaded little company, spreading their hair to dry in the wind and sunshine.

"It's simply delicious in the sea to-day," they called out; "quite warm, and as calm as possible."

The Chaddites had soon donned their bathing costumes, and went scampering down the causeway to take the coveted plunge into the waves.

"I don't know anything more glorious than the first few strokes of one's swim," said Lettice, floating for a moment or two by Honor's side. "I'm sure a frog couldn't enjoy it more, and a duck simply isn't in it!"

Honor seemed as much at home in the water as the fishes, and Miss Young, after watching her progress near the shore, gave her permission to go with the more advanced members of the class for a tour of the bay.

"I shall not be far off myself," she remarked, "and of course you must come back the instant I call to you."

"Miss Young generally stays close to the girls who aren't so much used to it, in case they should get cramp, or turn giddy," explained Lettice. "Beatrice Marsden and Ivy Ridgeway are only beginning, so I expect she'll paddle about with them in four feet of water. Janie Henderson never ventures very far either."

Once out in the bay, Honor began to distinguish herself, greatly to the delight of her admiring friends. She swam on her side and on her back, dived to pick up stones, and even contrived to make a wheel.

"How plucky you are!" exclaimed Lettice. "I should never dare to attempt such feats; but then, I haven't the sea to practise in at home. Look at Chatty; she's trying to do a wheel too. I know she'll come to grief. Chatty! Do you want us to have to practise life-saving?"

"No, thank you," said Chatty; "I was only seeing what I could manage. Look here! suppose we swim right round the bay. We can take a rest every now and then by floating and towing each other along."

Though there were no excursionists on the shore that day, the girls noticed a small boat bobbing about near the point of the cliffs. It contained three people, who were evidently visitors from Dunscar. A young man in his shirt sleeves, with a pocket-handkerchief tied over his head, was rowing in a very awkward fashion, as if it were the first time he had handled a pair of oars; while his companions, girls of about sixteen and seventeen, kept jumping up and changing places, or leaning suddenly over the side to catch pieces of seaweed.

"Vivian might complain of their laughing," said Lettice. "Just listen to them! Aren't they fearfully vulgar?"

"Cheap trippers come over for the day, no doubt," said Chatty. "Look! One of the girls is pretending to throw the young man's hat overboard, and he's trying to clutch it."

"The silly things! They're making that boat heel over far more than I should appreciate, if I were inside her," remarked Honor. "I don't believe they know there's any danger."

"I wonder they were allowed to go out without taking a boatman. I'm sure it's not safe," said Lettice.

The three young excursionists were still struggling and fighting over the hat when round the corner of the headland came the steamer from Westhaven, steering much closer to the shore than was her custom. She had started late, and her captain was trying to make up for lost time; and, in consequence, she was going at top speed. Her screw made such a tremendous wash that in a moment the sea was as rough as if there had been a storm. The bathers felt themselves tossed about like corks, and struck out as hard as they could for the shore, trying to keep abreast of the waves that threatened to overpower them. The next moment there was a chorus of wild, agonized shrieks, and the little cockle-shell of a boat whirled rapidly past, upside down, the young man and one girl clinging desperately to it, with white, terror-stricken faces. The other girl was nowhere to be seen. She rose in a few seconds, however, struggling violently, and sank again; then, when she came up for the second time, she had drifted a good distance farther on, and was strangely quiet.

The Chaddites had been separated by the sudden shock of the unexpected occurrence. Lettice found it as much as she could manage to keep her head above water, and Chatty acknowledged afterwards that she had never before felt in such danger of her life. Honor, however, was swimming fast in the direction of the drowning pleasure-seeker, and seized her just as she was on the point of going down for the third time. Luckily the poor girl had lost consciousness, and so did not grip her rescuer, or it might have ended fatally for them both. As it was, Honor was able to put her arm under her and keep her afloat while she called loudly for help.

But no one could come immediately. The heavy sea had got Ivy Ridgeway into difficulties, and Miss Young dared not leave her while she was still out of her depth; and the others were only able to save themselves: so Honor was obliged to do her best alone. By this time the steamer had stopped and was lowering one of its boats, but it took several minutes before the latter could be launched.

"Hold on a bit!" the sailors shouted encouragingly to Honor; and once they were clear of the vessel, they rowed with a will.

They reached the pair at last, and lifted the unfortunate girl, insensible and helpless as a log, over the gunwale.

"Better let us take you in too, miss!" said the coxswain to Honor.

"No, thanks; I'm all right," she replied, and, turning round, she swam straight back to the shore.

The passengers on the steamer gave cheer after cheer as they watched the little figure making its way so pluckily; and more than one person heaved a sigh of relief when it arrived in shallow water, and walked out on to the beach.

Meanwhile, the boat had picked up the young man and the other girl, who had clung to their upturned craft till they were in the last stage of exhaustion.

Poor Miss Young actually shed tears when she saw all her class safe and sound on dry land once more—a weakness of which her pupils never knew her to be guilty before or after.

"I'm not sure if I don't feel a little bit weepy myself," said Maisie Talbot. "Lettice is not a remarkably strong swimmer, and when I saw her so far out in the bay I thought—But there! it's over now, and I won't imagine horrible tragedies."

"It was a near shave for several of us," said Chatty soberly.

Honor took the whole affair with the utmost coolness; indeed, she insisted upon treating it almost as a joke.

"One doesn't always have the luck of picking up a mermaid," she declared. "I may find Father Neptune, or the Sirens, if I go a little farther; or perhaps I might drag back the sea serpent, as a neat little specimen for the school museum. If the trippers are often going to provide us with such entertainment, we shall have very lively times at bathing."

"All the same, I'm sure she's more upset about it than she pretends," said Lettice. "Her hands were trembling so much when she was dressing, she could scarcely button her blouse. It's just like her, though; she'd rather say something funny any time, than look serious."

Miss Young praised Honor highly for her "splendid bravery and presence of mind", and Miss Maitland added warm words of commendation. As for the Chaddites, they could scarcely make enough of her.

"No other house can show such a record," said Maisie enthusiastically. "We've beaten St. Hilary's hollow!"

"And even the School House," added Chatty, "though their monitress once stopped a runaway donkey on the shore."

"Paddy, we're proud of you!" said Lettice.

"Please don't say any more about it!" protested Honor. "I was only enjoying myself. I feel a great deal prouder when I've finished a sum in cube root, because I simply hate arithmetic. Swimming is as easy to me as walking, and I'm sure you'd each have done the same if you could."

Naturally, Honor was the heroine of the school, especially as the affair got into the newspapers, and the Royal Humane Society wrote to say that she would be presented with a medal in recognition of her courage. The father and mother of the girl whose life she had saved called with their daughter at the College, and begged to be allowed to express their gratitude, so Honor was sent for by the head mistress. She would have been glad to avoid what seemed to her an embarrassing interview, but there was no escape.

"These people have come on purpose to see you," said Miss Maitland; "it would be not only discourteous but unkind if you were to refuse to speak to them."

Honor had not been in Miss Cavendish's study since the memorable occasion when she had so injudiciously sported the shamrock, and as she entered the beautiful, old-world room again she could not help a feeling of wonder at how much had happened since she had first set foot there, and of relief that this second summons should be for approbation, instead of blame.

She would give no account afterwards of what took place, or what the girl's parents said to her, though Lettice was full of curiosity and pressed her for particulars.

"Look here!" she exclaimed; "if anybody says another word to me about this business, I shall leave St. Chad's and go across to St. Hilary's. I should be sorry to desert you all, but I'm sick of the very sound of 'life-saving'! As for the medal, I'm thankful to say it will be sent to me by post during the holidays, so there'll be no dreadful ordeal of presentation. Now, I've told you as much as I intend, so please go away, and let me do my preparation in peace!"

CHAPTER XI

A Relapse

Towards the end of June there was a burst of very warm weather, so sultry and hot as to make games, or any form of violent exertion, almost an impossibility. Ruth Latimer fainted one day when she was fielding, after which Miss Cavendish absolutely prohibited cricket in the blazing sun, and set to work to devise other means of occupation. The girls themselves would have been ready enough to lounge about all the afternoon in the grounds, chatting and doing nothing, but of that the head mistress did not approve; she considered it might tend to encourage habits of gossip and idling, and much preferred that everyone should have some definite employment. She temporarily altered the hours of work, setting preparation from two until four, so that in the evening the school might be free to go out and enjoy the breeze that often rose towards sunset. In the circumstances, this really seemed a better division of time, for during the early afternoon it was actually cooler in the house, with sunblinds drawn to protect the windows, than out-of-doors; and though there were many groans at having to learn lessons and write exercises immediately after dinner, on the whole the change was regarded with favour. General public opinion would have decided on swimming as the most suitable occupation in the state of the thermometer, but since the events related in the last chapter Miss Cavendish would not allow more than eight girls to go into the sea at once.

"It is as many as Miss Young can undertake to be responsible for," she said. "Steamers are frequently passing between Westhaven and Dunscar, and they seem to take a course nearer the coast than formerly. The wash from them is so exceedingly strong that it is wiser to run no risks."

Bathing, therefore, was conducted in small detachments, and though fresh relays went each day to the cove, it took so long to work through the whole school that nobody seemed to have the chance of a second turn. Miss Cavendish, however, was never at a loss. Everyone with the slightest aptitude for drawing was provided with paper and pencil, and taken out to sketch from nature. Those who possessed paint-boxes were encouraged to work in colours, and the head mistress, who had herself no little skill, gave many useful hints on the putting-in of skies and the washing of middle distances. Janie Henderson, who was naturally artistic, and had been accustomed to try her 'prentice hand at home, found herself at a decided advantage, and won more credit in a single week than she had hitherto gained in a whole year at Chessington.

"You've scored tremendously, Janie," said Honor, who revelled in her friend's brief hour of triumph. "Vivian Holmes was most impressed by your sketch of the cliffs. I heard her telling one of the Aldwythites about it. She said you were quite an artist. There, don't blush! I'm particularly rejoiced, because Vivian is so superior, and always does everything so much better than everybody else, and yet her picture wasn't half as good as yours, and she knew it."

"Vivian paints rather well, though."

"Oh, yes, tolerably! But she hasn't your touch. She muddles her greens, and her trees get so treacly! She's not really clever, as you are."

Honor had not brought a paint-box to school, but Janie lent her a brush and a tube of sepia and a china palette that she had to spare, so that she was able to attempt studies in monochrome, if she could not try colour.

"They're horrid daubs," she declared. "I don't pretend to have the least atom of talent; I only drew these because Miss Cavendish said I must. It's art under compulsion."

"Like the man who painted the pictures for some Moorish sultan," said Janie. "I've forgotten the exact facts of the story, but I know he was taken prisoner, and was marched with a long line of other wretched captives to learn his fate. The sultan asked the first on the list: 'Can you paint?' and when he answered 'No', ordered his head to be chopped off. Seven more were asked the same question, and given the same doom. Then, when it came to an Englishman's turn, he said 'Yes', although he knew as much about drawing as the man in the moon. The sultan spared his life, and ordered him to begin at once to decorate the walls of the palace, so he was obliged to try. I believe the pictures are still there, and people go to look at them because they're so extraordinary. I wish I could remember where the place is!"

"I should certainly like to see it," said Honor. "My productions would have been unique. I think I should have represented battle scenes, and put smoke to hide everything, and then have said it was impressionistic! The sultan was as bad as the Queen in Alice in Wonderland, who cried, 'Off with her head!'"

"They're absolute autocrats," said Janie. "I read a story of another who had a pet donkey, and sent for a philosopher and commanded him to teach it to talk. The poor old sage expected his last hour had come, but luckily an idea occurred to him. He said he would do so, but it would take seven years. He thought that in the meantime either the sultan might die, or the donkey might die, or he himself might die."

"And what happened?"

"Oh, I don't know! Like all good stories, it ends there."

"How disappointing! I want to hear the sequel. I suppose the philosopher might have poisoned the donkey."

"Or, perhaps, somebody poisoned the sultan. It was an amiable little way in those days of getting rid of an unpopular monarch. By the by, to go back to the subject of drawing, Miss Cavendish says there's to be an exhibition of all the sketches at the end of the term. They're to be pinned up round the gymnasium, and she'll ask an artist friend to come and judge them, and mark them first, second, and third class. Perhaps she may even set a special competition for a prize."

"You'll win, then, if she does. I'm certain Marjorie Parkes's painting is no better, though the St. Bride's girls have been crowing tremendously over her."

"Don't pin your hopes to me! I'm a broken reed. If I want to do a thing particularly nicely, I never can. All my most successful hits have been made when I wasn't trying."

"Yes, that's often the way. I always say my highest scores at cricket are really flukes. Here's Lettice coming to criticize. Don't look at my sketch, Lettice, it's abominable! You may admire Janie's as much as you like."

"I think you've both been very quick," said Lettice. "I've only drawn in about half of mine yet. But I can generally manage to make a little work go a long way! I came to tell you that it's time to pack up. And I have a piece of good news as well; it has been so much cooler to-day that Miss Cavendish says we may be more enterprising to-morrow. I don't know what's arranged for the other houses, but St. Chad's is down for a botany ramble. Isn't it jolly? I shall like it much better than sketching. Miss Maitland is to take us, and we're to walk along the hills towards Latchfield.

There's to be an archery tournament as well, and we may go to that instead, if we like, only we must put our names down to-night. The lists for both will be hung up in the hall. I know which I shall choose."

"So do I," said Janie. "I've never hit the target yet, so it's not much use my entering against Blanche Marsden and Trissie Turner and Sophy Williams. A ramble sounds lovely. Honor, do come! I'm sure you're not keen on bows and arrows!"

"I haven't tried, so I can't tell. A tournament doesn't seem exactly the place, though, to make one's first wild shots, and I've no time even for an hour's practice. If it's to be botany versus archery, I think I'll put my valuable autograph on the side of science."

No one could be more capable of leading a botanical ramble than Miss Maitland. She was a close student of nature, and not only loved plants and flowers herself, but could make them interesting to other people. The beautiful collection of pressed specimens in the school museum was mostly her work, and she was regarded as the best authority on the subject in the College.

"I'm often so glad we're at St. Chad's," said Janie. "Miss Maitland is a thousand times nicer than any of the other house-mistresses. The Hilaryites are very proud of Miss Hulton because she writes for the Scientific World, the Aldwythites plume themselves on Miss Paterson's double first, and the Bridites worship Miss Daubeny since she did that splendid climb in the Alps last summer; but Miss Maitland is so jolly all round, I like her by far the best. Of course, the School House girls say the very cream of Chessington is to be with Miss Cavendish, but I think a head mistress is pleasanter at a distance, one always feels so much in awe of her."

"Yes; I'm afraid I should never feel quite at ease with Miss Cavendish," avowed Honor. "At St. Chad's we seem almost like a big family."

The College stood in the midst of a pretty country, and there was no lack of walks in the neighbourhood. At exactly half-past four on the following afternoon a party of sixteen Chaddites set off under the wing of Miss Maitland, and turned at once in the direction of the woods that led to Latchfield, by a deliciously green and shady path. The warm sun, pouring between the thick leaves, made little radiant patches of golden light among the deep shadows under the trees; the whole air seemed alive with the hum of insects; and here and there rang out the sharp tap of a woodpecker, or the melancholy "coo-coo-coo" of a wild pigeon.

"The birds are generally very silent in such sultry weather," said

Miss Maitland. "They sing at dawn and again at sunset, but you hear little of them in the heat of the day. Those doves probably have a nest at the top of that tall ash. I think I can see some sticks among the leaves on that big bough."

Some pieces of honeysuckle twined round the low undergrowth of bushes, and tall foxgloves reared their purple spikes in every small, open glade. The girls gathered these as their first specimens.

"I wonder why they're called foxgloves?" said Lettice. "They've nothing to do with foxes."

"It's simply a corruption of 'good folks' gloves', meaning 'fairies' gloves'," said Miss Maitland. "People gave the plants much more romantic names in olden days than modern scientists do. I confess I like 'Queen of the Meadows' better than Spiræa Ulmaria, and I think 'poor man's weather-glass' a far better description of the scarlet pimpernel than Anagallis arvensis. We shan't find many flowers here, among the trees; but I'm hoping we may come across some orchids when we get on to the moors."

They had been walking uphill all the time, and, as soon as they were clear of the woods, found they had reached a high table-land, covered with pastures, through the midst of which flowed a stream, whose rushy banks were gay with purple loosestrife, Ragged Robin, and yellow spearwort. It was a famous place in which to botanize, and the girls were allowed to disperse and hunt about for specimens, and came back every now and then to show their finds to their teacher.

"Adeline Vaughan is the only one who knows much about the natural orders, or the proper scientific terms," said Lettice. "It seems rather funny, because she's a Londoner, and doesn't belong to the country."

"Country people aren't always the best authorities on the subject," said Miss Maitland. "I know some who go through life with deaf ears and blind eyes, and never hear or see what is all around them. The main thing is to have enthusiasm, and then, it doesn't matter where your home is, you'll manage to enjoy nature, even if it is only at second-hand, from books."

"And there are always the holidays," said Adeline. "We went to Switzerland last August, and I found twenty-seven different specimens just in one walk."

"Before I came to St. Chad's," confessed Lettice, "I used to think daisies were the flowers of grass, and not separate plants—I did indeed!"

"You certainly know better now," laughed Miss Maitland. "We

can get so much pleasure from things when we have learnt even a very little about them. Every leaf or blade of grass becomes a marvel, if we begin to examine its structure, and look at it through the microscope. There is nothing so wonderful as the book of nature, and it is always there, ready to entertain us when we wish to read it."

It was much cooler and breezier up on the hills, though even there the air had a sultry feeling, and a dull, heavy haze was creeping up from the sea.

"It looks like thunder," said Miss Maitland. "I should not be surprised if we were to have a storm to-night. We had better turn towards home now; but we'll go back by the cliffs above Sandihove, instead of through the woods."

It was rather a difficult matter to get the girls along, so many interesting discoveries were made on the way—first a patch of pink-fringed buck-bean, growing at the edge of the stream; then a clump of butterfly orchis; and last, but not least, a quantity of the beautiful "Grass of Parnassus", the delicate white blossoms of which were starring the boggy corner of a meadow. Miss Maitland was kept quite busy naming specimens, and everybody had a large bunch of treasures to carry home. Janie Henderson and Adeline Vaughan, being the two chief enthusiasts of the party, walked on either side of the teacher, discussing matters botanical; and the others straggled in little groups behind. Honor found herself walking with Lettice Talbot, who was in a more than usually sprightly frame of mind, bantering and teasing, and turning everything into fun.

"I've learnt the names of so many new flowers," she declared, "that I'm sure I shall get a bad mark for history to-morrow. My brain is small, and only capable of holding a certain amount. When fresh things are put in, out go the old ones, or else I mix them completely up. I shall probably say that Oliver Cromwell was born at Marsh Cinquefoil, and that Charles the First belonged to the family of Ranunculaceæ. Paddy, you look rather glum! What's the matter? Don't you like botany? Or are you longing for your native wilds in Kerry? Is that a surreptitious tear trickling down your cheek?"

"Surreptitious rubbish!" laughed Honor. "I wasn't thinking of anything so romantic. I was looking at that little white village below us, and wondering if it can boast of possessing a shop."

"Then I can satisfy you on that point. It does—a very small shop, where they sell tea, and red herrings, and tinned provisions."

"Do they sell peppermint humbugs, or raspberry drops?"

"I dare say. I believe I remember some big bottles in the window."

"Then let us go and buy some. I haven't had any sweets since I came to St. Chad's. I'm simply yearning for butter-scotch or chocolates!"

"Don't talk of them! So am I! There's only one slight drawback, and that is, that we're not allowed!"

"Why not?"

"How can I say why? It's one of the rules: 'No girl to enter any shop, or make purchases, without special permission from her house-mistress'."

"Then run on and ask Miss Maitland if we may. She's in a particularly good temper tonight, so she'll probably say 'yes'. I have some pennies in my pocket."

"All right. One can but try!" replied Lettice, and hurrying after the teacher, who was a little distance in front, she made her request.

She came back to Honor shaking her head gloomily.

"As I thought!" she announced. "Miss Maitland says 'No'. We're not to pass the shop at all; we're to keep to the upper road that skirts above the village."

"How disgusting!" grumbled Honor. "It would only have taken a minute longer. I'm sure there's no need to be in such a tremendous hurry. Lettice! Suppose we were to dash down this lane, we could go to the village and catch the others up at the crossroads. I can see the path quite plainly from here. We couldn't possibly miss it, and we could run all the way."

"Whew! But how about breaking rules?"

"Bother rules! Miss Maitland shouldn't make so many, and then they'd be better kept. It is ridiculous if girls of our age mayn't walk five yards by themselves. We're not infants in arms!"

Lettice hesitated, glanced to see if anyone in front was looking, or whether anybody was close behind, then yielded to the voice of the temptress.

"It's horribly risky, but it would be a joke!" she said.

Honor was in one of her self-willed moods that evening, ready to dare or do anything. In her heart of hearts she was offended because Janie should have walked on with Adeline and Miss Maitland, and left her behind. She was of a jealous temperament, and had enjoyed keeping her friend as her own private and particular property. It seemed quite a new state of affairs for Janie to be conversing in so animated a manner with anybody but herself, and the change was the reverse of pleasant.

"They're so interested in their talk, they've completely forgotten me!" she thought. "Very well; so much the better! They won't notice what we're doing. I'm not going to keep all these silly regulations. One might be in the nursery, to have to ask leave for such an absurd little thing as buying a pennyworth of sweets."

The two girls ran as fast as they could along the lane, Honor looking reckless and rather stubborn, and Lettice decidedly guilty. It was certainly a most deliberate act of disobedience, and one that, if they were caught, would involve them in very disagreeable consequences. The discipline at Chessington was so perfect that it was seldom any pupil ever dreamt of even questioning a mistress's orders; and Lettice, in her two years at St. Chad's, had never done such a naughty thing before. She felt almost frightened at her own daring, but very excited, and ready to follow Honor to the end of the adventure. They hurried into the little shop and made their purchases as quickly as possible, though the old woman who served them did not understand the meaning of the word "haste", and weighed out butterdrops and caramels with exasperating deliberation. The pair stood by almost dancing with impatience, and when the packets were at last ready, snatched them up and rushed off with all speed.

"This way!" cried Honor, turning sharply to the left through an open gate. "I noticed the path particularly when we were on the hill above, and this is a short cut back to the road."

"It looks as if we were going into an orchard," objected Lettice.

"No; I'm sure I'm right. We shall get out through those apple trees at the top of the bank."

The pathway, however, merely seemed to lead to a field, and ended at a gate that was securely fastened by a piece of wire.

"I believe there's a stile across there," panted Honor, hot and out of breath with running. "Don't bother to undo that wire! We'll climb over. Here, take my hand!"

It was a vain hope. On closer examination the supposed stile proved to be only part of a fence. The meadow was surrounded by a quickset hedge, so thick as to be an insuperable barrier.

"I must have taken the wrong turning, after all," said Honor blankly. "What a fearful nuisance! We shall have to go back."

"It's all very well to say 'go back'!" exclaimed Lettice, turning and clutching at Honor's arm. "Look at what is in front of us!"

Honor stopped short as suddenly as her companion. Directly facing them was a large bull: it had been feeding in the ditch when they entered the field, and thus they had not perceived its presence; but now it had walked across, and was standing exactly opposite the gate, completely cutting off their return to the footpath.

"Perhaps it mayn't be really savage," said Honor, with a slight quiver in her voice. "Shall we walk a little nearer, and see if it takes any notice of us?"

"No! No! Don't!" implored Lettice. "I'm terrified even of cows, and this is a monster. I'm sure it's dangerous—it has a ring in its nose!"

Honor looked round the pasture in dismay. She felt as if they were caught in a trap. How were they to make their escape while that huge beast stood between them and safety?

"We'd better go to the hedge again," she said. "Perhaps there may be some little hole where we can scramble through into the next field."

They beat a cautious retreat, not daring to run from fear that they might attract the bull's attention. But the farmer had mended his fences only too well; they did not find the smallest opening, search as they would.

"What are we to do?" demanded Lettice distractedly. "We can't stay all night in the field, yet if we call for help that creature will come rushing at us. Oh, Honor, look! It's seen us now!"

The bull had certainly become aware of their proximity. It was gazing at them in an uneasy fashion, sniffing the air, and pawing the ground restlessly. It gave a roar like the growling of thunder, and began to walk slowly in their direction. With white faces, the girls backed nearer the fence. Perhaps the heat, or the flies, or the unusual appearance of two strangers in its meadow irritated the animal, for again it gave a loud, rumbling bellow, and, lowering its horns, made straight for the intruders. Shrieking with fright, Honor and Lettice plunged into the hedge, scrambling anyhow through quickset and brambles, scratching their hands and faces and rending their dresses in the struggle, their one object being to escape from the horror behind them. With torn blouses and fingers full of thorns they issued from the opposite side, and rolled down a bank before they were able to stop themselves.

Honor sprang up promptly, and looked anxiously back. Fortunately, the bushes were far too thick and high for the bull to leap over.

"We're quite safe now!" she exclaimed, with a gasp of intense relief.

Lettice, sitting on the bank, indulged in a private little cry. She was very agitated and upset, and was trembling violently.

"I thought we were going to be gored to death," she quavered.

"Oh! has it gone away? It's dreadful to feel it's still so near us!"

"We'd better get on as fast as we can, and put another field be-tween it and us," said Honor, pulling her companion to her feet. "There are some hurdles over in that corner that we can climb, and then we shall be absolutely out of danger."

Honor's short cut proved a very long one before the two girls once more found themselves on the high road. There was not a sign of the rest of the party to be seen, so they began to walk home as briskly as their shaken nerves would allow. They had not gone far, however, before they met Miss Maitland, who, with Janie Henderson and Maisie Talbot, had come back to look for them.

"You naughty girls! Where have you been?" the house-mistress exclaimed, in righteous wrath, as the dilapidated pair made a conscience-stricken approach.

There was nothing for it but a full confession, and a very disa-greeable ten minutes followed for both. Miss Maitland knew how to maintain discipline, and would not overlook such a flagrant breach of orders.

"I had distinctly forbidden you to go," she said. "I am extremely disappointed, for I thought I could have depended on your sense of honour to behave as well behind my back as if you had been walking in front. You may be most thankful to have escaped from a danger into which your own disobedience led you. I am sorry that our pleasant ramble should have ended so unfortunately; it will be very difficult for me to rely on either of you again."

CHAPTER XII

St. Kolgan's Abbey

After what happened on Latchfield Moors," remarked Vivian Holmes, one afternoon about a week later, "I think it is extremely good of Miss Maitland to allow Honor Fitzgerald and Lettice Talbot to go to the picnic to-morrow. I shouldn't have been in the least surprised if she had left them both out, and I should certainly have said it served them right."

Vivian was at an age when stern justice appears more attractive than mercy. She kept rules rigidly herself, and had scant patience with those who did not, serving out retribution in her capacity of monitress with an unsparing hand. She was perhaps too hard on prodigals, but her influence and authority undoubtedly did much to maintain the high standard of St. Chad's; and if she were not altogether popular, she was, at any rate, greatly respected.

Honor's last delinquency had placed her more than ever on Vivian's bad list. The monitress considered that it completely cancelled the bathing episode, and regarded "that wild Irish girl" as the black sheep of the house, ready to lead astray such innocent lambs as Lettice Talbot who were impressionable enough to be influenced by her example. Miss Maitland, though grieved at such a relapse from the marked improvement that Honor had shown, was fortunately a better judge of character. She knew that old habits are not overcome all at once, and that it takes many stumblings and fallings and risings again before any human soul can struggle uphill. She did not want Honor to be discouraged, and hoped that if the girl felt herself trusted she would make an effort to be more worthy of confidence.

"I put you on your parole," she said to her. "It would be impossible for me to take you to Baldurstone if I imagined you were capable of a repetition of what occurred last week. I think, however, that I need feel no anxiety on that score."

"I promise faithfully," said Honor, and she meant it.

Vivian's opinions largely led popular feeling, and as Honor did not hold a high place in her estimation, the other Chaddites also, in consequence of the affair on the moors, slightly ostracized "Paddy", letting her understand that they did not altogether approve of her. Lettice Talbot suffered a severe snubbing from her elder sister, in addition to Miss Maitland's censure.

"It was such shockingly bad form!" declared Maisie. "Why, you might have been two little Sunday-school children, running away from your teacher to buy common sweets at a small village shop! I'm utterly ashamed of you. We don't do such things at Chessington. No wonder Miss Maitland was amazed and disgusted. Yes, I know Honor Fitzgerald is listening; I'm very glad, because she'll hear what I think of your fine adventure."

Honor undoubtedly felt much crestfallen to find that what she had regarded as spirited independence was labelled "bad form" at the College. On reflection it struck her that, apart from all rules, it had perhaps been scarcely polite to rush away, in direct opposition to the expressed wishes of one who had been taking so much trouble to make their walk interesting. In common with all the Chaddites, she keenly appreciated both Miss Maitland's personality and her knowledge of nature lore, and had enjoyed the expedition on the hills immensely.

To be left out of the picnic would have been a bitter disappointment. It was the great event of the summer term. Each house took its excursion on a separate day, as Miss Cavendish considered that the whole school made too formidable an invasion for any place. St. Hilary's and St. Aldwyth's had already respectively visited Weyland Castle and Eccleston Woods, and it was now the turn of St. Chad's to choose a destination. Miss Maitland had made a list of several interesting spots, which were well worth seeing, and had put the matter to a general ballot, with the result that by a majority of eight the votes fell in favour of St. Kolgan's Abbey at Baldurstone.

"It's the nicest of all, and Miss Maitland's favourite," announced Lettice.

"I chose it for three reasons," said Honor: "first, because it's the farthest off, and I like to have a long journey; secondly, because we're to go most of the way by steamer, and I love being on the sea; and thirdly, because Flossie Taylor wanted Haselmere Hall."

"What a very intelligent and desirable motive!" sneered Vivian Holmes, who happened to overhear. "You evidently go on the principle of pig philosophy. As a matter of fact, Miss Maitland said she had no preference."

"I was speaking to Lettice," retorted Honor. "I suppose my motives are my own business?"

"Oh, certainly! They're not of the slightest interest to me."

"Vivian's rather snappy this evening," whispered Lettice, as the monitress stalked away. "I believe she voted for Haselmere herself."

"Then I'm doubly glad it's to be Baldurstone. Even if people are monitresses, they've no need to think it's their mission to squash everybody else perpetually. I can hardly make the least remark without Vivian sitting upon me."

"You always answer her back, you see, and she thinks that's cheek in a new girl."

"I'm not new now."

"Yes, you are—you're not through your first term yet. Vivian says it takes a whole year to become a full-blown Chaddite, and until you've thoroughly assimilated Chessington ideas you oughtn't to presume to air outside opinions."

"What bosh!"

"No, it's not bosh. You see, we all think that Chessington is the only girls' school in England, and that St. Chad's is the one house at Chessington. One must keep up the traditions of the place, and it wouldn't do to let every fresh comer take the lead. You'll have to knuckle under, Paddy, and eat humble pie. Vivian has been here for five years—she's simply a 'Chaddite of the Chaddites'. That's why she was chosen monitress. You'll have your chance when you get to the Sixth Form."

"Shall I ever climb so high up in the school? If I were head of the house, though, I'd be rather less hard on new arrivals."

"Oh, no, you wouldn't! By the time you've gone through the mill yourself you'll want to grind everybody else. There's an attraction about the St. Chad's code; you'll like it better when you're more used to it, and when you've forgotten any pettifogging notions you may have brought from anywhere else."

"You're outspoken, at any rate!"

"Certainly! I believe in plain, unvarnished truths."

Honor had already discovered that fact, and also the further one that whatever a girl's position might be at home, it made no difference to her standing at the College, where each was judged solely and entirely on her own merits. She had once unfortunately alluded with a touch of pride to her family pedigree, but she rued her mistake in a moment, for Vivian, with uplifted eyebrows, had enquired in a tone of cutting contempt: "Who are the Fitzgeralds?"

A large public school is indeed a vast democracy, and members are estimated only by the value they prove themselves to be to the commonweal: their private possessions and affairs matter little to the general community, but their examination successes, cricket scores, or tennis championships are of vital importance. All, to use an old phrase, must find their own level, and establish a record for themselves apart from home belongings. Honor was beginning to realize that among two hundred girls she was a mere unit, and that her opinions and prejudices counted as nothing against the enormous weight of universal custom. It was quite a new aspect of life, so new that she was not sure whether she liked or disliked it; although, if she had been given her choice of remaining at the College or returning to the old, slipshod, do-as-you-please régime of her schoolroom at Kilmore, she would have decided most emphatically, despite strict rules, scoldings, snubs, and unwelcome truths, in favour of Chessington.

Nobody wished to lie in bed on the morning of the picnic; even Honor, to whom early rising was still one of the greatest banes of existence, actually woke up before the bell rang, and had the triumph of rousing her sleeping companion, a reversal of the customary order of things that afforded her much satisfaction.

"It's delightful to think that St. Chad's is going off for a jaunt, while all the other houses will have lessons just as usual," she remarked. "I'm sure I shall enjoy it twice as much when I think of Christina Stanton and Mary Nicholls toiling through equations and physics."

"It will be their turn to chuckle next week, when St. Bride's has its holiday," said Janie. "You'll feel rather blue then."

"No, I shan't—not if we've had our fun first. I shall turn philosophical, and say: 'You can't eat your cake and have it', and 'Every dog has his day', or any other little platitude I can think of. In the meantime, it's our day, and I'm glad to see it's a particularly fine one."

At precisely nine o'clock, just when the rest of the Chessingtonians were filing into classes, the Chaddites were assembled in the quadrangle, and at a signal from Miss Maitland started off, two and two, to walk to Dunscar, where they were to catch the steamer to Avonmouth, the nearest point for Baldurstone. Everything seemed delightful—the brisk march in the fresh morning air, the bright sunshine, the glinting, sparkling sea, the foam churned up by the steamer's revolving screw, the cries of the seagulls, and the steady motion of the vessel as she headed out of the bay. The breeze in the Channel was exhilarating, and so cool as to make the girls appreciate Miss Maitland's wisdom in having insisted upon all bringing wraps.

"I thought it seemed as foolish as carrying one's winter fur and muff on a broiling day like this," commented Lettice, "but I really think I should have been cold without my coat. It's marvellous what an enormous difference there is when you get well away from land."

Lunch was taken on the steamer, and they did not arrive at Avonmouth until half-past one. They were landed in small boats, for there was no pier, and vessels of any considerable size could not cross the harbour bar. Miss Maitland counted up her forty pupils as they stood on the jetty—a precaution that seemed more of a formality than a necessity, as everyone had taken good care not to be left behind.

"We have exactly three and a half hours here," she said. "The steamer will be back at five o'clock. That gives us plenty of time to walk to the Abbey, and enjoy the ruins. I have ordered tea to be ready for us as soon as we return on board. We shall be very hungry by then, I'm afraid, but there is nowhere to buy refreshments in this tiny place."

Avonmouth was, indeed, only a little fishing village, composed of an irregular row of cottages, huddled together on the beach, and a small, not-too-clean inn, which looked as if it would be quite incapable of providing even seats for a party of forty-three, to say nothing of cups and saucers.

"We're such an army!" said Vivian. "If we were to have tea here we should clear the whole place of provisions. I don't suppose there'd be enough milk and bread and butter to go round."

"Couldn't they have been ordered beforehand?" asked Lettice, who had a leaning towards picnic meals. "We might have sat on the grass outside the inn."

"Yes, no doubt. But suppose the day had been wet and we hadn't come, then all the things would have been wasted. A steamer is generally prepared to cater for any number of people."

St. Kolgan's Abbey stood about two miles from the village, on a headland overlooking the sea. It was a steady toil uphill the whole way, but the glorious view at the top was ample reward for the hot climb between high walls. The beautiful old ruin faced the Channel, and commanded a wide prospect of blue waves, flecked here and there with little, foamy crests.

"I wonder if that's the coast of Ireland, on the other side?" remarked Honor, shading her eyes with her hand to gaze over the dancing water.

"I'm afraid the wish is father to the thought," said Ruth Latimer.

"I don't honestly see anything that can possibly be construed into a distant coast line, and I've about as long sight as anybody in the school. Don't you want to come and listen to Miss Maitland? She's going to tell us a story about St. Kolgan, who founded this place."

Honor followed to the corner of the fallen transept, where Miss Maitland was installed on a fragment of broken column. The girls, in various attitudes of comfort, had flung themselves on the grass within earshot, prepared to listen lazily while revelling in the calm, tranquil beauty and the old-world atmosphere of the scene. It seemed so peaceful, so far removed from the bustle and noise of our hurrying, pushing age, that they could almost throw their minds back through the centuries, and imagine they heard the vesper bell tolling from the tower overhead, and the slow footfalls of the monks pacing round the cloister to those carved seats in the choir of which the very remains were so exquisite.

"Yes, Baldurstone is a wonderful spot," began Miss Maitland. "I don't believe any place in the neighbourhood has older traditions. St. Kolgan was a British saint, and his legend has come down to us from the very earliest times. You know that there was a thriving and orthodox Celtic Church in Britain long before St. Augustine's 'introduction' of Christianity—a Church that was so important and vigorous that it contributed three bishops to the Council of Arles in a.d. 314, and several to the Council of Nicæa in 325, thus showing that it formed a part of united Christendom. It sent missionaries both to Ireland, where St. Patrick preached the Faith, and to Scotland, where St. Ninian spread Christian teaching in the north. Then came the invasion of the heathen Norsemen, the Angles, Saxons, and Jutes of history, who burnt and plundered every sanctuary they could find, slaying the priests at the altars, destroying both prelates and people, and forcing the Britons to take refuge in the woods and mountains. Though driven westward, the Celtic Church did not perish, and every now and then some devoted monk would try to establish himself among the worshippers of Thor and Odin. Such a mission was extremely dangerous, for so intense was the hatred of the pagan conquerors for the religion of the New Testament that it was almost impossible for a Christian teacher to show himself among them and live.

"At about the beginning of the seventh century, when the Saxons had spread so far westward as Dunscar and Avonmouth, and were practically masters of all the country round, a monk called Kolgan came over from Ireland with a little band of brethren, and prevailed upon Osric, the chief, or 'under king', of the district, to allow him to settle at Baldurstone. Those Celtic pioneers built a small monastery, and worked very earnestly among the people, some of whom they persuaded to become adherents of the Cross. Osric, though a pagan himself, tolerated them for the sake of his British wife, Toura, and for a while they went unmolested. When Osric died, however, the chiefdom fell to Wulfbert, a fierce warrior, who was determined to annihilate by fire and bloodshed any faith that had taken root among his subjects. In daily peril of their lives, Kolgan and his monks stayed on, knowing that if they deserted their post the last light of Christianity in the district would flicker out. One day a cowherd, who had been cured of a dangerous wound at the little settlement, came running to warn the brethren that Wulfbert and a band of armed men were advancing against them; and he besought them at once to flee into the woods. Kolgan marshalled his trembling companions, and, giving them the altar vessels to carry into a place of safety, sent them straightway to seek refuge in the vast forest that stretched ever northward and westward beyond the dominion of the Saxons.

"He himself was determined to remain. He knew that many of those who were coming with Wulfbert had, in Osric's time, been converts, either openly or secretly, of the Church; and he hoped, even at the eleventh hour, that he might recall their lost allegiance. Alone, with a cross uplifted in his hand, he stood at the door of the monastery to meet the Norsemen. The fierce band paused in amazement at the sight of his temerity; it was something those savage men had not known before. The swift rush through the battlefield of the warrior who hoped by slaughter to gain Valhalla, they could understand; but this calm courage in the face of death was beyond their experience. Kolgan seized the opportunity of the moment's respite to appeal to them in the name of the Trinity, and thundered out a denunciation against those who forsook the Faith. A few trembled, but Wulfbert, rallying his ranks, cried: 'Cowards! Are ye afraid of the empty words of an unarmed priest?' and rushing forward, he struck the first blow with his battle-axe.

"Kolgan fell where he stood, the little settlement was plundered and ravaged, and for the time it seemed as though his work had been of no avail. But brighter days were in store for the Church; slowly and gradually Christianity had begun to spread, not only from Celtic, but from Saxon sources, and before many years were past Wulfbert himself had accepted baptism. The monastery was by his special desire rebuilt in honour of St. Kolgan, and became afterwards one of the greatest centres of learning in the west country. For nine hundred years it flourished, till at last it was suppressed in the reign of Henry VIII, and the buildings, untended and neglected, fell into the state that we see now."

"And is this actually the place built by Wulfbert?" asked Ruth Latimer.

"Oh, no! That must have been a very rude and primitive erection; probably it had wattled walls, and a thatched roof. The Abbey was reconstructed more than once, and the present ruins are the remains of fourteenth-century work."

"What a shame that it should have been destroyed!" said Dorothy Arkwright.

"Yes and no. One much regrets the ruin of so lovely a place, but the monks had grown idle and self-indulgent, and were as different from the founders of their order as could well be imagined. The old, self-sacrificing spirit had passed away; and the days were gone, too, when the monastery had stood as the sole centre of light in a dark age, at once the substitute for school, college, hospital, and alms-house, as well as the home of painting, literature, music, and all the refined arts. When any custom or institution, however beautiful, becomes effete, the ruthless hand of progress sweeps it away, and supplants it with something else, leaving us only ivy-covered ruins to show us what our forefathers loved and valued."

"How grand St. Kolgan was!" said Vivian. "I think it was simply splendid the way he stood at the door and braved the Saxons!"

"Yes; but to me the truest part of his heroism was not his death, but his life. It needed far greater self-denial and true courage to spend each day in trying to teach a wild and hostile people, making long and fatiguing journeys, and suffering the loss of every joy that earth could offer him, than it did to summon up the supreme spirit to meet martyrdom. It is just the same in most of our lives," continued Miss Maitland, with a glance in Honor's direction; "it takes more real and strenuous effort to do plain, ordinary things, obeying rules and keeping our tempers, than one occasional very brave thing; and, though I would not for a moment depreciate the latter, I think that in the aggregate the others are of greater importance. Anybody, however, who can do a courageous deed is capable of living up to it every day, and thus rising to a still higher level. We must consider ourselves as failures unless we are trying to develop the very best that is in us."

When Miss Maitland and the girls had dispersed to explore the ruins more thoroughly, Honor lay still on the grass, gazing hard at the wide, shining expanse of sea. Janie stayed too, and sat abstractedly plucking daisy-heads and pulling them to pieces, or crumbling little pieces of mortar from the wall. For a long time neither spoke.

"I believe Miss Maitland was having a shot at me," said Honor at last; "only, I don't understand exactly what she meant."

"I do," returned Janie. "She thinks that you're capable of very much more than ordinary people."

"I can't imagine why!"

"Because it's in you. You've brains, and pluck, and 'go', and all kinds of things that other folks haven't. You might do such a splendid amount in the world some day!"

"I, my dear girl!" cried Honor in amazement. "Why, I'm sure I'm not up to much!"

"You could be, if you tried."

"There are some things that aren't possible, however hard one tries. I can no more be really and truly good than you could win the Atalanta race at the sports!"

The colour flushed into Janie's thin cheeks. Her lack of physical prowess was sometimes rather a sore subject to her. Though she did not enjoy games, she would, nevertheless, have dearly liked the credit of excelling in them. For a moment or two she did not reply. She was considering hard, and making up her mind on a difficult point. When she spoke, it was with a touch of diffidence and hesitation in her voice.

"Suppose I could win the 'Atalanta', would you think it possible to be what Miss Maitland wants you?"

"Indeed, I'd think anything possible!" replied Honor, with more truth than politeness.

"Then shall we make it a bargain—if I win the race, you're going to try your very hardest?"

"Turn over a new leaf, in fact?"

"Yes."

"All right; I've no objection. I should like to see you flying round the quad!"

"And I should like to see you doing other things! Will you promise, then?"

"On my honour, if you want."

"Very well. Give me something as a pledge."

"You can have this small compass," said Honor, rummaging in her pocket. "It's rather a treasure. Brian brought it me from Switzerland, and it's made of agate."

"All the better, because you'll want to have it back. I'll give you my silver fruit-knife, which I'm equally loath to part with. We must each keep each other's token until after the sports."

"And then?"

"Ah! that remains to be seen," said Janie, as she rose and strolled leisurely away.

All the Chaddites agreed that the visit to Baldurstone was one of the most interesting excursions they had ever taken, and that the ruins were the most picturesque in the neighbourhood, far exceeding Weyland Castle, favoured by the Hilaryites; and Clayton House, the destination of St. Bride's. The memory of their delightful day was sufficient to carry them through the ordeal of recapitulation that always preceded the examinations, necessitating an extra half-hour of preparation in the evenings, and, as Lettice described it, "concentrating one's unfortunate brains to absolute splitting point".

Whether Lettice's mental exertions were sufficient to bring her to such an unhappy crisis was a question on which her class mistress might have expressed some doubt, though she herself thought she had proof conclusive one afternoon during the week following the picnic. She ran in from the grounds in quite a state of excitement, and hailed a group of friends assembled in the recreation room.

"Girls!" she exclaimed, "I've seen a vision, a most extraordinary and peculiar sight! You wouldn't believe what it was! I happened to be at the bottom of the garden, and in that quiet path behind the laundry I actually saw Janie Henderson tearing up and down, as if she were doing the last spurt of a Marathon."

"Janie Henderson! Impossible!" cried everybody.

"Just what I said. I rubbed my eyes, and came to the conclusion that I'd been overstudying, and must be suffering from a delusion. Do I look queer?"

"Not in the least; your cheeks are as red as peonies."

"Well, my eyesight must be defective, then, for I certainly thought I saw her."

"You've been dreaming!"

"It's about as likely as seeing Miss Cavendish performing with a skipping rope."

"Yes, it's absurd on the face of it. It must have been somebody else."

"A case of mistaken identity."

"There are heaps of girls the same height, and with long, light hair."

"No doubt. I was a fairly good distance off too. And yet," added Lettice to herself, as she went to change her cricket shoes, "I verily believe it was Janie Henderson, after all!"

CHAPTER XIII

Miss Maitland's Window

While the weather continued to be so hot and close, Miss Maitland allowed the girls to spend their evening recreation in the garden, so that they might have a blow of fresh, cool air before they went to bed. They enjoyed sitting under the trees with books or fancy work, though as a rule their tongues wagged so fast that there was little display of industry with their needles.

"I hate sewing," confessed Honor, "and it's no use pretending I like it."

"This piece of embroidery has lasted me three terms, and it isn't finished yet," said Maisie Talbot, leisurely snipping off a thread, and pausing before she chose another piece of silk.

"I don't have to look at my knitting," said Chatty Burns; "but then, I'm Scotch, and every Scotchwoman knits."

"You're getting on so fast, it will do for me as well," said Honor, lying comfortably on the grass with her hands clasped under her head, and watching Chatty's rapidly growing stocking. "It's a 'work of supererogation', and that always leaves a little virtue over, to count for somebody else."

"I didn't say I'd hand the extra merit on to you," retorted Chatty.

"You can't help it. If there's so much to spare it must go somewhere, and I'm the idlest person; it will naturally fly to make up my deficiencies."

"What a fallacious argument!" declared Maisie.

"Do you know," interrupted Ruth Latimer, "that it's exactly a fortnight on Friday to the end of the term?"

"Know! I should think we do know!" replied Lettice. "I expect each one of us is counting the days, and longing for the time to come, if I'm any sample of the rest of the school. I say, 'One more day gone', every night when I get into bed."

"It's glorious to think the breaking-up is so near," said Pauline Reynolds. "What are you all going to do in the holidays?"

"We're starting for the Tyrol at the beginning of August," said

Ruth. "We want to have a walking tour. We shall leave our heavy luggage at Botzen, and then tramp off up the mountains with just a few things in knapsacks on our backs, and stop at chalets and little inns ('guest-houses', as they are called there) on the way. We shall feel most delightfully free, because we can go any distance we like, and shall not be bound to arrive at any special place by any special time. That's the beauty of a walking tour."

"How far can you go in a day?" asked Honor.

"It just depends. If one is in the hot valleys, quite a short distance knocks one up; but when one gets the real mountain air, one can march along without feeling the least scrap tired. I once did twenty miles in Switzerland, but that's my record."

"And a pretty good one," said Pauline, "particularly as one oughtn't to reckon miles in Switzerland; one counts mountain climbing in hours."

"Yes, I've sometimes been deer-stalking at home," said Chatty, "and it's a very different affair toiling uphill over the heather from walking on a flat road. We're not going away this summer. Father has taken some extra shooting, and we're to have a big house-party instead. It's great fun! I like helping to carry the lunch in the little pony trap on to the moors; and we have jolly times in the evening—games, and music, and dancing. Have your people settled any plans yet, Pauline?"

"They talk of Norway. It would be glorious to see the midnight sun, and the lovely pine forests. I've wanted to go ever since I read Feats on the Fiord."

"You won't find it so romantic as that," laughed Ruth Latimer. "Things have changed since the time Harriet Martineau wrote about it. There are no pirates nowadays, to try to kidnap bishops and burn farms. You might, perhaps, find Rolf's wonderful cave, but I'm sure there isn't a peasant left who believes in the water sprite, and the Mountain Demon, and Nipen, and all the rest of the spirits of which Erica was so afraid."

"Perhaps not; but the country's just as beautiful, and I shall see the fiords, if I haven't any adventures there. I didn't say I wanted to meet pirates among the islands; on the whole, I should prefer their room to their company."

"Well, I wish you just one adventure, to keep up the element of romance. Perhaps your boatman will row you into the middle of the fiord, and demand your purse before he consents to take you back to the vessel; or you may be shipwrecked on a sunken rock, and left stranded in the Arctic Circle, dependent on the hospitality of the Laplanders!"

"No, thanks! I believe their tents are disgustingly dirty. I hope I may see a Lapp settlement, all the same, and also a few seals. I'm afraid a whale, or an iceberg, is too much to expect."

"Where are you going, Lettice?" enquired Chatty.

"Nowhere in particular, unless Maisie and I are asked to our aunt's. But we shall have jolly fun at golf and tennis. When one has been at school the whole term, one likes to be at one's own home, and to meet all one's friends again. It feels such ages since one saw them."

"Yes; the middle part of the term always seems to drag dreadfully, and then the last comes with a rush, and the exams. are on before one knows what one is doing."

"Don't talk of exams!" cried Pauline. "I expect I shall fail in every single one. I'm completely mixed up in chemistry, and I never can remember dates and names properly. My history paper will be a series of dashes: 'War with France was renewed in ——, when the English gained the decisive battle of ——, in which the Prince —— was slain and the Duke of —— taken prisoner. By the Treaty of —— a truce was concluded', &c."

"Perhaps Miss Farrar will think it's a guessing competition," remarked Honor.

"I dare say she will. I wish we needn't have exams., or marks, or any horrid things, to show whether we've done well or badly."

"I can get on tolerably with facts," said Lettice, "but I'm always marked 'weak' for composition. Miss Farrar says I use tautology and repeat myself, and that my grammar is shaky and my general style poor. She told me to take Macaulay as a model, but I can no more copy other people's ways of writing than I could improve my features by staring at the Venus de Medici."

"Poor old Salad! You're not cut out for an authoress."

"I'm certainly not; I'd rather be a charwoman! I don't aspire to be editress of the school magazine, I assure you, nor even a contributor. By the way, Honor, why don't you send something? I'm sure you could."

"I did think of it," replied Honor. "I was going to make a nice little series of acrostics on all of your names. I did one about Chatty, and showed it to Janie; but she said that it was far too slangy, and Vivian would never pass it, so I tore it up, and felt too squashed to go on."

"Oh! what was it?" exclaimed the girls. "Can't you remember it?"

"I'll try. I believe it went this way:

"C hatty Burns is just a ripper!
 H air's the colour of a kipper;

A nd her face so round and red is
T hat you'd think her cheeks were cherries.
T hough we often call her 'Fatty',
Y ou depend we're nuts on Chatty."

"What a shame!" cried the indignant original of the acrostic. "My hair's auburn, it's not the colour of a kipper!"

"We certainly call you 'Fatty', though," laughed Lettice. "I think the poem is lovely!"

"It's a good thing you tore it up, all the same," said Ruth. "Vivian would have been simply horrified. We have a crusade against slang at Chessington, and 'ripper' is one of the words absolutely vetoed. We only say 'jolly' by stealth."

"I'm sure 'jolly' ought to be allowable. I saw it in a book in the library: 'as jolly as a sandboy', was the expression."

"What is a sandboy?" asked Lettice. "The phrase is always quoted as the high-water mark of bliss."

"I've never been able to find out," said Ruth. "I suppose it's either one of those wretched little urchins who dive for pennies, or an ordinary donkey boy. But this is what Miss Farrar calls 'a digression from the subject'. I want to hear if Honor has written any more acrostics."

"I made one on Lillie Harper," replied Honor. "It had an illustration, too, done very badly, in just a few crooked strokes, like little children draw:

"L illie is a dab at cricket;
I depict her at the wicket.
L ook how tight her bat she's grasping,
L eaving all the fielders gasping!
I have done this sketch in woggles,
E specially to show her goggles.

"It ought to have the picture to really explain it," said Honor regretfully; "I'm sorry now that I tore it up. I began a piece on the exams. too; it was a parody of 'The boy stood on the burning deck', but I can't get beyond the first verse:

"The girl sat at the hard, bare desk,
Whence all but she had fled;
Her fingers they were stained with ink,
And aching was her head."

"Oh, go on! It would be so nice!"

"It's impossible to think of any more."

"The time rolled on, she could not go
Without her teacher's word,"

improvised Ruth.

"That teacher, taking tea below,
Her sighs no longer heard,"
finished Honor. "Only, Miss Farrar wouldn't be taking tea in the middle of an exam. No, it can't be done!"

"Then we must put 'To be continued'," said Ruth.

"Make another acrostic, Paddy!" urged Lettice.

"Acrostics are too hard, because one is hampered by keeping to the letters of the girls' names," objected Honor. "Limericks are much easier. How would this do for Vivian Holmes?—

"There was a head girl of St. Chad's,
Who was subject to fancies and fads;
When we tried to talk slang,
She declared it was wrong,
And said she considered us cads."

"Good!" laughed Ruth. "Only, of course, Vivian wouldn't dream of using such a word as 'cad'. Now, I've got one about you:

"There's a girl at our house we call 'Paddy':
She's not 'goody-goody', but 'baddy';
She loves practical jokes,
Or to play us a hoax,
Though we tell her such tricks are not 'Chaddy'."

"Very well, Miss Ruth Latimer! I'll return the compliment," said Honor. "How do you like this?—

"There's a girl at our house who's called Ruth:
She is fond of an unpleasant truth;
She says she is seeking
To practise plain speaking,
But we think she is merely uncouth."

"I don't mind in the least," declared Ruth; "in fact, I'm rather flattered than otherwise."

"Make one about Maisie or me," implored Lettice. "You can say as nasty things as you want."

"Nothing could possibly rhyme with Lettice," announced Honor after a moment's cogitation, "or with Salad either. I might do better with Maisie. Let me see—crazy, hazy, daisy, lazy—I think those are all. Will this suit you?—

"There's a girl in this garden called Maisie;
At lessons she's horribly lazy,
But she's splendid at sports,
And at games of all sorts,
While o'er cricket she waxes quite crazy."

"What are you all laughing at?" enquired Flossie Taylor, sauntering up to join the group, and taking a seat on the grass.

"Limericks. Honor is winding them off by the yard. Now, Paddy, let us have one about Flossie! Quick, while your genius is burning!"

"It's only flickering," laughed Honor, "but I'll try:

"There's a girl at St. Chad's who's named Flossie;
She tries to be terribly 'bossy',
She sets us all straight
(Which is just what we hate),
And makes us exceedingly cross(y)."

"Oh, what a fearfully lame rhyme!" said Lettice.

"I know it is, but I couldn't think of any other word. If you're offended, Flossie, you can go away."

"I'm not silly enough to care about such trifles," replied Flossie loftily.

"You've quite left out Janie," said Lettice, "and there she is sewing all the time, and as usual never offering a single remark. Janie Henderson, why don't you talk?"

"You don't give me a chance to put in a word," protested Janie. "Perhaps I'm like the proverbial parrot, which couldn't talk, but thought all the more."

"You mean that I do the talking, and not the thinking?"

"I didn't say so."

"But you implied it. You deserve a horrid Limerick, and I shall make one myself. Wait a moment, while I rack my brains. Oh, now I've got it!—

"Miss Henderson, otherwise Jane,
May think very hard with her brain,
But it never comes out,
So she leaves us in doubt
If there are any thoughts to explain.

"There! You can't retaliate, because, as Honor says, there isn't a rhyme for Lettice."

"It's a good thing, for we might get too personal," interposed Chatty. "I think we've been over the margin of politeness as it is. Suppose we change the subject. Do you know, the honey dew is dropping from this lime tree overhead and making my knitting needles quite sticky!"

"It would be a lovely tree to climb, the boughs are so regular," said Honor, gazing into the green heights above.

"I don't believe I could go up a tree if a mad bull were after me," asserted Pauline. "I should just collapse at the bottom, and be gored to death, I know I should!"

"It isn't difficult," declared Honor. "You've only to catch hold of the branches, and keep swinging yourself a little higher. I've climbed ever so many trees in our garden at home."

"I should like to see you do it here, then."

"Very well! I'll show you, if you don't believe me."

The lime tree in question stood close to the house—so near, in fact, that some of its boughs brushed the windows. Miss Cavendish had several times decided to have it cut down, thinking it interfered with the light; but Miss Maitland had always begged that it might be spared a little longer, saying she loved its cool shade.

Honor swung herself quite easily from branch to branch, while the group of girls below watched her with admiration.

"You look like a middy going up the main-mast," said Ruth.

"Or a monkey at the Zoo," added Lettice.

"That's the voice of jealousy," remarked Chatty. "Lettice is green with envy because she can't do it herself."

"A squirrel would be a happier simile," suggested Ruth.

"She's getting along very quickly," said Pauline.

Half-way up the tree Honor paused and looked down.

"Hallo!" she cried, "I'm just by Miss Maitland's study. I shall go in, and pay her a call. Ta-ta!" and she disappeared suddenly through the open window.

"What will Miss Maitland say if she's there?" exclaimed Lettice.

"I don't believe she'd be cross," said Maisie. "She'd be amused to see anybody come in so funnily."

Honor was absent only about a minute, then her beaming face peeped from the window once more.

"Miss Maitland's not at home," she announced. "I've left my card with the footman, and said I'd call again another day, in my aeroplane. Keep out of the way down there—I'm coming!" and down she came, with a rush and a scramble, arriving quite safely, however, with only her hair ribbon untied and her hands a little grazed.

"You see, it's really a very easy matter," she explained; "we do far harder things in the gym."

"Can you find a good foothold?" asked Flossie.

"Oh, yes! There are heaps of places that seem made on purpose to put your toe in. It's almost like a ladder."

"Here's Vivian!" said Chatty. "I'm afraid she's come to call us in."

"What a nuisance! I don't want to go to bed."

Chatty had accurately guessed the monitress's errand.

"It's nearly nine o'clock," proclaimed Vivian. "Didn't you hear the bell? I rang it at the side door."

AN UNLUCKY ESCAPADE

"We didn't hear a sound," replied Lettice. "But then, we were all laughing so much. Honor Fitzgerald has just been climbing the lime tree, and she went right through the window into the study."

"Honor Fitzgerald is a hoyden, then," said Vivian. "And what business had she to go inside Miss Maitland's room? It was a piece of great impertinence."

"I'm sorry I told you," said Lettice ruefully.

"I wish Vivian could have heard the verse you made about her!" whispered Pauline to Honor. "Is hoyden a dictionary word, or not? I'm afraid I should have said 'cheek' instead of impertinence, but I'm not a monitress."

The girls had entered the dressing-room, and were putting away books and sewing materials in their lockers, when Maisie exclaimed:

"Oh, what a bother! I've left my work-basket on the grass. It was open, too, and if there's a heavy dew my scissors and crewel needles will be covered with rust. Lettice, do go and fetch it for me!—there's just time."

Lettice was so accustomed to wait upon her elder sister that she did not even remonstrate, but turned straightway and ran into the garden to fetch the lost property. It had grown suddenly very dusk, almost dark. The lime tree stood out tall and black by the side of the house, and the bushes were dense masses of shadow. Lettice had to grope for the basket, but found it at last, and began to retrace her steps along the hardly-discernible path. She was about twenty yards away from the lime tree when a slight noise made her look back, and she noticed the figure of a girl swinging herself down by the branches in the same way as Honor had done. Whoever it was alighted on the ground gently, and rushed off into the bushes before Lettice could see her face, though it would have been too dark, in any case, to distinguish her features. It was all done very quickly, and so silently that, except for the first sound, there was scarcely a rustle.

Lettice was in a great hurry, and did not stop to make any investigation; indeed, she did not trouble to give the matter a thought. It seemed a trifling little incident, not even worth mentioning to the others; yet it was one that she was to remember afterwards, in view of certain events that followed, for it was destined to make a link in the strangest chain of circumstances that ever occurred at St. Chad's.

CHAPTER XIV

A Stolen Meeting

Honor had hurried with the other girls from the garden, laughing and joking as she went, and was almost in the act of running into the house when quite unexpectedly something happened, something utterly amazing and out of the common, and which was to be fraught with entirely unlooked-for consequences. As she put her foot on the first of the steps that led to the side door a figure moved silently from under the shade of a lilac bush close by, and, tapping her upon the arm, drew her aside with a whispered "Sh-sh!"

Honor suppressed an exclamation of astonishment, and, peering through the dusk to see who thus accosted her, recognized Annie, an under-housemaid who had only lately come to St. Chad's.

"I've been waiting to catch you alone, miss," whispered the girl, "and a difficult matter it's been too. I didn't dare speak to you before the other young ladies. I'm to give you this letter, safe into your own hand. I'd never have done it if I hadn't promised so faithful—it's almost as much as my place is worth!"

"What is it? Who sent it?" asked Honor, taking the note.

"It's from one of the young gentlemen at Orley Grange, and I was to be sure you got it secretly. Put it in your pocket, miss, and run indoors! I must be off to the kitchen," and without another word Annie turned and fled, as if relieved to have accomplished her errand. Full of curiosity, Honor entered the house. The clock had not yet struck nine, so, seeing that the light was on in the dressing-room, she peeped inside. Fortunately, nobody was there, and she was able to go in and read her letter free from all observation. Its contents appeared to occasion her no little perplexity and dismay, for she knitted her brows and shook her head as she replaced the envelope in her pocket. She went, however, to the recreation room, where the rest of the girls were assembled waiting for the bell that always rang to proclaim bedtime; but she was in such an absent and abstracted frame of mind that several of her friends noticed and remarked upon it.

"What's wrong with Paddy?" asked Lettice. "She's shut up suddenly, like an oyster. I can't get a word out of her."

"I can't imagine," said Pauline. "I spoke to her just now, and she didn't seem to hear me."

"It's most unlike her," commented Ruth. "She generally goes to bed with so many jokes and parting shots."

To-night Honor walked upstairs with unwonted staidness and gravity. She went quietly into her cubicle and drew the curtain, and answered so briefly when her room-mate spoke to her that the latter was almost offended.

"Perhaps she's only tired though," thought Janie charitably. "This hot weather is enough to wear anybody out. I don't always care to talk myself."

Janie was certainly not a girl to push conversation where it was evidently not wanted, so the pair undressed in absolute silence. From Honor's cubicle came sounds that suggested that its occupant was fumbling with a key and unlocking a box, but as she did not volunteer any explanation, her room-mate made no comments. When Vivian arrived at half-past nine to switch out the light, both girls were in bed.

Next morning Janie woke suddenly just as the grey dawn was growing strong enough to show faintly the various objects that were in the room. Some unusual noise had disturbed her, and she lay listening intently. She could hear stealthy movements in the next cubicle, and wondering what her friend was doing, she popped out of bed and peeped round the curtain. There was Honor, fully dressed, and in the act of putting on her hat.

"What's the matter?" asked Janie anxiously. "Honor! where are you going?"

"I hoped I shouldn't waken you," replied Honor in a whisper. "Hush! Don't talk loud, because with all the windows so wide open the girls in No. 6 can hear quite plainly when we speak in this room."

"All right. But do tell me why you're getting up at this extraordinary hour?" said Janie, in a subdued tone.

"I'm in a dreadful fix! I must meet Dermot down on the beach soon after five o'clock."

"Meet Dermot! Your brother? But why?"

"He's in such a scrape, and I have to get him out of it."

"How do you know?"

"One of the servants slipped this note into my hand last night, as we came in from the garden. You can read it if you like."

Janie took the letter, which was written in a scrawling, boyish hand on a piece of paper apparently torn out of an exercise-book. It ran thus:—

"Orley Grange,

"Tuesday.

"Dear Honor,

"I am in the most awful row, and if I can't get a sovereign by to-morrow morning I shall be done for. I owe it to Blake. I haven't time to tell you the whole affair, but I have been an absolute idiot. Blake wants the money, and he's a mean sneak. He says if I don't pay up he'll let on about something that I'm trying to keep dark. He really means it, too, and if it gets to the Head's ears I shall be expelled. Can you possibly lend me anything? I'd have written to the Mater, but I hear she has one of her bad attacks, so it wouldn't do to upset her. As for the governor, he'd be furious if he knew. He told me last term that if I ran into debt I needn't trust to him to get me out of it, for he wouldn't stir a finger to help me, and would give me a thrashing for my pains. He must not know on any account. It is of no use writing to Brian or the others, because it is so near the end of the term they're sure to have no money left. Have you spent all yours? I am going to get up before five o'clock to-morrow and climb out through the dormitory window, and go along the shore to the beach below Chessington, just by your bathing-place. Can you manage to do the same, and bring me any cash you can gather? Perhaps Blake might take something on account, if you haven't the whole. The janitor has promised to go with this letter to St. Chad's; he says he thinks he can get it smuggled in through his niece, who is a servant there. But he won't have time to wait for an answer, so the only way to give me the money is to meet me on the shore. I am awfully sorry to have to ask you to do this, but it is the one chance I have left, and if you knew what a hole I am in I think you would be sorry for me. I must stop now. The bell is ringing.

"Your loving brother,

"Dermot."

"Oh, Honor! Are you going?"

"Of course I am. I wouldn't fail Dermot at such a pinch. Luckily I have the money too. I shall let myself out by the dressing-room window, and climb over the fence at the end of the cricket field. It won't take very long. I shall be back before any of the servants are stirring."

"But it's such a frightfully risky thing! Suppose you were caught, you'd certainly get into a scrape."

"I shall have to take the risk. Dermot will get into a far worse scrape if I don't go. I couldn't bear to think of him waiting for me on the shore, and finding I never came. Hush, Janie! Please don't ask me any more. I've made up my mind."

Honor had put on her tennis shoes, and now stole very softly out of the room and down the passage. Janie went to bed again, though certainly not to sleep. She heard the stairs creak, and wondered if anyone else were awake in the house, and would notice the compromising sound.

"Oh, dear! What is to be done?" she thought anxiously. "It's fearfully naughty of Honor, yet I sympathize with her wanting to help Dermot. I believe I should have gone myself, if I'd had a brother of my own in trouble. Major Fitzgerald must be a very stern man; they both seem too frightened of him to tell anything, and their poor mother is so ill she mustn't be disturbed. I'm sorry for Honor. I hope she won't be long away; I shall be wretched till she comes back. Somebody might see her from a window, even if no one hears her in the passage, and then—I don't like to think of the consequences!"

Honor was indeed determined to do her utmost for Dermot. Of all her five brothers, he was the dearest. Rather younger than herself, he had been her inseparable companion in nursery days, when the pair had shared everything, from sweets to scoldings, with strictest impartiality. Honor had never forgotten the terrible parting when her father had decreed that Dermot was old enough to go to school—how she had cried herself sick, and how absolutely lonely and deserted the Castle had seemed when she was obliged to wander about and amuse herself alone. She had grown accustomed in time to solitary rambles, but she had always looked forward to her brother's return with keenest anticipation, and regretted bitterly that holidays were so short.

That Dermot was in trouble and wanted her was now the one thought uppermost in her mind, and rules were entirely ignored in her desire to see him and speak with him. Though she was determined to carry out her project she knew, however, that it was a most unorthodox and unwarrantable proceeding to leave St. Chad's at such an hour, and on such an errand, and she had no desire to be caught and prevented from going.

She stole along the landing, therefore, as softly as possible, pausing every now and then to listen if all were quiet. The whole house seemed to be sound asleep, and not a door opened as she passed. Once down the stairs and in the hall she felt safer, and hurrying quickly into the dressing-room, she easily unbolted a

French window that led into the garden.

Was that a step on the stairs? Honor was not sure. She dared not go back to ascertain, but, rushing outside, fled as fast as she could round the corner in the direction of the cricket pitch.

"Whoever it was will find the bird flown," she said to herself. "Perhaps I was mistaken, though, and only imagined I heard somebody."

A glance at the little watch pinned to her blouse told her that she had not much time to lose. She did not wish to keep Dermot waiting, for she knew he would be in a fever of anxiety until she made her appearance.

"I hope he has managed to get off safely," she thought. "It must be more difficult to leave a large dormitory than a small bedroom; still, I don't suppose any of the other boys would try to stop him, or would tell afterwards."

She had now reached the playing-fields, and she climbed over the fence that separated them from a neighbouring pasture. A few hundred yards, and a stile brought her to a path along the cliffs that led to the bathing-place.

Dermot was first at the tryst. Even before Honor began to descend the flight of steps she caught sight of his familiar figure on the beach below. He was pacing impatiently up and down, glancing first one way and then another, until at length he happened to look upwards in the right direction, and saw her. He waved his hat, and came eagerly along the shingle to meet her.

"All right, Dermot! I've brought you the sovereign!" she cried, anxious to relieve his mind at once.

"Really? Oh, I say, Sis, it is good of you!"

There was no long line of grinning schoolboys to jeer, nor sedate Chaddites to disapprove, so Honor hugged her brother this time to her heart's content. It seemed so delightful to see him again that she almost forgot for the moment upon what errand she had come, only realizing that he was there, and that she had him all to herself. The remembrance of his trouble, however, quickly returned to her.

"Come and tell me everything," she said, drawing him towards the bathing-hut. "We can sit on these steps and talk."

"I was rather doubtful whether my letter had reached you," began Dermot; "I'd to settle with the janitor, and at first he said that the College was so strictly kept, it would be quite impossible. Afterwards he gave way and said he'd try, but I couldn't see him again to ask if he'd really managed the affair; I had just to come to the cove on chance. I can tell you I was glad when I saw you coming down the rocks. Oh, Honor, I've got myself into the most awful mess!"

"How is it? I don't understand. Who is this Blake?"

"He has a place in Dunscar, a kind of second-rate veterinary surgeon's business; and he sells dogs, and rats, and rabbits, and even does a little mole-catching, I believe—rather a low-class sporting chap, in fact. Roper took me to the kennels one day, to see a spaniel. Some of our fellows keep dogs there, and Blake looks after them. Well, I liked the spaniel; it was a perfect beauty! Roper said Blake only wanted ten shillings for it, and it was an absolute bargain. He advised me to buy it and keep it at the kennels. I'd run through all my cash by then, but Blake said I could go on tick if I cared; and I thought it was a pity to miss the chance, because if I didn't have the dog, Jarrow was going to take him."

"I suppose you mayn't keep dogs at school?" said Honor.

"Rather not! You'd have liked this one, Honor! His name was Terry, and he was as jolly as poor old Doss used to be. He got to know me directly, and he'd come jumping and trying to lick my face. He was clever, too; he could do all kinds of tricks—trust for a biscuit, and lie down and die, and give three barks for the King. I grew so fond of him, and I meant to take him home with me in the holidays. Well, I hadn't been able to go to the kennels for several days, and when at last I managed to run down there Blake told me that Terry was dead and buried. He looked so shifty when he said it that I had my suspicions at once. I don't believe Terry died at all; I'm sure Blake sold him to somebody else, who has taken him away."

"Oh, what a shame!" exclaimed Honor.

"It's just like the fellow, though—he's an atrocious cad! Of course, I couldn't prove anything. I could only say that Terry had looked all right when last I saw him, and it seemed a queer thing for him to pop off so suddenly; but then Blake rounded on me with all sorts of medical terms, and said he'd made a post-mortem examination, and could give me a written certificate. As if that would have been of any use! Well, the long and short of it was, we had a quarrel, and Blake turned nasty. He said he wanted the money I owed him for the dog, and he gave me an immense bill for its keep. It was quite ridiculous; he made out it had eaten pounds and pounds of Spratt's biscuits every week, and that he'd bought fresh meat for it too. I'm sure he hadn't! I disputed every item; but he said if I wasn't satisfied I could refer the matter to the Head. The whole affair came to exactly a sovereign. I couldn't possibly pay it—I hadn't more than a few shillings left in the world. I tried to get him to give me tick for a little longer, but he was as surly as a bear, and threatened that if I didn't turn up with the money by Wednesday, he'd send in the bill to the Head."

"I suppose that would mean a big row?"

"Simply terrific! You see, the kennels are out of bounds; besides which, we've all been warned we're to have nothing to do with Blake. The Head said he was a rascal, and any fellow who went to his place would do so at the risk of expulsion. I was an idiot to let myself get mixed up in such a business, but Roper, and Graveson, and several others had dogs, and I was so taken with that black spaniel! I thought and schemed how I could find a way out of it. I didn't dare to write home to the Mater: if she's well enough to read her own letters, she'd be in quite a nervous state of mind about it; and if she's ill, then the governor will open them all for her, and you know what he'd say!"

"It would be as bad as when I bought Firefly," replied Honor. "He was most fearfully angry that time."

"And he'd be harder on me than on you, because you're a girl. He couldn't thrash you, however much he might scold you. I've had a little experience of his hunting-crop before, and it's not exactly pleasant."

"Yes, I remember—when you took the cartridges out of his gun cupboard."

"Well, I say, Honor, I mustn't stay here too long; I've got to be back before anyone's about the place, you know."

"Did you get off all right?"

"Oh, yes! I dropped out of the dormitory window on to a piece of roof near, and let myself down by the spout. It was quite simple."

"How about climbing up again?"

"Easy as A B C."

"Well, here's the pound, at any rate."

"Thanks immensely! How is it you're so flush of cash?"

"I'm not. I've hardly any of my pocket-money left. This is my Jubilee sovereign."

"Not the one Uncle Murtagh gave you?"

"Yes."

"Oh, Honor, I am sorry! I scarcely like to take it."

"Don't be absurd! You must!"

"But you had the thing as a locket, and vowed you'd never part with it."

"It can't be helped. Vows are sometimes better broken. Uncle Murtagh told me to keep it until I happened to want it very badly, and I'm sure we need it to-day."

"Well, I do, at any rate, though it seems rather a swindle to commandeer your particular, pet treasure. I'll have to borrow it now, I'm afraid; but I'll get you another some time, I promise you faithfully."

"I don't care in the least, so long as you get out of this scrape," protested Honor.

The sun was already so high that its bright rays, reflected in a little pool near their feet, warned the pair that it was no longer safe to delay their parting.

"It's a quarter to six!" exclaimed Dermot, looking at his watch. "I must absolutely fly. I'll run all the way to Dunscar. I hope you'll get back quite safely into the College. You were a perfect trump to come. Good-bye; I'm off!"

Honor stood watching him until he had disappeared round the rocks at the end of the cove, then half-regretfully she climbed up the steps again on to the headland. She returned to St. Chad's the same way as she had come, walking across the pasture and climbing the fence of the cricket ground. She found the French window in the dressing-room still ajar, and bolted it on the inside before she went upstairs. All was still quite quiet in the hall and on the landing, and she was able to regain her room without any alarms.

Janie looked up nervously as the door opened. She had been lying awake, suffering far more anxiety on her friend's behalf than Honor had experienced for herself, and she gave a sigh of intense relief on hearing that the interview was successfully accomplished.

"I've been thinking it over," she said, "and I really believe it would have been much the best to go straight to Miss Maitland and tell her about it. She's very kind and sympathetic; perhaps she would have let you meet Dermot, and then you could have gone openly, and without all this dreadful stealing up and down stairs."

"I daren't risk it," replied Honor. "Suppose she had said 'No'? I should have been far worse off than if I hadn't asked. Besides which, she might have insisted upon telling Dr. Winterton. That's quite within the bounds of possibility; and then I should have given poor old Dermot away."

"On the whole, wouldn't it be more satisfactory for Dr. Winterton to know?"

"Janie! How can you suggest such a thing?"

"Well, if, as you say, this man Blake is a scamp, and has really sold the dog, it ought to be enquired into. If it were all exposed, perhaps he would be obliged to leave Dunscar and go to some other place, and that would be much better for the boys at the Grange."

"But in the meantime Dermot would be the scapegoat."

"I don't believe Dr. Winterton would expel him, if he went and owned up himself. He'd be rather angry, I dare say, but then the thing would be over, and there'd be no more fear of being found out. If Blake is such a dishonest man, he may send in the same bill again."

"Dermot said he should make him give a receipt for the money. No, Janie! You don't quite grasp the case. You've no brothers of your own, so how can you understand boys?"

"Then couldn't you have asked your father?" pleaded Janie desperately. "It seems—please don't be offended!—not quite straight to be suppressing the whole affair like this."

"You don't know my father, or you wouldn't suggest it. He can be very stern, particularly with the boys. They always say he's more of a martinet at home than ever he was in the Army. Yes, I know you tell your mother everything, but mothers are much more lenient than fathers. I'd tell mine, if she weren't ill. It's no use arguing, Janie! I'm sorry if it isn't all on the square, but Dermot was in a very tight place, and I felt bound to help him, even if I had to do something rather wrong."

CHAPTER XV

Sent to Coventry

Though Honor had seen nobody, either in leaving or re-entering St. Chad's, her morning adventure had not been so entirely unobserved as she imagined. Vivian Holmes, who was a light sleeper, had awakened by the unfortunate creak that had been made by the stairs. Always mindful of her duties as monitress, she had jumped up and cautiously opened her door, and was just in time to peep over the banisters and catch a glimpse of Honor's back disappearing down the hall. She hurriedly returned to put on her dressing-gown and bedroom slippers, then followed as rapidly as she could. When she arrived downstairs, she found the French window leading into the garden open; but Honor was well round the corner, and running fast towards the cricket field. Vivian was very much disturbed and distressed. She scarcely knew what she ought to do. She ventured a little way into the grounds, but not a trace of any truant was to be seen, so she thought it useless to search far. One of the girls must have gone out; on that point she was absolutely certain.

"I'm almost positive it was Honor Fitzgerald," she said to herself. "It looked exactly like her, although I only saw her back for a moment."

Vivian was extremely conscientious, and felt personally responsible for all under her charge at St. Chad's. She was apt to err on the side of severity, but she honestly strove to do her duty, and to see that the rules were duly kept. In this case, however, she was in a difficulty. There was no rule to prevent a girl getting up early and going into the garden, because it had never occurred to Miss Maitland that anyone would wish to rise before the usual dressing-bell. Vivian knew that Honor had been accustomed to much liberty in her Irish home, and that she greatly chafed against the constraints of school life. What was more probable than that, waking at dawn, she had longed for a breath of the cool morning air, and was taking a stroll round the grounds?

"She may have a headache, or have slept badly," thought the monitress, with an endeavour to be charitable. "These hot nights are very trying, even with both one's bedroom windows wide open."

After all, it was not a very desperate offence, and there seemed no need to report it to Miss Maitland. Vivian determined to listen for Honor's footsteps and catch her on the stairs as she came back, or, at any rate, to tax her with the affair later during the day, and point out that in future such early rambles could not be allowed. In the meantime, she went back to bed, and, in spite of her resolution to intercept the returning wanderer, fell asleep again, and heard nothing until the bell rang at a quarter to seven. In the busy whirl of occupations that followed, there was no opportunity for any private conversation with Honor, either before or after morning school; and immediately dinner was over, all the Chaddites rushed off to watch a croquet tournament between mistresses and monitresses, in which Vivian herself was taking part. The day, therefore, passed exactly as usual, and it was not until after tea, when the girls were just going to preparation, that anything particular occurred.

At precisely half-past four o'clock Janie Henderson chanced to be walking down the passage when she saw the door of Miss Maitland's study suddenly open, and Vivian Holmes come out, looking so greatly agitated and upset that Janie stopped in amazement.

"Why, what's the matter?" she exclaimed, for she was on sufficiently friendly terms with the monitress to venture the enquiry.

"A great deal's the matter!" replied Vivian. "The worst thing that has ever happened at St. Chad's, or in the whole College. I'd give all I possess in the world to have nothing to do with it! I wish I weren't monitress! Where's Honor Fitzgerald? I have to find her."

"She's practising," said Janie. "Shall I fetch her?"

"Look here!" returned Vivian. "Honor sleeps in your room; did you hear her get up very early this morning and go out?"

Janie's tell-tale face betrayed her at once, though she would not have attempted to deny the fact, in any case.

"Then I'm sorry, but you'll have to come to Miss Maitland too," said Vivian. "It's a hateful business altogether, and after our splendid record at St. Chad's, and the way we have all tried so hard to keep up the standard, it hurts me more than I can tell you. I can't bear to get Honor Fitzgerald into trouble! I simply couldn't have believed it of her, though I'm afraid it's only too plain. She's been very naughty sometimes, but she always seemed extremely straightforward, and I never dreamt she could be capable of an affair like this. We shall have to tell the exact truth, Janie; there's nothing else for it, and she must clear herself as best she can. I'm afraid she's bound to be expelled. It's a terrible disgrace to the house. Yes, go and fetch her now; the sooner we get it over the better."

Janie walked down the passage in the utmost perplexity. She could not account for Vivian's excited diatribe. What had Honor done to bring disgrace upon St. Chad's? It was, of course, a very irregular thing to run away at daybreak to meet her brother, but it was no worse than many of her other scrapes, and did not seem an offence of sufficient gravity to warrant such an extreme measure as expulsion from the school.

"Vivian is always hard on Honor," thought Janie. "Perhaps, after all, she's making an unnecessary fuss, and it won't turn out to be so dreadful as she says. Tell the truth! Of course I shall do so; Vivian needn't remind me of that!"

Janie called her friend as quietly as possible from the piano. There were several other girls in the room, and she did not wish them to know anything about the affair. She only whispered therefore that Honor was wanted in Miss Maitland's study at once, and did not add any explanation, thinking it better not to mention Vivian's remarks, as she had not understood them herself. Honor put her music away calmly enough, and closed the piano. She knew that the summons must have reference to her morning adventure, and anticipated a scolding; but it was not the first she had received at St. Chad's, and she thought the punishment would probably not exceed two hundred lines, or, perhaps, a few pages of poetry to be learnt by heart.

The two girls hurried to the study, and, after knocking at the door, entered in response to Miss Maitland's "Come in". The house-mistress was seated at her writing-table, talking to Vivian, and turned round at their approach. She looked worried, and had a sterner expression on her face than they had ever seen there before.

"Honor Fitzgerald," she began, "I have sent for you because a very unpleasant thing has occurred, which I hope you may be able to explain to me. Last evening I was sitting writing at this table, and laid a sovereign down just at this corner. I was called away, and left the room for about ten minutes, or a quarter of an hour. When I returned, I found to my astonishment that the money was gone. I searched everywhere, and it had certainly not fallen on to the floor, nor was it amongst my papers; so I can only conclude that someone must have come in and taken it. I have made careful enquiries as to who was seen near my study last night, and I hear that you climbed up the lime tree and entered the room by the window shortly before nine o'clock. Is that so?"

"Yes, Miss Maitland," replied Honor, without any hesitation. "I did come in, but I only stayed a minute. I didn't go near the table, and I didn't see the sovereign. If I had, I certainly shouldn't have touched it."

Miss Maitland sighed.

"I was afraid you would say that, Honor! My dear child, it would be better to tell me the truth, and confess at once. We have the clearest proof that you, and only you, must have taken it, so it is no use denying it any more."

"I should like to know what proof you mean, Miss Maitland?" said Honor, in a strained voice.

"This letter," replied the mistress, producing Dermot's note. "It was found on your bedroom floor this morning by the upper housemaid, who brought it at once to me. It was given you, I find, by one of the under servants, who much regrets now that she was persuaded to deliver it secretly. It shows me, of course, your motive for taking the money."

"But I did not take it!" said Honor. "I said before that I didn't see it, and I mean it."

For answer Miss Maitland turned to Janie.

"Janie Henderson, did Honor Fitzgerald leave her bedroom before five o'clock this morning?"

Poor Janie whispered, "Yes", though the word almost choked her. That she, of all people, must be a witness against her friend seemed too cruel to be endured.

"Did Honor mention to you where she was going?"

"To the bathing cove."

"And her errand?"

"To meet her brother."

"Did she say that she meant to take him the money he needed?"

"I believe—yes—I remember she did," stammered Janie, almost bewildered by this cross-questioning.

"Did she seem to you in any way conscious that she was doing wrong?"

Janie paused. She recalled only too plainly Honor's words: "I'm sorry if it isn't all on the square, but Dermot was in a very tight place, and I felt bound to help him, even if I had to do something rather wrong".

"I am waiting for your answer, Janie."

"I—I—think she seemed—sorry!"

"Did she mention to you where the money came from that she was taking to her brother?"

"No, she said nothing about it."

"That will do for the present, Janie. Now, Vivian, I wish you to tell me if you saw Honor Fitzgerald go along the hall early this morning?"

"It looked like Honor; I could be nearly certain," faltered Vivian, rather hesitatingly.

"It was, so you needn't mind saying so!" interrupted Honor, who had been listening attentively to this evidence. "I admit that I went out, and ran down to the beach, and met Dermot. I never wanted to deny that. But I certainly didn't even see the sovereign, much less take it."

"Let us have the truth, Honor," urged Miss Maitland. "I believe that you yielded to a sudden temptation, and I am very sorry for you, since I think you did it entirely for your brother's sake. If you will confess now, I will promise to deal leniently with you."

"I can't confess what I haven't done," said Honor. She had turned very white, but she did not flinch in the least.

"Nevertheless, you handed money to your brother on the shore?"

"Yes. I gave him a sovereign, but it was my own, and not yours."

"Honor! Honor! It is no use holding to such a palpably false story. Where could you get a sovereign? You banked your pocket-money with me at the beginning of the term, like the rest of the girls; it was only a small amount, and you have spent it weekly."

"I had a sovereign, all the same," answered Honor. "It was a Queen Victoria's Jubilee one, with a hole in it, which my uncle had given me. I wore it as a locket, and kept it inside my green work-box. Last night I took it off the chain. That was the piece of money I gave to Dermot."

"Did Honor ever show you this locket?" asked Miss Maitland, turning to Janie.

The latter shook her head sadly. How she wished that she could have replied in the affirmative!

"Then the only way in which your words can be proved, Honor, is to trace your sovereign. Possibly your brother has not parted with it; or we could find the man to whom he paid it. A Jubilee gold coin with a hole in it is so uncommon that it could easily be identified. I am personally acquainted with Dr. Winterton, so there will be no difficulty in calling and asking his co-operation in the matter."

"Oh, don't ask Dr. Winterton—please don't!" implored Honor in much agitation. "I'd rather leave things as they are than that!"

Terrible as was the indictment against her, she felt she would not clear herself at her brother's expense. To allow Miss Maitland to call at Orley Grange would expose Dermot's peccadillo to his headmaster, and involve him in as serious a trouble as her own. If one or other must be expelled, she would rather it were herself. She, of the two, had less to fear from her father's anger; and, besides, there was a further reason. Dermot was destined for the Navy, and was very shortly to take the entrance examination for a cadetship; were he expelled from his training school, he would be prohibited from competing, and by another year he would be above the required age, and therefore no longer eligible as a candidate. To put any hindrance in the way of his success might ruin his whole future career. At all costs she must shield him, come what might.

"Then you wish me not to pursue the enquiry, Honor?" continued Miss Maitland. "Remember, it is the only way of clearing up this most unfortunate affair."

"I can't help it! The sovereign mustn't be traced. It was my own, all the same. Indeed I am telling the truth!" blurted out Honor, in great distress.

"I am sorry I cannot believe you," returned Miss Maitland coldly. "I thought better of you than this. You have given much trouble during your term here, but I considered you at least to be strictly honourable. I am most bitterly disappointed, and even now I will offer you a last chance. I perhaps took you by surprise, and you were not prepared to acknowledge what you had done. I will let you think the matter over until to-morrow morning. If you come to me then, before chapel, and confess the truth, I will forgive you; but if you still persist in denying it, I shall be forced, though sorely against my will, to take sterner measures. For the credit of our house and of our school, we cannot allow such things to happen at St. Chad's."

"I have told you the truth now, Miss Maitland," answered Honor, with a certain dignity in her manner. "I can only say the same to-morrow and every day. I don't know who has taken your money. I may do naughty things sometimes (indeed, I often do), but if you knew us Fitzgeralds at home I think you would scarcely have accused me of this."

Honor walked into preparation outwardly calm, but inwardly she nursed a burning volcano. She had great pride of race, and had often gloried in the honourable name which she bore. That a Fitzgerald should be suspected of so despicable a crime as stealing a sovereign seemed little short of an affront to her whole family. It was a blot on their good repute such as had never been placed there before. In days gone by her ancestors had fought duels for far less insults; now, however, she was obliged to submit to that horrible charge without making any attempt to defend herself. The one means of proving her innocence was closed to her. For Dermot's sake she must endure to be thought a thief! Yes, a thief! She repeated the word under her breath, and the very sound of it seemed to sting her. A Fitzgerald a thief! Oh, it was impossible to bear the reproach! Surely even Dermot's future could not compel her to such a sacrifice? Yes, it must and should. She knew it was the dream of his life to become a Naval cadet, and that her father and mother also cherished hopes for their youngest son's success. She seemed, like the Argonauts of yore, "'twixt Scylla and Charybdis". Which was the worse she could hardly decide, for Dermot to miss his examination, or for herself to be sent home under the slur of such a false accusation. Both seemed equally bad, but she reasoned that the former would involve more disastrous consequences, and, therefore, was the greater evil of the two.

She sat with her French grammar before her, mechanically looking at the pages; but her thoughts were so busy that she did not take in a single word of what she was reading, and would scarcely have known, if asked, whether she was studying French or geometry. What must she do? Some answer must be given to Miss Maitland to-morrow morning, and only one was possible. At all costs she would persist in her determination not to allow the affair to be mentioned to Dr. Winterton.

Janie, meanwhile, was in a hardly less disturbed state of mind. Never for a moment was her faith in her friend shaken. The mass of evidence was certainly strong, but it did not convince her. She knew Honor too well for that, and would have taken her word against all the world. Though she could not understand the particular reason for screening Dermot at such an enormous cost, she appreciated the fact that Honor was prepared to brave anything sooner than allow enquiries to be made at Orley Grange.

"It's that that looks so bad," thought Janie. "Of course, Miss Maitland thinks she made up the tale about her own sovereign, as she seems so afraid of having to produce the proof. Oh, dear, what a terrible tangle it all is! I wish that Honor had trusted me more at the very beginning, when she first received the letter. She didn't even want to let me know she was stealing out to meet her brother, only I happened to wake. I was so taken by surprise I didn't say half what I should have liked! If I could have persuaded her last night to go and tell Miss Maitland, she couldn't have been suspected. It's too late now, unfortunately, and I can't imagine how the affair will end."

Vain regrets were futile, so Janie with an effort concentrated her mind upon her lessons, and the two hours of study dragged slowly to a close. The evening was wet, and it was impossible to go into the garden, therefore all filed into the recreation room, with the sole exception of Honor, who lingered behind, putting away her books. Ill tidings fly apace, and within two minutes of the close of preparation every girl in the house had heard that Honor Fitzgerald had taken a sovereign from Miss Maitland's room, and refused to "own up". The news made the greatest sensation. Such a thing had not occurred before in the annals of the College. It seemed a stain on St. Chad's that could never be wiped out, and for which no amount of tennis shields, champion cups, or other triumphs would ever compensate. How could the Chaddites hold up their heads again? They, who had ranked in reputation next to the School House, would now sink to a lower level than St. Bride's! A hush fell over the whole community, as if some dreadful calamity had taken place. The girls stood in little groups, whispering excitedly; consternation and dismay were on all faces, for the honour of the house appeared a personal question to each. Maisie Talbot suddenly voiced the universal verdict.

"Anyone who's capable of bringing this disgrace upon us deserves to be sent to Coventry, and cut dead!" she announced, loudly enough to be heard by everybody.

There was a common murmur of assent, which stopped instantly, however, for the object of their opprobrium walked into the room. As she entered the door, Honor became aware of the hostile feeling against her. All eyes were turned in her direction, but there was recognition or welcome in none. It was a terrible thing to meet the cool stare of nearly forty companions, and feel herself thus pilloried for general contempt, yet not for a moment did she flinch. White to the lips, but with her head held up in silent self-justification, she moved slowly down the room, running the gauntlet of public disdain. Did I say all had abandoned her? No, there was one who remained faithful, one who was, not merely a fair-weather friend, but ready to believe in her and stand by her through the severest ordeal. Janie, the shyest girl at St. Chad's, who never as a rule raised her voice to venture an opinion or a criticism on any subject, came boldly to the rescue now. Stepping across to Honor, she took her firmly by the arm; then, almost as white and haggard as her friend, she turned and faced the rest.

"I think you will be very sorry for this afterwards," she began, in a voice that astonished even herself by its assurance. "It is not right to convict anybody without a trial, and Honor has not yet been proved guilty. I'm absolutely certain she is innocent, and that in time she'll be able to establish her good name. We've known her for a whole term now at St. Chad's, and she has gained a reputation for being perfectly truthful and 'square'. The charge against her is so entirely opposite to her character that I wonder anyone can credit it."

"Let her clear herself, then!" replied Maisie Talbot. "It ought to be easy enough, if she is really innocent. In the meantime, the honour of St. Chad's is being trailed through the dust!"

Excited comments and indignant accord greeted these words. All evidently were in agreement with Maisie, and determined to blackball Honor as a vindication of their zeal for the credit of their house. The supper-bell fortunately put an end to the unpleasant scene, and nobody was surprised when Honor, instead of walking into the dining-hall with the others, marched straight upstairs to her cubicle. Miss Maitland noticed her empty place at table, but made no remark. Perhaps, like the girls, she felt her absence to be a relief.

When Janie went to No. 8 at nine o'clock she found her friend already in bed, and feigning sleep with such persistence that she evidently did not wish to be disturbed. Always tactful and thoughtful, Janie drew the curtain again without attempting any conversation. She knew that Honor's heart must be too full for speech, and that the truest kindness was to leave her alone.

CHAPTER XVI

A Rash Step

Honor's sleep was undoubtedly of a very pretended description. She lay still in bed, pressing her hand to her burning head, to try to calm the throbbing in her temples and allow herself to think collectedly. She must decide upon what course she meant to take, for matters could not go on thus any longer. Before nine o'clock to-morrow morning she must again face Miss Maitland, and take her choice between betraying Dermot and her expulsion from St. Chad's. In either case, the danger to her brother seemed great. If Miss Cavendish wrote to Major Fitzgerald, asking him to remove his daughter from the College, he would naturally come over to Chessington and make full enquiries as to the reason. She would not be able to face her father's questions, and Dermot's secret would come out, after all. How might this most fatal consummation be avoided?

"If I were only at home, instead of here, then Father wouldn't be able to go and call at Orley Grange," she said to herself.

It was a new idea. She wondered she had not thought of it before. She would solve the problem by running away! She would thus meet her father at Kilmore Castle, instead of in Miss Maitland's presence at St. Chad's; and could avoid many awkward questions, simply saying she had been accused of taking a sovereign, and leaving out Dermot's part in the story altogether.

The prospect was immensely attractive. She felt scarcely capable of once more confronting the cold scorn of her companions. Home seemed a haven of refuge, an ark in the midst of a deluge of trouble, the one place in the wide world where she could fly for help. Perhaps her mother might be better, and well enough to see her, and she could then pour out her perplexities into sympathetic ears. But how to get to Ireland? It was impossible to travel without money, and she had less than a shilling left in her purse. She knew, however, that a line of steamboats ran from Westhaven to Cork; if she could walk to the former place she thought she could persuade the captain of one of the vessels to take her to Cork by promising that her father's solicitor, who lived there, would pay for her when she arrived. Mr. Donovan had often been on business at Kilmore Castle; she knew the address of his office, and was sure that he would advance her sufficient to pay for both the steamer journey and her railway ticket to Ballycroghan.

The first thing, therefore, to be done was to leave the College as early and as secretly as she could. She did not dare to go to sleep, but lay tossing uneasily until the first hint of dawn. Sunrise was at about four o'clock, so soon after half-past three it was just light enough to enable her to get up and dress. Miss Maitland had sent a glass of milk and a plate of sandwiches and biscuits for her supper the night before, but she had left them untouched on her dressing-table. Now, however, she had the forethought to drink the milk and put the biscuits and sandwiches in her pocket. The face which confronted her when she looked in the glass hardly seemed her own, it was so unwontedly pale, and had such dark rings round the eyes. She moved very quietly, for she was anxious not to waken her room-mate.

"Janie mustn't know what I intend, or she'll get into trouble for not stopping me," she thought. "It's a comfort that she, at any rate, doesn't believe I've done this horrible thing, and that she'll stand up for me when I'm gone."

She listened for a minute, till the sound of her friend's even and regular breathing reassured her; then, drawing aside the curtain, she crept into the next cubicle. Janie was lying fast asleep, her head cradled on her arm. With her fair hair falling round her cheeks, she looked almost pretty. Honor bent down and kissed the end of one of the flaxen locks, but too gently to disturb its owner; then, with a scarcely breathed good-bye, she left the room. She had laid her plans carefully, and did not mean to be discovered and brought back to school; so, instead of going downstairs, and thus passing both Vivian Holmes's and Miss Maitland's doors, she went to the other end of the passage, where the landing window stood wide open, and, managing to climb down by the thick ivy, reached the ground without mishap. She crept through the garden under the laurel bushes, and, avoiding the cricket field, scaled the wall close to the potting shed, helped very much by a large heap of logs that had been left there ready to be chopped. Once successfully over, she set off running in the direction of the moors, and never stopped until she was quite out of sight of even the chimneys of St. Chad's. Then, hot and utterly breathless, she sat down on the grass to rest.

It was still very early, for the sun had only just risen. The air was fresh and pleasant. Behind her lay green, round-topped hills, and in front stretched the sea, smooth as glass, with a few small, white sails gleaming in the distance. Innumerable rabbits kept scuttling past. One small one came so near that she almost caught it with her hands, but it dived away into its burrow in a moment. She brought out her sandwiches and biscuits, and began to eat them. She was hungry already, and thought wistfully of breakfast. The bread had gone rather dry and the biscuits a little stale, but she enjoyed them, sitting on the hillside, especially when she remembered all she had escaped from at St. Chad's. She felt that, once back in dear old Ireland, her difficulties would be nearly at an end, and she registered a solemn vow never to cross the Channel again, except under the strictest compulsion. The last fragment of biscuit having vanished, she got up and shook down the crumbs for the birds; then, turning towards the hills, she struck a footpath which she thought must surely lead in the right direction. West-haven, though twenty-five miles away by the winding coast road, or the railway, was only twelve miles distant if she went, as the crow flies, over the moors. The authorities at the College, she imagined, would never dream of looking for her there. When they discovered her absence they would probably suppose she had gone to Dunscar, and would enquire at the station, and search the main road; but, of course, nobody would have seen her, and there would be no clue to her whereabouts.

She was so pleased to have such a good start that she felt almost in high spirits, and strode along at a fair pace, keenly enjoying the unwonted sense of freedom. It was very lonely on the moors, and not even a cottage was to be seen. The path was hardly more than a sheep track, sometimes nearly effaced with grass, and she had to trace it as best she could. After some hours she began to grow tired and desperately hungry again. She wondered how she was to manage anything in the way of lunch; then, hailing with delight the sight of a small farm nestling in a hollow between two hills, she turned her steps at once in that direction. She had a six-pence and two pennies in her pocket, and thought that she might perhaps be able to buy some food.

The farm, on nearer acquaintance, proved a rather dirty and di-lapidated-looking place. Honor picked her way carefully through the litter in the yard, and was about to knock at the door, when a collie dog flew from the barn behind, barking furiously, show-ing his teeth, and threatening to catch hold of her skirt. Much to her relief, he was called off by a slatternly, hard-featured woman, who, hearing the noise, came out of the house with a pail in her hand, and stood looking at her visitor in much amazement.

"I want to know," said Honor, "if you can let me have a glass of milk and some bread and butter, and how much you would charge for it."

"We don't sell milk here," replied the woman, shaking her head. "I've just put it all down in the butter-pot, so I'm afraid I can't oblige you."

"Oh!" said Honor blankly. Then, "I should be so glad of a little bread and butter, if you can let me have it."

"Are you out on a picnic?" asked the woman. "Where are the rest of you?"

"No, I'm by myself," answered Honor. "I'm walking across the moors to Westhaven."

"To Westhaven? You're on the wrong road, then. That path will lead you out at Windover, if you follow it."

Poor Honor was almost dumbfounded at such unexpected bad news.

"Have I gone very far wrong?" she faltered. "I must get on to Westhaven as fast as I can. Perhaps you can tell me the right way?"

"Aye, I can put you on the path, if you want," replied the woman; "but you'll have a good long bit to go."

"Is there any village where I could buy something to eat? I've had nothing since breakfast," said Honor, returning again to her first and most pressing need.

"No, there ain't," said the woman; then, apparently softening a little, "Look here, I don't mind making you a cup of tea, if you care to pay for it. The kettle's boiling. You can step in if you like."

Glad to get a meal in any circumstances, Honor entered the squalid kitchen, and tried not to notice the general untidiness of her surroundings, while the woman hastily cleared the table and set out a teacup and saucer, a huge loaf, butter, and a pot of tea. The dog had made friends, and crept up to Honor, snuggling his nose into her hand; and a tabby cat, interested in the preparations, came purring eagerly to join the feast. Honor did not know whether to call it late breakfast, dinner, or tea, but she told Janie afterwards she thought she must have eaten enough to combine the three, though she only paid sixpence for it all. She finished at last, and got up to go; then, remembering the long walk still in store for her, she gave the farmer's wife her remaining twopence for some extra slices of bread and butter to take with her.

"It's a tidy step for a young lady like you, and a-going quite alone too," said the woman, eyeing Honor keenly as she led her round the side of the cottage, to point out the right path. "You've come from over by Dunscar, I take it?"

"Oh, I'm a good walker!" replied Honor, who did not wish to encourage enquiries. "I shall soon get along. Thank you for coming so far with me."

"You're welcome," said the woman. "I hope you'll keep the path, and reach there safe; but if you'll take my advice, you'll turn round the other way and go straight back to school. You'd just get there by tea-time."

Honor started at this parting remark, and hurried on as fast as she could. How did the woman guess she had run away from the College? Of course!—she had forgotten her hat. Everyone in the neighbourhood of Chessington knew the unmistakable "sailors", with their coloured ribbons and badges. She might have remembered they would easily be recognized, and blamed her own stupidity and lack of forethought. She hoped no message would be sent to Miss Cavendish, and looked round carefully to see if she were being followed. Yes, she could certainly see the woman now, calling a boy from a field, and pointing eagerly in her direction. They would perhaps try to take her back against her will, and she would be marched ignominiously, like a prisoner, to St. Chad's.

"That they shall never do!" she thought, and choosing a moment when the pair were passing round the front of the house, she turned from the path and scrambled up the bed of a small stream on to the hills again. She decided that so long as she knew the right points of the compass, it would be quite easy to find her way, as she could walk in a line with the path, only higher up on the moor, where she would be neither seen nor followed. She flung her hat away, determined that it should not betray her again; and, on the whole, she liked to have her head bare, the wind felt so fresh and pleasant blowing through her hair. For a while she went on briskly, then, coming across a spring, which rose clear and bubbling through the grass and sedges, she took off her shoes and stockings, and sat dabbling her feet in the water, watching a pair of dragon flies, and plaiting rings from the rushes that grew around.

She stayed there so long that when she happened to look at her watch she was startled to find it was nearly half-past four.

"I must push on," she said to herself. "I've a long way to be going yet. I wonder what time the steamer starts for Cork, and if I shall find it waiting in the harbour?"

She was quite sure that she had come in exactly the same direction as the path, but somehow she did not seem to be getting any nearer to civilization. On and on she wandered, hour after hour, seeing nothing before her but the same bare, grass-covered hills, till she began to grow alarmed, and to suspect that after all she had completely missed her way. The sun was setting, and as the great, red ball of fire sank behind the horizon, her spirits fell in proportion. What was she to do, alone and lost on the hills? Even if she could reach Westhaven in daylight, she would not like to be obliged to go to the quay in the dark; and suppose there were no night boat, like the mail steamer in which she had crossed from Dublin to Holyhead, where could she go until morning? She had not foreseen any of these difficulties when she set out, it had all appeared so easy and simple; but she saw now what a risky adventure she had undertaken. She was almost in despair, when luckily she came across a track sufficiently trodden to indicate that it probably led to some human habitation. It was growing very dusk indeed now, but she could just see to trace the path, and she hurried hopefully on, till at length the lights of a farmhouse window shone out through the gathering gloom.

At first Honor thought of knocking boldly at the door and asking for food and shelter; but then, she reflected that the people of the house would think it most strange for a nicely dressed girl to present herself so late in the evening with such a request, and would be sure to ask awkward questions, and might possibly send a messenger to the College to tell of her arrival, detaining her there in the morning until Miss Cavendish or Miss Maitland arrived to fetch her. Even supper and a bed, welcome though they might prove, would be too dearly bought at such a price; and she determined, instead, to spend the night in a barn, the door of which stood conveniently open. It was half-filled with newly made, sweet-smelling hay, on to which she crept in the darkness; and flinging herself down, she drew some of it under her head for a pillow. A strange bed indeed, and very different from the one in her cubicle at St. Chad's! But at least she was free to go when she pleased; she meant to be up at daybreak, before anyone on the farm was astir, and to-morrow she would surely reach Westhaven and the steamer, and be able to start for that goal of all her wanderings—home.

It is easy enough before you go to sleep to resolve that you will rouse yourself at a certain time, but not quite so simple to carry it out, especially when you happen to be dead tired; and Honor's case was no exception to the rule. Instead of waking at dawn, she slept peacefully till nearly eight o'clock, and might even have slept on longer still if the farmer and his son had not chanced to

"STARTLED BY THE VOICES, SHE JUMPED UP"

stroll into the barn on their way to the stable. The boy was walking to the far end to hang a rope on a nail, when he suddenly ran back, with his eyes nearly dropping from his head with surprise.

"Dad!" he cried. "Dad! Come and look here! There's a girl sleeping on the hay!"

Honor, newly aroused, was just raising herself up on her elbow; she had not quite collected her senses, nor realized where she was. Startled by the voices, she jumped up, with the instinctive impulse to run away; then, seeing that two strangers stood between her and the open door, she sat down again on the hay and burst out crying.

"There! There!" said the farmer. "Don't you take on so, missy; we ain't a-goin' to hurt you. Tom, you'd best run in and fetch Mother hither!"

"Mother", a stout, elderly woman, arrived panting on the scene in a few moments. No lady in the land could possibly have proved kinder in such an emergency. She kissed and soothed poor Honor, took her indoors and gave her hot water to bathe her face and wash her hands, and finally settled her down in a corner of the delightfully clean farm-kitchen, with a dainty little breakfast before her.

Honor felt sorely tempted to unburden herself of her story to this true friend in need, but the dread that she would be sent back to St. Chad's kept her silent, and she only said that she had been lost on the moor, and was anxious to get to Westhaven, and to go home as speedily as possible, all of which was, of course, absolutely true. Mrs. Ledbury, no doubt, had her suspicions; but, seeing that questions disturbed her guest, with true delicacy she refrained from pressing her, and suggested instead that, as her husband was driving into Westhaven market that morning, he could give her a lift, and save her a walk of nearly seven miles.

Honor jumped at the opportunity; she felt stiff and worn out after her yesterday's experiences, and much disinclined for further rambles; so it was with a sigh of genuine relief that she found herself seated in the high gig by the side of the old farmer.

"Good-bye, dearie!" said Mrs. Ledbury, tucking a shawl over Honor's knees, and pressing a slice of bread and honey into her hand, from fear that she might grow hungry on the road. "You run straight home when you get to Westhaven! They'll be in a fair way about you, they will that! It gives me a turn yet to think of you sleeping in the barn all night long, with rats and mice scrambling round you, and me not to know you was there!"

Mr. Ledbury was evidently not of a communicative disposition; he drove along without vouchsafing any remarks, and Honor was so lost in her thoughts that she did not feel disposed to talk to him. Her great anxiety now was to catch the steamer to Cork; she wished she had some idea of the time of its starting, and only hoped that it did not set off early in the morning, for to miss it would seem almost more than she could bear. The gig jolted slowly on over the uneven road, till at length the moor gave way to suburban villas and gardens, quickly followed by streets and shops; and they finally drew up in the busy market-place of Westhaven.

Mr. Ledbury helped Honor to dismount, and having thanked him and said good-bye, she turned round the nearest corner; then, once safely out of his sight, she set off as fast as she could for the harbour. Partly, perhaps, because she enquired chiefly from children, whose directions were not very clear, and partly because it is generally difficult to find one's way in a fresh place, it was a long time before she saw the welcome gleam of the water and the masts of the shipping; and then, after all, she found she had come to the wrong quay, and it was only by dint of continual asking that at last she arrived at the particular landing-stage of the Irish steamers.

"Want the boat to Cork, miss?" said the weather-beaten seaman to whom she addressed her question. "Why, she's bin gone out an hour and a half ago. She was off at eleven prompt. When will there be another, did ye say? Not till eight to-night, and she's only a cargo."

Honor's hopes, which had managed to sustain her spirits so far, dropped to zero at this bad news. There she was, penniless, in a strange town; and how could she get through all the long, weary hours until the evening? Gulping down a lump in her throat, she asked the sailor if the cargo vessel were already in the harbour, and if it were possible that she might go on board now, and wait there till it should be time to set sail.

"We're expecting of her in every minute," said the man, looking at Honor curiously. "You can speak to the captain when she comes. Maybe he'd let you, maybe he wouldn't; I shouldn't like to give an opinion"—which, to say the least, was not consoling.

Honor walked on a little farther down the landing-stage, trying to wink back her tears. She was in a desperate strait, and almost began to wish she had never left St. Chad's. Suppose the captain would not take her without the money for her passage? Possibly he might not know Mr. Donovan's name, and would think she was an impostor; what would she do then? She turned quite cold at the idea, and had to sit down on a bulkhead to recover herself, for she felt as though her legs were shaking under her.

She did not remember how long she sat there. A noise and bustle behind presently attracted her attention, and turning round, she saw that a steamer was arriving, and that the sailors were busy catching the thick cables and fastening the vessel to the wharf. The gangway was thrown across, and a few passengers stepped on shore. They had evidently travelled steerage—two or three women, with babies and bundles, and a party of Irish labourers come over for the harvest, with their belongings tied in red pocket-handkerchiefs; but after them strode a tall figure, with a grey moustache, at the sight of whom Honor sprang up from her seat with a perfect scream of delight, and raced along the quay like a whirlwind, to fling herself joyfully into the gentleman's arms.

"Father! Father!" she sobbed. "Oh, is it really and truly you?"

CHAPTER XVII

Janie turns Detective

Honor being safely in her father's charge, we must leave her there for the present, and return to Chessington, to see what was happening in the meantime at St. Chad's. Janie's slumbers had been quiet and undisturbed until half-past six, when she woke with a start, feeling almost ashamed of herself for being able to sleep when her friend was in trouble. She got up at once, and peeped round the curtain into the other cubicle, only to discover, too late, that the bird had flown. She looked on the dressing-table to see whether a note might have been left, but to her disappointment there was nothing. Honor had vanished mysteriously, leaving not the least sign or clue behind her. Where had she gone? Janie could scarcely venture a guess. Such a daring scheme as a return to Ireland did not even suggest itself to her less enterprising mind. Perhaps, she thought, Honor might have set out to try to find the man Blake, and ask him to come and show the Jubilee sovereign to Miss Maitland; but this seemed so at variance with her determination of last night that Janie could hardly consider it probable. She wondered if it were her duty to go and tell Miss Maitland immediately, but came to the conclusion that, as the bell would ring in a few minutes, she might put off giving the information until she had dressed.

Her news naturally caused the greatest consternation at head-quarters. Steps were taken at once to institute a search for the runaway. Miss Cavendish communicated with the police, who, exactly as Honor had anticipated, enquired at the railway station and the pier at Dunscar, in case she had taken the train or the steamer; and caused the high roads to be watched. It did not occur to anybody that she would have ventured on such an undertaking as to cross the moors, and she had the advantage of several hours' start, so that, from her point of view, her plan was a success.

"You should have come to me instantly, Janie, when you made

the discovery that she was gone," said Miss Maitland reproach-fully. "We have lost at least three-quarters of an hour through your delay."

Poor Janie burst into tears. It had been very hard to be obliged to reveal the fact of her room-mate's flight at all. She felt that, utterly against her will, she had the whole time been the principal witness in Honor's disfavour, and that every word she had spoken had helped to confirm unjust suspicion. She would have made an attempt to plead her friend's cause if Miss Maitland had looked at all encouraging, but the mistress was anxious to waste no further time, and dismissed her summarily from the room.

Janie had taken the affair as much to heart as if the disgrace were her own. It seemed so particularly unfortunate that it should have happened, because, since their talk at St. Kolgan's Abbey, she had thought that Honor was making increased efforts, and that Miss Maitland had noticed and approved the change. Now all this advance appeared to be swept away, and in the opinion of both teachers and girls her friend was not fit to remain any longer on the roll of Chessington.

Although the Chaddites tried to keep their shame hushed up, the news leaked out somehow, and very soon spread through the entire College, where it instantly became the one absorbing topic of conversation. Owing to her prowess at cricket, and her friendly, amusing ways, Honor had won more notice than most new girls among her two hundred schoolfellows; but, in spite of her undoubted popularity, she was universally judged to be guilty. The general argument was that the money was missing, that somebody must have taken it, that Honor was known to have needed it desperately, and that her action in running away showed above everything that she dared not stay to have the matter investigated.

Janie thought that no day had ever been so long. The hours seemed absolutely interminable. Her lessons had been badly prepared the night before, and won for her a reproof from Miss Farrar; and her thoughts were so constantly occupied with wondering where Honor had fled that she could scarcely attend to the work in class, and often answered at random. Her head was aching badly, and her eyes were sore with crying, neither of which was conducive to good memory, or lucid explanations; so she was not surprised to find at the end of the morning that her record was the worst she had had during the whole term.

The afternoon was cool after the rain of the previous evening, and games were once more in full swing. Dearly as she would have liked to shirk her part in them, Janie was not allowed to absent herself; but she played so badly that she drew Miss Young's scorn on her head, to say nothing of the wrath of the Chaddites.

"You missed two catches—simply dropped them straight out of your hands! You're an absolute butter-fingers!" exclaimed Chatty Burns indignantly.

Janie was too crushed by utter misery to mind this extra straw. She retired thankfully to the pavilion as soon as she was allowed, feeling that missed catches or schoolmates' scoldings were of small importance in the present state of general misfortune.

"If I could only find out who took the sovereign!" she thought. "Honor certainly did not, so somebody else must have. Who? That's the question. I wish I were an amateur detective, like the clever people one reads about in magazines. They just get a clue, and find it all out so easily, while the police are on quite a wrong tack. The chief thing seems to be to make a beginning, and I don't know in the least where to start."

Neither tea nor preparation brought her any nearer to solving the difficulty. After supper she went into the garden, taking her work-basket and crochet with her. She was in the lowest of spirits, and blinked away some surreptitious tears. Weeping was not fashionable at St. Chad's, being classed as "Early Victorian", and she wished to hide her red eyes from the other girls; for this reason she hurried down the long gravel path behind the rows of peas and beans, and found a snug place by the tomato house, where there was a convenient wheelbarrow to sit upon. She had not been there more than five minutes when, to her surprise, she was joined by Lettice Talbot.

"I've been hunting for you everywhere, Janie!" announced Lettice. "I shouldn't have found you now, only I caught a glimpse of your pink hair ribbon through a vista of pea-sticks. Is there room for two on this barrow? Thanks; I'll sit down then. Look here! I want to tell you how glad I am that you stuck up for Honor last night. I know Maisie and all the rest think she took that wretched sovereign, but I declare I don't. Poor old Paddy! I'm certain she never could; I would as soon have done it myself."

"I'm so thankful to hear you say this," exclaimed Janie. "I was afraid I was the only one who believed in her."

"A few of our set are beginning to come round; Ruth Latimer is certainly wavering, and so is Pauline Reynolds. But naturally they all say: 'If Honor didn't take it, who did?'"

"That's exactly what I should like to find out," sighed Janie.

"Miss Maitland is absolutely certain that she left it on her table, and that it was gone when she came back within a quarter of an hour; also, that it hadn't fallen down anywhere in the room," said Lettice, with the air of a judge weighing evidence. "Where is it, then?"

"I've thought and thought," replied Janie, puckering up her forehead, "but I can't get any nearer. If we could prove, now, that someone else had been in Miss Maitland's room, it might quite alter the case."

"Why, what an idiot I am!" exclaimed Lettice, suddenly bouncing up from the wheelbarrow.

"What's the matter?"

"It's only just occurred to me! I suppose a really clever person would have thought of it at once. I'm afraid my brains don't work very fast. Oh, what a jubilee!"

"Lettice Talbot! Have you gone mad?"

"Not quite, but a little in that direction."

"Do explain yourself!"

"Well, you recollect when Honor climbed up to the window? We all went into the house afterwards, and then I ran back to fetch Maisie's work-basket. I saw a girl climb down the lime tree, and run away into the bushes."

"Are you sure?"

"I could not be mistaken."

"Then this is most extremely important."

"I know it is. I can't imagine how I never remembered it before. They may well call me 'Scatterbrains' at home! I certainly shouldn't have done for a barrister, if I'd been a boy."

"Could you tell who it was?"

"No, I wasn't near enough. I only saw her for a moment. If I had caught a glimpse of her face, it might have been of some use; but everybody wears the same kind of blue skirt and white blouse at Chessington, so it's quite impossible to recognize any particular girl when you see nothing but her back."

"Unless you could find somebody else who happened to have seen her too."

"No one else was there at the time."

"We must make enquiries," said Janie excitedly. "It really seems a clue. We won't leave a stone unturned, if we can help it."

"I should be very glad to get poor Paddy out of trouble," replied Lettice. "The slur on our house will be just the same, though, whichever Chaddite may be the culprit. It's only moving the disgrace from one person to another."

"We must see that the blame is put on to the right pair of shoulders, though; it's not fair for Honor to bear it unjustly."

"Indeed it isn't. What would be the best way to begin?"

"We need a witness. I wonder if Johnson was about at the time, and noticed anything?"

"A good idea! We'll go and find him. I believe I saw him just now, shutting up the greenhouse."

After a rather lengthy search, the girls at last discovered the old gardener putting away his tools in the potting shed.

"Johnson, please, we want to ask you a question," began Janie. "Were you near St. Chad's at nine o'clock on the night before last; and did you happen to see anyone climbing the lime tree that stands close to the house?"

Johnson stroked his chin reflectively.

"It couldn't have been last night," he replied, after a few moments' consideration. "I was in Dunscar then. It must 'a been the night afore that. Aye; I did see one of you young ladies go up that lime tree. I remember it, because she climbed that smart you'd have thought she was a boy. In at the window she gets, and I watches her and thinks it's well to have young limbs. It's not much climbing you'll do when you're nigh sixty, and stiff in the joints with rheumatism besides!"

"What was she like?" enquired Janie eagerly.

"Had she long, dark hair?" added Lettice.

"Nay, it was fair hair. There was a light in the room, so as she comes back through the window I sees her as plain as I sees you now. I knows her in a minute. It was the young lady as every Sunday morning pesters my life out of me to cut her a rose for her buttonhole: Miss Taylor, I think she's called."

"Flossie!" exclaimed Janie. "I know she always begs for roses."

"Then it was Flossie!" said Lettice. "I had an uneasy feeling in the back of my mind all the time that it was she—it looked like her figure. It seemed too bad to suspect her, though, when I had absolutely no proof."

"There can be little doubt about it now."

"Shall we go straight to Miss Maitland, at once?"

"I don't know. I'm not sure if it wouldn't be better to ask Flossie herself about it. She may be able to explain it; and, at any rate, I think we ought to warn her before we say anything, and then we shan't seem to have told tales behind her back."

"She doesn't deserve any consideration," grumbled Lettice.

Janie's conscience, however, required her to be scrupulously fair. She could not bear to take an advantage, even of one who must be shielding herself at the expense of another.

"We'll give her a chance," she decided emphatically.

The next step evidently was to search for Flossie. She was not in the garden, but after a diligent quest through the house they eventually found her in her own cubicle, engaged in the meritorious occupation of tidying her drawers. It was an unpleasant task for the two girls to voice their suspicions, but one that nevertheless had to be done.

Somewhat to their surprise, Flossie sat down on the edge of her bed, and burst out crying.

"Oh, I knew it would come! I knew it would!" she sobbed. "What am I to do? Oh, I've been so wretched all day! I believe I'm quite glad it has come out at last."

"Flossie, did you take that sovereign?" asked Janie.

"Yes—no—at least—yes! Only, I didn't know I was taking it!" groaned Flossie, trying in vain to find her handkerchief, and mopping her eyes in desperation with a corner of the sheet instead.

"What do you mean?"

"I'll tell you. Oh, it's such a relief to tell somebody! Of course, I was there when Honor climbed up the lime tree, and after you had all run indoors I thought it would be fun to see if I could go up too. It was quite easy, and I jumped through the window without any difficulty. There was nobody in the study, but the electric light was turned on. I walked over to the writing-table, and I remember noticing the sovereign lying at the corner, on the top of a pile of letters. There were ever so many papers strewn about, and some of them were our house conduct reports for the term, which Miss Maitland was evidently just beginning to fill in. I was so anxious to see if mine was there that I stretched over and took some of them in my hand, to look at them. Then I thought I heard a step in the passage, and I didn't want to be caught, so I popped them quickly back, and went down the tree a good deal faster than I had gone up. I took off my blouse as usual that night, and put it away in my middle drawer, and next day I wore a clean one. Then this morning, when I was dressing, I looked at the first blouse, to see if it were really soiled and ready for the laundry. To my horror, out tumbled a sovereign on to the floor! I can only suppose it must have slipped inside my turnover cuff, when I reached across the table; I certainly hadn't the least idea it was there. I couldn't think what to do! I hoped I might be able to smuggle it back on to the table, and I've been watching all day, but there has never been the slightest opportunity to go into the study. I didn't dare to tell Miss Maitland, from fear she would think I'd taken it on purpose. She wouldn't believe Honor, so I thought she wouldn't believe me either. Oh! isn't it all dreadful?"

"It is indeed," said Janie; "especially as Honor has had to bear the blame. It isn't the first time she has acted scapegoat for you!"

"I know what you mean," sobbed Flossie. "Vivian thought it was she who shammed ghost that night when I played a trick upon Evelyn Fletcher. I didn't intend to get Honor into trouble. I was very sorry about it; still, what could I do?"

"Do! Why, you ought to have told Vivian at once. Any girl with a spark of honour would have known that."

"You'd better make a clean breast of everything now," suggested Lettice.

"I daren't! I daren't!" cried Flossie, in an agony of alarm.

"I don't believe you need be afraid of Miss Maitland," said Janie. "You've only taken the sovereign by accident. She would be far more angry with you for not owning up."

"If you don't tell her, I shall go to her myself," threatened Lettice.

It was dreadfully difficult to screw Flossie's courage up to the required point. She declared she could not and would not make the necessary confession.

"I'll write to my mother to send for me to go home, and it can come out after I'm gone," she declared.

Lettice lost her temper and indulged in hard words, which, so far from altering Flossie's decision, only made her more obstinately determined. Fortunately, Janie had greater patience.

"I'm sure you'll be brave enough to do it for Honor's sake," she said. "You'll feel far happier and more comfortable when it's over. I know it's hard, but it's right, and we shall all think so much better of you afterwards than if you shirked telling, and went home. You could hardly come back again here if you did that. Be a true Chaddite, and remember our house motto: 'Strive for the highest'. I'll go with you to Miss Maitland, if you like."

In the end, Janie's counsel prevailed, and Flossie, very tearful and apprehensive, allowed herself to be led to the study, to return the sovereign and explain how it came into her possession. Miss Maitland proved kindness itself. She was immensely relieved to find that the whole affair was due to a mischance, and that none of her girls had been capable of committing a dishonest act. It wiped a blot from St. Chad's, and restored the house to its former high standing.

"If we could only find Honor Fitzgerald," she declared, "my mind would be at rest."

CHAPTER XVIII

The End of the Term

Major Fitzgerald's astonishment at meeting his runaway daughter on Westhaven Quay was great, but he was extremely thankful to find her safe and sound. He had received a telegram from Chessington informing him of her flight, and had started immediately for the College, coming from Cork to Westhaven by a night cargo vessel, as he thought that a quicker route than by the ordinary mail steamer from Dublin to Holyhead.

He at once took Honor to a hotel, where he engaged a private sitting-room and ordered luncheon; then he set to work to demand an explanation of what was still to him an absolute puzzle and mystery. In spite of her determination to suppress all mention of Dermot's embarrassments, Honor speedily found herself pouring out the whole of her troubles into her father's ears. She was no dissembler, never having been accustomed to concealment, and possessing naturally a very open character; so, with a few skilful questions, the Major easily drew from her the entire story.

She had prepared herself to expect a stern rebuke, but to her surprise her father seemed far more pained than angry.

"I thought my children could have trusted me!" he said. "You will find, Honor, as you go through life, that no one has your interest at heart so truly as your own father. Perhaps I have erred on the side of severity, but it is no light responsibility to keep five high-spirited lads under control, to say nothing of a madcap daughter. My father brought me up on the rule of 'spare the rod, spoil the child', and I thought modern methods produced a less worthy race, so I would stick to his old-fashioned principle. I have taken far harder thrashings in my boyhood than I have ever bestowed on Master Dermot. All the same, I believed you knew that, though I might sometimes appear harsh, I meant it for your good, and that I was the best friend you had in the world."

"You are, Daddy, you are!" cried Honor, clinging round his neck.

"Well, little woman, you must have more confidence in me another time, and come boldly and tell me your scrapes. I would rather forgive you a great deal than feel that you kept anything back from me. You've been a very foolish girl, and have got yourself into sad trouble. Your mother is wild with anxiety about you."

"How is Mother? Is she still so ill?" quavered Honor.

"She was much better until yesterday, when we received Miss Cavendish's telegram. Naturally, that upset her very much. I have wired to her already, to say that you are safely here with me."

"Oh, Daddy, let us go home to Mother at once!"

"No, my dear!" said Major Fitzgerald decidedly. "I couldn't let you return to Kilmore with such an accusation resting against your name. We must face that, and get it cleared up. I shall have a talk with both Miss Maitland and Miss Cavendish. Don't you see that by running away you are practically admitting yourself to be guilty? It was the silliest thing to do! Come, don't cry! We'll get to the bottom of the matter somehow."

"But you won't tell Dr. Winterton?" implored Honor, whose tears were more for her brother than for herself.

"I won't promise. It may be necessary to do so. You needn't fear Dermot will miss his exam.; I should of course stipulate that he must take it. I don't believe, however, that he would be expelled. It is so near to the end of the term, and if he secures a pass he will be leaving the Grange in any case, to join his training ship. The young rascal! He certainly deserves his thrashing. He's always up to some mischief! There, dry your eyes, child, I won't be too hard on him! In the meantime, we must think of getting back to Dunscar. We can just catch the 2.40 train. The sooner we arrive at the College and ease Miss Cavendish's mind, the better. I must buy you a hat as we walk to the station, and then perhaps you'll look more respectable."

It seemed to Honor as if an immense weight had been lifted from her mind. She began for the first time to understand her father, and to realize how much he thought of and cared for his children's welfare. The knowledge drew her nearer to him than she had ever been before. Her troubles seemed over now that he had taken the responsibility of them; she wished she had trusted him sooner, and felt that he was indeed, as he had said, her best and truest friend.

Miss Maitland was greatly relieved that afternoon when her missing pupil was restored to her, and congratulated herself that the mystery had been solved, and that she was able to give a full explanation to Major Fitzgerald of what had occurred.

The latter listened with close attention to her account.

"Pray don't apologize for having accused Honor falsely," he said. "As house-mistress, it was your plain duty to act as you did, and the evidence seemed overwhelming. I don't exonerate my little girl altogether; she had no right to take the law into her own hands and meet her brother in defiance of rules, and, still worse, to run away from school; neither had she any business to climb through the window into your study. She deserves a thorough scolding, but I think she is truly sorry, and that the consequences of her foolishness have been punishment enough."

"We will say no more about it," replied Miss Maitland; "it is an unpleasant episode, which we shall be only too glad to consign to oblivion. Honor has shown us already that she is capable of better things, and I shall expect much from her in the future."

The runaway received a warm welcome from the Chaddites, who much regretted their hasty action in condemning her without sufficient proof.

"I'm afraid I misjudged you before, Honor," said Vivian Holmes. "Flossie has told me that it was she who shammed ghost. It's a pity there have been so many misunderstandings, but I'm glad you weren't responsible for Evelyn's fright."

Vivian spoke kindly, but without enthusiasm. She was ready enough to acknowledge Honor's innocence, but she still did not altogether approve of her, and considered that there was much room for improvement before she became a worthy member of St. Chad's. The monitress had no sympathy with lawlessness, and preferred girls who upheld the school rules, instead of breaking them. Undue exuberance of spirits during a first term was in her eyes presumption, and not to be countenanced by a monitress who did her duty.

She need not have been afraid, however, that the black sheep of her flock was going to indulge in any more lapses from the strict path of convention. Honor had returned in a very subdued frame of mind, and gave no further occasion for reproof.

She took the girls' apologies for sending her to Coventry in excellent part.

"If you really believed I'd stolen the sovereign, you were quite right," she remarked briefly. "Anyone who'd done such a thing would have richly deserved that, and worse. I care quite as much as you all for the honour of the house."

To Janie alone, the one friend who had taken her part and stood up for her when the whole school was against her, could Honor turn with a sense of absolute confidence; the bond between them seemed closer than ever, and she felt she owed a debt of gratitude that it would be difficult to repay. Janie's joy at this happy ending to what had appeared a scholastic earthquake was extreme; and, though she gave Lettice the credit that was due, she could not help experiencing a little satisfaction at her own share in elucidating the mystery. She had worked hard to clear her friend's name, so it was delightful to reap her reward.

The sensation caused by the events of the last few days was soon forgotten by the majority of the girls in the excitement of the examinations. For the next week the whole College lived in a whirl of perpetual effort to marshal scattered facts, or recall forgotten vocabularies. The classrooms, given over to pens, ink, and sheets of foolscap paper, were the abodes of a silence only disturbed by the occasional scratching of a pen, or the sigh of a candidate in the throes of attacking a stiff problem. To Honor the experience was all new. She tried her best, but found it difficult to curtail her statements sufficiently to allow of her answering every question, in spite of Miss Farrar's oft-repeated warning against devoting too much time to one part of the paper. She was, of course, at a great disadvantage, as she had spent only one term at Chessington, and the examinations were on the work of a whole year; but she nevertheless acquitted herself creditably, and actually gained higher marks than several girls who had come to school the preceding September.

"I feel as if I'd been in a battle!" she announced, when at length the ordeal was over and the last set of papers handed in. "My fingers are soaked with ink, for my fountain pen leaked atrociously; but it wrote so much quicker than an ordinary one that I didn't dare to abandon it."

"You'll soon get the ink off," said Lettice. "Miss Maitland always puts plenty of pieces of pumice stone and slices of lemon in the dressing-room at examination time. I'm sure I've failed in geometry, and I shall be very much surprised if I find I've scraped through in physics."

"I feel just as doubtful over English language," said Chatty Burns. "But it's no use worrying ourselves any more; we can't correct mistakes now, whatever stupid ones we may have made."

"And we can just have a few peaceful days until the sports," added Lettice.

The end of the term was always celebrated by a gathering of parents and friends, at which the girls gave exhibitions of their skill in running, jumping, or some of the physical exercises that they had learnt with Miss Young. This year the programme was to include military drill and flag signalling. The latter was a new departure in the school, but one that everybody had taken up with enthusiasm. Little bands of the most expert performers had been selected, and these practised diligently in the playing-fields, waving their messages with great accuracy and dispatch.

"It might come in useful if there were a war," said Lettice; "and, at any rate, it will be very convenient at home. I mean to teach some friends who live at a house close by, and we shall be able to stand at our bedroom windows and talk with our flags."

"It will be fun out yachting," said Madge Summers. "We can signal any vessel we pass, and ask her name, and where she is going, and all kinds of questions."

"I wish Miss Young would teach us heliography next term," said Honor. "I should like flashing messages with looking-glasses."

"We'll ask her; but we shall have to wait nearly a year. We only have hockey in the winter term, with gymnasium work when it's wet. Are any of your people coming over on Thursday?"

"I'm afraid not—it's such a long way from Kerry! My mother is still ill, and my father is busy."

"That's a pity!" said Lettice. "We all like our parents to turn up for the sports. There's generally an absolute crowd."

As Lettice had indicated, a large number of visitors made their appearance on breaking-up day. The quadrangle and playing-fields were gay with summer dresses and parasols, and everywhere girls might seen conducting little parties of friends over the College buildings.

"The whole place seems topsy-turvy," remarked Honor. "You can go where you like, and actually speak in the laboratory without forfeits! Even the library is turned into a tea-room!"

"Yes, there are no rules this afternoon," replied Janie.

The sports were held in the cricket ground, and began punctually at half-past four. Forms had been brought from the school, to make seats for the spectators and for those of the girls who were not taking part in the proceedings.

"I like a large audience," said Chatty Burns; "it's rather inspiring. Of course, it makes one nervous, but, at the same time, it puts one on one's mettle. I always do better when there are plenty of people to watch."

"Especially when one feels that one is working for the credit of one's own house," said Ruth Latimer. "We all want to see the orange ribbon to the fore to-day."

"I'm afraid we've very little chance of winning anything," groaned Madge Summers. "The Hilaryites are almost sure of the long jump. Mona Richards beats the record. They call her 'The Kangaroo'!"

"And the School House will get the high jump," said Lettice. "We haven't anybody so good as Lois Atkinson."

"How about the Atalanta race?"

"Doubtful. I expect it will go to Aldwyth's, or Bride's. They've been training their champion runners the whole term, while we were concentrating our energies on cricket. No Chaddites have even entered, I believe! Chatty, you ought to be in it."

"It seemed no use putting down my name. I was practising last week—you remember, we had a general trial of all the houses?—and I soon found I hadn't a ghost of a chance."

"Well, St. Chad's must content itself with its cricket laurels. We've got the cup for this year, at any rate."

The first portion of the programme consisted of military drill and physical exercises, in which the whole school took part, showing a readiness and promptitude of action worthy of a regiment. Miss Young had prepared a little surprise for the visitors. At the end of the display, the girls suddenly ranked themselves so that their sailor hats, viewed from a distance, formed the College motto: "United in effort"; then, at a sign, they moved again, and the greeting, "Welcome to Chessington" appeared instead. Naturally, this caused much applause, and many congratulations were offered to Miss Cavendish on the excellent discipline prevailing throughout.

The flag signalling was confined to a picked band, so the greater portion of the girls now joined the spectators, only those who had entered for the various competitions remaining in a separate corner of the field.

"I'm glad we have five Chaddites at flag work," said Chatty Burns; "it's a larger proportion than any other house. But there our triumphs are likely to end."

"We won't give up too soon," said Lettice. "There's an old proverb: 'You're never killed till you're dead'. We might manage to score, after all."

In spite of Lettice's sanguine anticipations, St. Chad's did not appear likely to win any triumphs on this occasion. The long jump, as everyone had expected, fell easily to Mona Richards, who thoroughly justified her nickname of "Kangaroo", and caused the Hilaryites to hold up their heads with the proud consciousness of victory. The high jump seemed at first of more doubtful issue; both Dorothy Saunders, of St. Bride's, and Rachel Foard, of St. Aldwyth's, ran Lois Atkinson very close, and the School House had almost made up its mind to a beating when the luck suddenly turned, leaving Lois mistress of the event.

The next item was the "Atalanta Race", so called because each competitor was obliged to pick up three apples during its course, and present them duly at the winning post—not an easy feat to accomplish, as it was possible to drop the first and second in the hurry of snatching at the third.

"There are eleven in for it," announced Lettice, as the candidates began to take their places at the starting-point. "Five scarlet ribbons, two pinks, three violets, and one blue. Not a single Chaddite, alas! Yes, I believe there actually is! Look, there's an orange hat walking up, to make a twelfth!"

"Who can it be?" asked several of the girls, straining their eyes to catch a glimpse of the last comer, who was rather hidden behind the others.

"She's about Pauline's height," said Lettice. "No; Pauline is over there, with Madge and Dorothy. It's not tall enough for Effie Lawson, nor fat enough for Claudia Hammond-Smith. Can it possibly be Adeline? Why, girls, by all that's wonderful and marvellous, it's Janie Henderson!"

Janie's appearance among the trained runners in the Atalanta race was indeed sufficient to cause the most unbounded astonishment. Her general dislike of active exercise was proverbial. It was well known that she only played games under the strictest compulsion, and throughout her school course she had earned the not unmerited reputation of a "slacker". That she, the most unathletic and altogether unlikely girl in the College, should have calmly taken her place as the sole champion of St. Chad's in so difficult a race seemed nearly incredible.

"I wonder Miss Young let her!" gasped Ruth Latimer in horror. "She's bound to fall out immediately."

"And it will bring more discredit on the house than if no one had tried," added Chatty Burns. "I'd have gone in for it myself, only Vivian begged me not to."

"I call it a regular swindle!" said Maisie Talbot. "Honor, did she tell you of this mad scheme?"

"Not a word!"

There was a curious expression on Honor's face as she answered, a look of mingled surprise and enlightenment. She had not forgotten the talk at St. Kolgan's Abbey, and she alone of the whole school knew the motive that had prompted Janie to such an amazing action, and could account for this apparent inconsistency of conduct.

"I never dreamt of her really doing it!" she murmured, under her breath.

"Someone ought to stop her in time!" exclaimed Lettice indignantly.

So far, however, from placing any hindrance in the way of Janie's attempt, Miss Young, on the contrary, appeared to be giving her a few words of encouragement and final advice.

The course was to be three times round the cricket ground, an apple to be picked up in each circle. Heaps of early green codlins from the orchard had been disposed at regular intervals, and competitors might select from which pile they wished, so long as they took neither more nor less than the one required specimen in every round, the object being to prevent a general scramble. There were to be no handicaps, so the twelve girls were drawn up in even rank, each girl with one foot on the white line, and her eyes fixed on Miss Young, in readiness for the signal to start. It was an anxious moment.

"One! Two! Three—off!"

They were gone, a row of young athletes, each bounding forward in the ardent hope of outstripping the rest, and gaining the coveted silver cup of victory. The race was always a great feature of the Chessington sports, but to-day, to the members of one house at any rate, it afforded a spectacle of more than ordinary interest. The eyes of all the Chaddites seemed riveted upon Janie, and they watched with frantic excitement to see how she would conduct herself in the struggle.

"She's keeping well up with the rest," whispered Lettice.

"And has a very light, swinging pace," replied Ruth.

"She's actually ahead of Connie Peters already!" said Chatty.

"And gaining on Christina Willoughby!"

"There! She's picked up her first apple!"

"And passed Blanche Hedley!"

"If she only goes on at this rate, St. Chad's may begin to hope."

"Too good to last, I'm afraid."

"She's begun the second round!"

"She's flagging a little!"

"No, she isn't! She's saving herself for a spurt. There! I told you so! She's passed Christina now!"

"I can hardly believe it's Janie Henderson who's running. It doesn't seem possible!"

"Well, of course, she's extremely light; that gives her a great pull over most of the others."

"But I didn't know she could run at all!"

"Perhaps she didn't either, until she tried."

"She's picked up her second apple!"

"And Alice Marsh has nearly knocked her over, through rushing to the same heap."

"Never mind! it hasn't really hindered her."

"She and Nettie Saville are almost equal now!"

"How well she keeps up!"

"There she goes, past the post again!"

"This is actually the last round!"

"And that's her third apple!"

"She'll let it fall!"

"No, she won't; she's got them quite tight!"

"She's up to Nettie!"

"No—Nettie is spurting, and gaining fast!"

"Janie must push on!"

"Hurrah! Nettie has dropped an apple, and she'll have to stop, and pick it up."

"Janie is ahead of everyone!"

"If she wins, it will be a triumph for the orange ribbon!"

Thus the girls, with continuous anxiety, followed the events of the race, all unknowing that Janie was playing for a far higher stake than they realized, and that on the result of that race hung, not only the honour of St. Chad's, but the future of a human soul, capable of infinitely so much more than it had yet achieved.

"They're all putting on steam! Oh, look! Alice Marsh is almost even!"

"And so is Christina!"

"And Connie Peters has gained what she lost at first!"

"Janie mustn't fail now!"

"Nettie has passed her!"

"Then she'll lose, for a certainty!"

"Oh, dear! I hardly dare look!"

"She won't! She won't! She's making a last dash! She's in front of Nettie! She's gaining—three feet—four feet! Well done, Janie! Go on! Go on! You're safe! Don't flag now!"

"Oh! Hurrah for St. Chad's! She's actually won!"

The wild delight of the Chaddites at this most marvellous and unexpected achievement was beyond all bounds. They cheered themselves nearly hoarse, and waved their handkerchiefs in the exuberance of their joy. To have gained the Atalanta race was a score for their house which, added to their previous cricket successes, would place it on the highest pinnacle of the athletic records of the year.

"And to think that my delicate Janie should be capable of such a feat!" exclaimed Mrs. Henderson, who had watched the contest with hardly less excitement than the Chaddites themselves. "Chessington has been the making of her, and I cannot thank you enough, Miss Cavendish, for your care of her general health. She is another girl from what she was two years ago. The doctor always told me that plenty of exercise would be her salvation, but I could never persuade her to run about at home."

"I am as delighted as you at the change," declared Miss Cavendish. "Janie has shown us quite a new phase to-day, and we shall take care that she keeps up to this standard."

Janie herself, panting and flushed with victory, heard the applause almost as in a dream. It was sweet to her ears, yet it was not the reward for which she had striven. Her eager gaze searched down the long line of clapping girls till she found Honor's face. For a moment their eyes met, but in that one swift glance she read all she wished to learn, and could interpret without the medium of language her friend's unspoken thoughts: "It was a bargain. You have kept your part of it, and I will keep mine."

The Honor who returned to Ireland next day was indeed changed from the one who had left home in disgrace only thirteen weeks before—so much more thoughtful, sympathetic, and considerate, with such higher ideals and nobler aspirations, that she scarcely seemed the same: an Honor who could tread softly in her mother's room, and give the required tenderness to that dear one who was to be spared so short a time to her; an Honor who, while keeping all her old love of fun, could forget self, and turn her merriment into sunshine for others. Character is a plant of slow growth, and she was not yet all she might be; but she had set her foot on the upward ladder, and whether at school, or at home, or in after years, life to her would always mean a conscious effort towards better things.

It seemed to her as if she had been away years, instead of only three months, when she and Dermot (who had passed his examination for a Naval cadetship) drove from Ballycroghan along the well-known road to Kilmore. The villagers stood at their cabin doors waving a greeting; her father, and actually her mother too, were waiting for her on the Castle steps when she arrived; and her four elder brothers had collected all the dogs of the establishment to join in a warm, if somewhat uproarious reception.

"I believe everything looks glad to see me," said Honor, "the very house, and the trees, and the birds, and the flowers in the garden! I'm going to have the most glorious holidays, and enjoy every hour of them. It feels almost worth while to have been thirteen weeks at Chessington, for the joy of such a coming home again!"

The following titles are available in print.

By Angela Brazil

- A Pair of Schoolgirls
- A Popular Schoolgirl
- A Fortunate Term
- A Fourth Form Friendship
- A Harum Scarum Schoolgirl
- A Patriotic Schoolgirl
- A Terrible Tomboy
- Bosom Friends
- For the Sake of the School
- For the School Colours
- Loyal to the School
- The Luckiest Girl in the School
- Monitress Merle
- The Fortunes of Philippa
- The Girls of St. Cyprian's
- The Head Girl at the Gables
- The Jolliest School of All
- The Jolliest Term on Record
- The Leader of the Lower School
- The Madcap of the School
- The Manor House School
- The New Girl at St
- The Nicest Girl in the School
- The Princess of the School
- The School by the Sea
- The Third Class at Miss Kaye
- The Youngest Girl in the Fifth

PRINTED IN THE UNITED STATES OF AMERICA
IBOO PRESS HOUSE